HE WAS CALLED JEAN, THE BASTARD

As Jean bore her down onto a heap of piled cushions, Simone cried out thickly, knowing that his wife would hear and understand the pleasure her husband was bringing to another woman. She wanted to scream out her triumph, but found her lips caught by the mouth of her lover, her words silenced in this wild flood of animal passion. Yet as she clutched him in wild victory, she saw in his eyes the hurt and longing for his wife, Marie.

And so, while Frenchmen died by English swords and a kingdom teetered on the edge of doom, a noblewoman and a blonde wench fought for the love of a man who was husband of one, lover of the other.

For Jean, bastard son of royalty and the greatest fighter of his day, life swung in a dizzying arc between the bloody battlefields of the Hundred Years' War and the eager arms of two fiery women.

The Bastard of

GARDNER F. FOX

Orleans

WILDSIDE PRESS

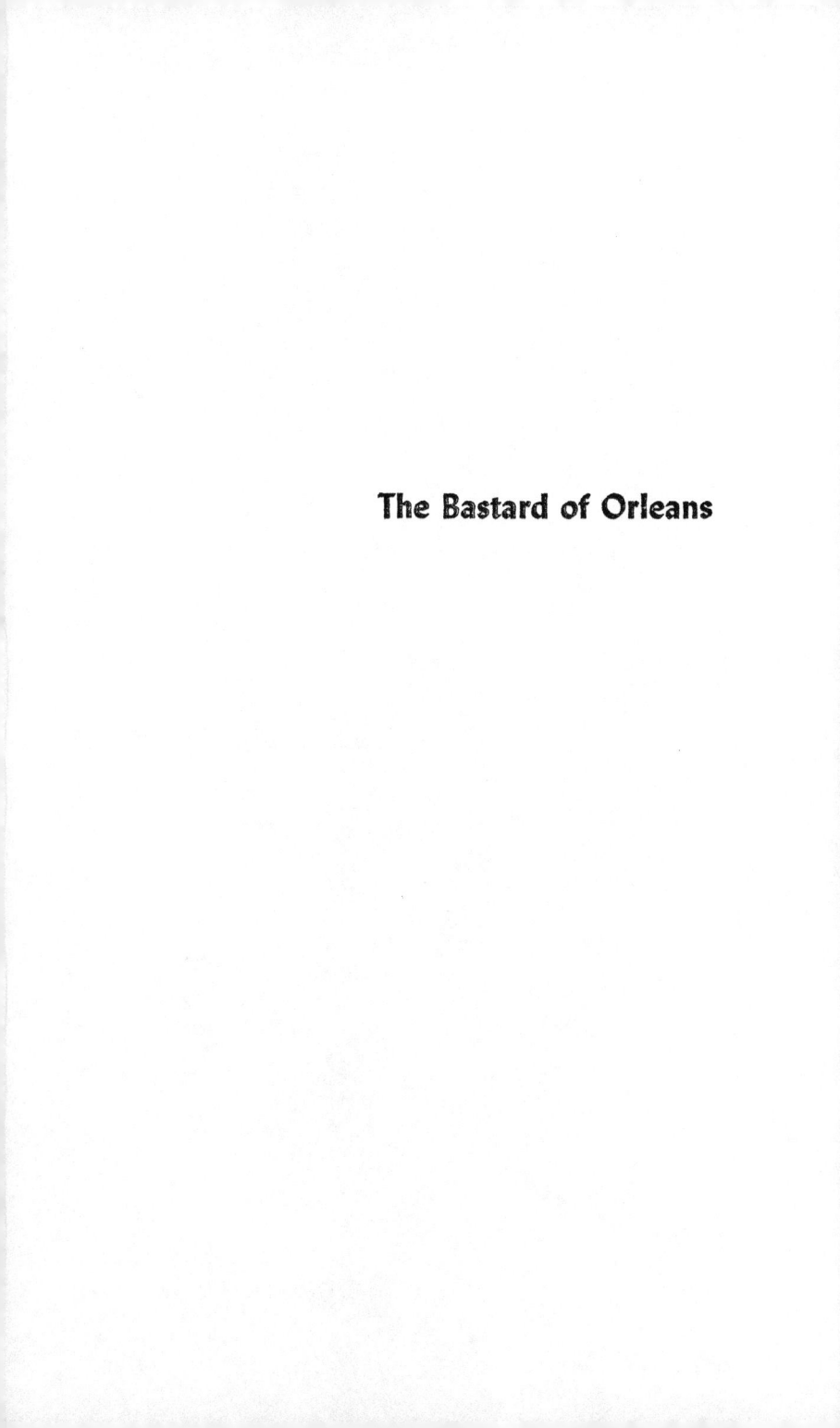

The Bastard of Orleans

Book One: *The Wanderer*

CHAPTER ONE

THE MAN WENT UP the rope hand over hand, swaying sideways with kicking feet, framed against the night sky. Below him the cold waters of the moat reflected the stars and crescent moon; above him loomed the dark battlements of the Château Neussy. Against the stone walls of the turret, where he climbed, a yellow rectangle of candlelight gleamed. Somewhere along the wall walks a viol scratched out an evensong.

The man smiled grimly. There would be a different sort of *serenata* sung in the tower apartment before the night was done. He went up the rope at a slightly faster pace. His breath labored in his throat, and his shoulders felt the weight of his body again and again. Then his hand edged over the stone coping of the inset window, and he rested.

He pulled himself onto the ledge, panting harshly.

As his eyes raked the moat and the lifted bridge, the portcullis chains and the twin turrets of the barbican, his hand closed over the horn haft of the hunting knife at his belt. His fingers tightened until the skin over the knuckles turned white. Hate burned in him with a slow, steady flame. He swung about and stared into the candlelit solar.

His breath caught in his throat.

Where he had expected a man, a woman stood. She was in the early years of her maturity, of middle stature, with a rounded perfection of limb and body that made the man purse his lips thoughtfully. She wore only a shift of sendal, a material so thin he could see the shapeliness of her white legs from the sloping hips to the red leather poulaines on her feet. When she turned slightly, he saw her profile and knew her for the Lady Alix of Bar, wife to Raoul d'Anquetonville, Lord of Neussy and Valclare.

It was D'Anquetonville he had thought to surprise in the tower solar, for whom the knife was intended, who was to die so that he, The Bastard, might have his vengeance. A growl of anger at this trickery of fate rose in his throat; as suddenly, it was gone. Where a scowl of fury had darkened his features, now a smile transfigured them. Revenge might be more than murder done to repay murder. A life for a life could have more than one interpretation.

He moved forward, and now the yellow radiance of the many candles revealed his face to be that of a young man in his early twenties, agile and strong as one of the great panthers on display at Arles. His hair was close-cropped and tawny above a face that possessed the handsome features of the Valois family. In leather jerkin and cavalier boots, he looked more the soldier down on his luck than the nobleman.

Patience was a voice inside him, counseling prudence. The hour was long past complin, which was the hour of bedtime.

Already the Château was half asleep. There was no footfall of guardsman or serving woman in the tower room, only the Lady Alix in her *camisa* before her wall mirror of Venetian glass, brushing the long brown hair which fell below her waist. At every stroke of the brush, her firm breasts trembled, loose under the thin sendal bodice. The young man crouching in the window niche became aware of an increased excitement in his breathing. It had been a long time since he'd looked upon a woman preparing for bed.

Placing the brush on a large chest that stood against the wall below the mirror, the Lady Alix moved with swaying body across the room toward the garderobe. When she was out of sight behind a standing screen, the man slid off the windowsill into the room and went silently to the big oaken

8

door. His hand slipped the thick iron bolt through its hoops and blessed the provost's clerk for greasing it.

A silver flagon of chilled wine caught his eye. He poured the rich red Bordeaux claret into a matching goblet and sipped, relishing the tart flavor. He was still sipping as Lady Alix came striding from the garderobe to pause in amazement at sight of him. Her chin lifted imperiously.

"Who are you? What are you doing in my bedchamber?"

Realizing how exposed her body must be in the thin stuff of her *camisa*, she looked about for her wrapper. Cheeks flushed, she reached for it only to find the handsome young invader a step before her, lifting the *peliçon* and holding it up between them. His smile was lazy, confident.

"Come, let me be your servant in the absence of your husband."

"Who are you?" she whispered. Her eyes studied him more closely now, noting the handsome face and powerful body, the warm blue eyes that roved so shamelessly between the low neck of her shift and its hem. She asked hesitantly, "Louis? But the Duke of Orleans has been dead so many years! And yet—"

"Jean, Lady Alix. His son—The Bastard."

"Ohhh!" Her hand went to her mouth, and her eyes grew wide. She had heard tales of this young hothead, of his duels with the Burgundian nobles he ran to earth between Bretagne and Calais, of the various ways in which he took his vengeance on those who had stabbed his father on the cobbles of the Rue Vielle du Temple in Paris. He wore a long hunting knife at his belt. Alix of Bar was not a stupid woman. Only the chance that had taken her husband to Rouen had prevented this firebrand from achieving his vengeance this night.

She said softly, "If you go now, I promise I'll not give the alarm. It will be our secret." The mistress of Château Neussy could be persuasive when she desired. She was very attractive and was ranked as one of the leading beauties of France.

Jean shook his tawny head, smiling faintly. "I didn't come to deal in secrets. I came to avenge myself on D'Anqueton-ville."

"My husband has gone to Rouen. It will be a disappointment, but you must forego your vengeance until another time." Triumph glistened in her eyes as a deep breath lifted the magnificent bosom under its sheer sendal covering.

The Bastard laughed and turned again to the wine pitcher. As the red Bordeaux flowed, he said casually, "I find vengeance to be a two-edged sword, milady. A man need not necessarily kill to take revenge."

The sharp glance that roved over her body made the Lady Alix take a backward step. She was older than this stripling who was sampling her claret—not so much older, however, that she might not prove attractive to him, she thought wildly. Yet she was certainly old enough to remember seeing his father Louis, Duke of Orleans and brother to King Charles VI of France, as a little girl. She could recall how handsome Duke Louis had been, how courtly of manner. This young cockatrice before her was just as fine a figure of a man.

"You talk in riddles," she snapped, anger making her flush.

"A riddle you understand only too well, *madame*. Your eyes betray your thoughts." He smiled down at her over the lowered goblet. "Your husband led the fatal attack on my father. Until this night I've never been able to get close enough to lay my mark on him—or on any of his possessions."

Her glance touched the great oaken door leading to the outer hall and its spiral staircase. She wondered if she might reach it and throw back the bolt before Jean could stop her. Uneasily, she realized she could not. With that knowledge came a stir of mounting excitement.

"Do you intend to kill me?" she whispered.

"For shame," he chided her, laughing softly. "I said before that vengeance has two sides. On one is the black swan of death, on the other the white egg of life."

He moved across the rush-strewn floor toward the massive ambry that held her gowns and kirtles. On a rack beside it stood a number of headdresses, conical hennins standing side by side with twin-horned escoffions and the more delicate atours. He lifted one of the escoffions. "Horns of the devil, these are named. It's the wife who flaunts them publicly,

10

but it should be the husband who wears them, morals being what they are these days."

Lady Alix shook her head. "I've been a faithful wife."

"Until tonight," he added, and lifted the headdress. "How would your Raoul look wearing horns, *madame?*"

"You wouldn't dare!"

"Wouldn't I? I've come this far to kill him. I can stay a little longer to give his wife a child. Face it, *madame.* Raoul D'Anquetonville is too old to sire further children. You're his third wife. I may be your only hope to—"

She whirled to run, but he was beside her before she had taken half a dozen steps on wobbling legs. An arm banded her back, held her soft body tight against his own. Then his mouth was warm on her lips, and his strength was such that she found herself welcoming his hard young body, his hungry mouth. She wanted desperately to struggle free, but a lethargy, on which a tide of desire began to rise, was in her flesh.

He kissed her soft white throat, her closed eyelids.

"We must not. Oh, I beg—" she breathed.

A kiss buried her words. Then she clung with starving arms—Raoul was an old man, not young and fiercely demanding like *le Bâtard*—and, even while she prayed to *le bon Dieu* for forgiveness, she aided him in slipping down the straps of her *camisa*. She moaned above his head, eyes closed, lost in a spill of pleasure. Only dimly was she aware of his hands tugging her thin shift to the floor.

She felt herself swung up in powerful arms and carried toward the canopied bed, lowered tenderly and admired first with ardent eyes and then with caressing lips. She writhed, her small white hands clenched into tiny fists. Her breasts were hard and her body receptive as he drew her to him.

The Lady Alix was not accustomed to the immoralities of court life and the casual manner in which noblemen and noblewomen bedded one another at whim. Oh, she knew enough of the goings-on which made the reign of the mad Charles VI a scandal in Europe. The father of this youth she held in her arms had seduced more than his share of highborn ladies, among them the queen herself, Isabel of Bavaria,

11

wife of Charles VI. Gossip said he had also seduced the Duchess of Burgundy, which caused her husband John the Fearless to have him slain outside the Hotel Barbette. Some even murmured that the Dauphin, who would be the future Charles VII if fate permitted, was not the son of Charles VI but of the Duke of Orleans.

In this springtime of the year 1425, no one gave any thought to the love affairs that made the court of the Dauphin such a gay and light-hearted menage. Virtue was a word with little meaning. She knew all that. But so far Alix of Bar had held herself aloof from this gay round of amoral intimacies.

She felt shame creep like a crimson tide above the fair white shoulders on which he rained his kisses, shame that fought with her heated blood, that made her whisper protests even as his caresses caused her to emit little cries of delight. For just a little while that shame troubled her; then it was drowned in the lifting tide of pleasure under which she shuddered.

"You are taking vengeance—without mercy, *seigneur!*"

"Is revenge ever merciful?"

"You have begun something I can never forget!"

Her arms about him, her kisses became as ardent, as searching as his own. There was a dormant flame in the Lady Alix which this young hothead was fanning into life. The thought occurred to her, as she gathered him against her body, that Raoul d'Anquetonville would never be enough to satisfy her from this night on. And in this knowledge the Lady Alix understood the terrible manner of his vengeance.

The Paris candles used to tell the time were guttering in their holders when she finally leaned above him, kissing the corners of his mouth with tender lips. "A devil you are, Jean. You've awakened me as a woman. Did you intend this or was it by the merest chance?"

As he stirred and would have rolled from the bed, her arms tightened, imprisoning him. Her smile was sensual. "Not yet. In all these years I never realized what a precious joy might be shared between a man and a woman. You came for vengeance. The horns are scarcely planted on my husband's brow. They need a firmer tamping."

12

Jean laughed. "It must be past the hour of lauds. Soon it will be dawn."

"And you'll go back to killing the men who murdered your father. But not for a little while. Not yet." She leaned above him, letting him know the weight of her breasts. "Is it so very important, this killing?"

"To me, yes. It's a goal giving purpose to my life."

She made a wry face. "A silly, stupid goal for such a wonderful young man. To slay your father's murderers is selfish. They have so many friends. All Burgundy! One man against so many? It's a task to dismay a Samson."

"Then don't play Delilah to my strength, Alix."

She collapsed in laughter on him. After a moment she turned her head sideways on his chest so she could look at him. "How long have you been away from your estates in Dauphiné?"

"Six months or more. I quarreled with the Constable of France over the policies of state. Richemont holds the Dauphin's ear. I retired from the field to pursue my own inclinations. I became a soldier of fortune."

She considered that, staring down into his handsome face, suddenly remembering that Jean of Orleans was a married man. "And your wife? What does Marie think of this vengeance trail you take?"

"No wife of mine, that one. At best, wife in name only."

"Oh? Can I believe what you imply? That a hot-blooded young stallion would permit such a pretty mare to run untended?"

"She came to the altar a virgin. A virgin she remains. She considers herself too good to bed a bastard."

Bitterness erupted in him, making his mouth thin and hard. Once there had been a time when his only goal had been to attain the woman he loved, Marie Louvet. Now that dream, like so many others of his life, was washed away by the fact of his bastardy. He would never forget her mocking laughter as she had confronted him following the wedding ceremony, when they were alone in the solar of the great hall of Vaubernais.

The unclothed body of this woman beside him was warming, even more warming than the flame of the oil lamps in

13

the solar that night three years before, when Marie had thrust him back, away from her. "You must be mad to think I'd let you take me in your arms, Jean. What difference does it make if a bishop has said a few Latin words over us?"

Amazement had held him speechless. True, their courtship had been a cold and formal affair, dictated by conventions and checkreined by the watching eyes of the Duchess Yolande of Anjou, who had arranged the match, but—

"Marie, you're tired. You don't know what you're saying!"

"Don't I? Have you ever heard me say I loved you? Never! I think I've always hated you, Jean. Actually hated!"

"But—but why? What did I ever do?"

The full red mouth he longed to kiss had curled in disdain. "It's what you didn't do that maddens me. You had the misfortune to be born under an unlucky star. Your half brother Charles was much more clever. He had the sense to have Valentina Visconti for his mother! Your father's wife, his duchess. You chanced to pick an adulteress to give you birth."

He had shaken with the fury consuming him. The fingers of his right hand had opened and closed convulsively, again and again. He had wanted very much to strike out with that hand, to put the brand of his blow across her lovely features. Jean had fought his anger with every last ounce of will power. Calm, be calm! She's overtired and doesn't know the meaning of the words she speaks. Marie Louvet was three years younger than himself, scarcely more than a child despite the early signs of the mature beauty which would be hers.

Her hair, a dark, rich brown, had hung from her wedding coronet in long, rippling waves. Her adolescent bosom had made tiny mounds in the white samite of her wedding dress, and her young hips had been scarcely more rounded than those of a boy. Yet her dark, brooding eyes and pouting, overripe mouth had hinted at the sensuality that lay hidden behind the samite, a sensuality that had attracted his Valois blood. There had been a physical ache in his strong young arms to hold her close, an emptiness in his middle that could be filled only by her nearness.

14

"Marie, let's not quarrel on our first night," he had pleaded.

Her shoulders had shrugged impatiently. "Quarrel? I'm not quarreling. I'm only telling you I've no intention of going to bed with you, that's all."

His hands had gestured outward. "Then why in the name of God did you marry me?"

"My father needed monies with which to repay certain loans advanced him by Jacques Coeur. His investments—especially those in Flemish cloth manufacturers, who turned to England for their raw materials rather than to Champagne as of old—were disastrous. The gold *écus d'or* my marriage brought have set him on his feet again."

"I can't believe that! I'm not a rich man."

Her lips had quirked. "Your adoptive mother—the Visconti woman—was wealthy beyond a greedy man's dreams. Your half brothers Charles of Orleans and Charles of Dauphiné—"

"You mean the Dauphin? The future king?"

"He's your half brother, isn't he? Didn't Louis sire all three of you?"

He had not been able to fight the flush that had mounted into his pallid face. His girl-bride had laughed at him, head thrown back. "Jean, Jean! Didn't I say you were born under an unlucky star? The two Charles are legitimate—or at least Charles of Orleans is! France needs a king, so Charles of Dauphiné is permitted to be."

She had come walking toward him with fluid ease, her boyish hips already swinging with a hint of the flirtatiousness that was to flower in later years. "The two Charles' and your mother gave you a royal dowry, Jean. To save my father, I agreed to stand before the bishop with you. But I don't consider myself your wife. *Comprenez?*"

His hand had lifted to strike, to lash back at her mockery with the only weapon he had, his physical strength. Never had he felt more alone in the world, more abandoned by fate and God. An emptiness inside him had made him reel; he had had to fight for composure. His arm had fallen to his side.

"I ought to beat you," he had snarled out of the despair

15

that gripped him. "I ought to raise that gown and lay on with a willow switch."

Her head had gone high. Twin red spots had darkened her cheeks. "You wouldn't dare! I'm the daughter of the Sieur Louvet, Seneschal of Provence!"

"And a callous, unfeeling swingtail!"

She had sprung to slap but had felt her wrist caught and turned so that she was flung off balance and fell against him. She had lain inside his arm like a wounded bird, trembling, filled with sudden terror, panting softly. Jean had been able to feel her lifting ribs against his front.

Her wide eyes had been inches from his own, staring up at him. Just as close had been that red fruit of a mouth, slightly parted. His arms had tightened slowly, holding her young body against his own until he could feel her from knees to throat. She could not stir so much as a finger.

It was then he had kissed her tenderly, as if he would have spoken silently to the womanhood inside her proud little body, telling her the love he had for her. Something inside him had called to whatever femininity she might be hiding behind the white samite.

Her mouth had firmed against his, suddenly, and had held the kiss.

When he released her, she had slapped him.

If he had known more of women during this period of his life, The Bastard might have recognized that Marie Louvet had been fighting not so much his love as the feelings storming into her virgin heart. Scarcely out of childhood, she had still been full of the imageries of the *Roman de la Rose* and the chivalrous ideals of Jean de Meun. A lover in her bemused eyes had been more ethereal than earthy, more heavenly than human.

As it was, he had read only disgusted rejection on her features. He had said wearily, "All right, I'll go. I love you too much to do what I suppose I ought, throw you down on the bedstead yonder and pay no heed to your maidenly modesty or your virginal screamings." His lips had twisted bitterly. "It's another misfortune of mine, my sentimentality."

She had watched, scarcely breathing, as he came and

caught her chin in a hand. "Be grateful I love you so much, Marie. And remember me in your prayers."

He had walked out of the room into the long gallery and closed the door behind him. He had never seen his wife again. . . .

The Lady Alix of Bar sensed his wandering thoughts and, as if to tempt him to the present, ran the tip of a forefinger about his mouth, which was so quick to respond to laughter and to anger, or to the shape of a kiss. "You and Marie were only children. She may feel differently now."

"Not that one! I swore I'd forget her, and I have."

"By slaying the men who slew your father?"

"It's a goal I set myself long ago. When Aubert de Flamency, the Sieur de Canry—the lawful spouse of my mother, Mariette d'Enghien, Madame de Canry—wanted to adopt me, I refused. I would be known as The Bastard, since that was the way God let me come into the world. I sought no other title. It reminds me of what I am."

"And what is that, Jean?"

"A hand to hold a dagger. No more."

They lay quietly while the glittering candles threw dark shadows across their naked bodies. Jean stared sightlessly at the canopy above them, seeing neither the heavy Spanish brocade nor the intricately carved oaken posts; instead he saw the handsome laughing man who had sired him. He had been only four years old when Burgundian daggers felled Duke Louis, and such young minds remember little of what they see and hear. Only fragmentary memories remained to him of hands tossing him high into the air, of bright blue eyes beaming down at him proudly. He thought bitterly, If he had lived, he would have made me legitimate by adopting me. Duke Louis' death removed all chance of that! Jean's hatred had begun in the first hour of his realization that bastardy was to make a difference in his life. It had crystallized in that hour of agony with Marie Louvet.

"You could be more than a hand and a dagger, you know," she whispered between nibbles at his ear lobe. "The Dauphin is your half brother, everybody says. Your father was his father."

17

His laughter was bitter. "My father had a way with women."

"Like father, like son."

Sometimes he wondered if he ought not hate his parent rather than those who wore the red cross of Burgundy. He knew the story only too well—how Duke Louis of Orleans had carried on a love affair with Queen Isabel of Bavaria, wife to the mad king Charles VI and leader of the court revels long before they put away her husband. Nobody knew how many of her children had been sired by Louis of Orleans. Rumor could only guess.

"As half brother to the future king, your fortune is assured," she went on, beginning to stroke him slowly with soft white hands.

"Future king? Of what? England and Burgundy rule France from the Channel to Orleans. And England rules Burgundy."

"Dispossess them, Jean. Your father was a soldier as well as a lover of fair ladies. You may have inherited more than one of his talents."

He looked at her as if she were as mad as King Charles. "Would you teach me ambition?"

"Only love," she murmured, and rose to hands and knees.

After a moment he gasped and stared up at her in surprised delight. "Who takes revenge now, milady?" Her eyes were closed, her white teeth sunk into her lower lip. When he put his hands on her she gave a wild cry and fell on him, trembling spasmodically.

The night became eternity and the bed a battlefield on which The Bastard achieved triumph and defeat in the arms of this frenzied woman, who whispered strange and broken words as her hands caressed his body. He was both victor and vanquished; he fought her and, in fighting, loved her until she cried out in sobbing tones to name him slave and master in the same breath.

"Thus might you—do with France—could you find the way! In this manner—might you reach the goal I dream for you! Jean? Jean, can you hear me? I am so far away—in another world entirely—yet so close. Oh, so very close! You are more than—a hand and dagger. You are!"

18

During her mad outcries, Alix of Bar wondered if she sought to justify her pleasure by making him more than he was, so that her surrender might be symbolical of something other than temporary lust. She did not know the truth. All she did was ask the question. Only Jean of Orleans and time itself might known the answer. . . .

Dawn was a red sky beyond the river Aisne as Jean dressed and moved to the recessed stone window. The rope he had hung from the tower merlons yesterday afternoon, after gaining entrance to the Château disguised as a wandering mendicant, was close to his hand as he leaned out.

Lady Alix said, "If a guard sees you, you'll be killed."

"Little risk, little gain—and I've gained much tonight." He drew her against him for a last kiss.

"Was it more than just revenge?"

He pinched a bared buttock and laughed, then caught the rope in his hands and stepped from the stone window. The moat lay two hundred feet below, dank with reeds, beginning to reflect the brightening light of day in its smooth surface. Jean could see himself in those waters like a spider crawling down its web. It would be the hour of primes very soon now, and the guard would be changing on the wall walks. Thirty feet above the moat he loosed his grip on the rope and fell.

The cold moat waters closed down over his head. He sank like a stone, waiting until his lungs seemed about to burst before swimming as swiftly as he could for the shelter of the drawbridge overhang. The dark wooden boards protected him from all eyes but those at a windowslit in the east wall, and that chance of discovery he would have to risk. He popped to the surface gasping, clinging to a rusty ringbolt until he was breathing normally once again.

He swam across the moat, underwater, and pulled himself up over the stone abutment. Without looking back he set off southward toward the forest of Compiègne. Last night he had tethered his black gelding to an oak tree in the forest. Momentarily he expected a crossbow quarrel to thud between his shoulder blades; he walked with his head held high, but behind his belt his insides were as weak as mush. Only when he reached the first stand of elm trees did he dare to turn and look back at the Château Neussy.

Something white fluttered in the tower window.

His arm lifted and waved back at the Lady Alix.

Then he was plunging between the thick boles of mighty oaks and chestnuts, smelling the fragrance of blooming hyacinth in this springtime of the year, tramping over clustering trilliums and hepaticas. Alix of Bar had said her husband was traveling the Rouen road, which ran through the forest of Compiègne. *Jean le Bâtard* did not want to be caught within chasing distance of the Château Neussy by Raoul d'Anquetonville.

Relief touched him when he saw the black gelding cropping grass at the end of its long tether. The horse lifted its head, as he approached, and whinnied. Jean grinned and clapped a hand to the shiny rump.

"Ha, *mon fidele!* You like the grasses of Compiègne? *Bien!* Then feast quickly, for we won't be here much longer."

He put his toe in the wooden stirrup and swung upward into the saddle, a plain wooden hull covered with black leather. His longsword dangled from a strap at the pommel. A coat of mail, tied by leather thongs and fastened tightly to his unadorned helmet, was thrown over the crupper, which held leather bags containing some extra clothes and a small sack of golden *livres tournois.*

Everything he owned in the world he carried on the gelding, or so he liked to feel. It gave him a sense of freedom to know there was no one dependent on him for his or her happiness or livelihood. Sometimes at night the thought came to him that he might be shirking a duty, but he put this notion aside hastily, for he was filled only with a sense of urgency to accomplish the task of revenge he had set himself.

He rode through the early morning sunlight, with the chirp of sparrows sounding from the berry bushes on either side of the wide dirt road. His belly was empty, but his heart and mind were alive with the knowledge that he had avenged himself on his greatest living enemy, Raoul d'Anquetonville. The old Duke of Burgundy, John the Fearless—he who had ordered his father cut down with cold steel—had been dead five years now, slain on the Montereaufault-Yonne bridge, with the Dauphin looking on, and so removed from the touch of the hunting knife at Jean's belt.

20

All he had left to his blade were four men.

His fingers counted them off—first there was Raoul d'Anquetonville, then Gaudry of Angers, Robert de Berri and Étienne Aymon. Three others were dead by his hand—François of Anjou and Guillaume the Fleming in alleyway duels, Roland of Uisel during a knife fight at an inn in Troyes.

Now D'Anquetonville was a cuckold.

Jean whistled the tune of a popular *balada*. Too bad those others had no wives as sensual as Alix of Bar. *Ma foi*, but the night had been well spent. She had been a revelation, the D'Anquetonville woman. It would be pleasant indeed to revenge himself upon those others as he had on old Raoul.

For a little while shame rode the saddle with him. I'm no better than a sneak thief skulking behind merchant's stalls or street door recesses to snatch a purse when a man's not looking! No, he must not begin thinking like that. His whole life was wrapped around his vengeance. If he had no such goal to sustain him, he would be no more than the villein laboring in the fields to produce turnips and wheat for the manor table—or even less, for the villein had a purpose in life, no matter how ignoble.

The dust rose in little puffs behind the clopping hoofs of his horse, and the sunlight was warm on his back. He drowsed a little in the high-peaked saddle, promising himself he would stop at the next wayside inn for cheese and bread and chilled wine.

A distant cry woke him to the moment.

The forest was thinning here, and rolling meadows lay like long green carpets on the land. A stone fence made a twisting path along a field of barley, and beyond this a thin line of poplars formed a windbreak to a field whose furrows sprouted beans and cabbages, lettuce and cucumbers. The blue spring sky was filled with fleecy clouds, and a lazy breeze made the yellow bellworts sway by the roadside.

Yet his eyes saw none of these.

His gaze was fastened instead on a thin black plume of smoke lifting upward beyond the tilled fields. An instant later he caught the red lick of flames at a distant haystack.

21

"Brigands," he muttered, and drove his toes into the gelding.

He went at a fast gallop across the meadow. The black soared over the low stone fence as Jean put a hand on the braided handle of his longsword, yanking it free of its scabbard. He could see several horses in the farmyard and two men struggling with a third. Again he heard the scream that had roused him from his reverie, as a woman appeared briefly in the open doorway of the hut before being dragged back into the interior.

The two men looked around at the sound of pounding hoofbeats. They yelled hoarsely to their fellow inside the hut and released the peasant they were restraining. Drawing their swords, they ran to meet the oncoming rider. Free of his captors, the peasant whirled and made for the low doorway of his hut.

Jean came down on the bandits at a headlong pace. His long blade glinted in the sunlight as he swung it in an overhand blow at the first man. Its edge went deep into a shoulder even as the gelding hit the second bandit and threw him offstride. Jean reined in and turned. The unwounded brigand was standing on spraddled legs, indecision written on his loutish face.

Then the gelding was looming above the bandit, who struck at the rider with flailing sword. Jean turned its edge and almost in the same motion brought his own blade around in a savage sideswipe. The steel caught the man at the base of the neck and sheared deep. He stood a moment, dead on his feet, eyes white and staring before he began to topple.

Jean leaped from the saddle and ran for the hut.

A red-headed man came into the doorway and stood grinning at him, sword in one hand, left fist tightly clenched. This was no stupid clodpoll as the others had been. Slyness looked out of those pig eyes, and shrewd cunning pursed thin lips. The sword in his right hand was red with blood. Jean wondered whether it was the man or woman he had killed—probably the man. Dead, the woman was no use to him.

"No need for us to fight," the redhead said. "The woman's strong enough for both, and I'll share the jug of coins they have put away."

"Filth," said Jean, and leaped.

Too late he saw the clenched fist open and hurl dirt and straw into his eyes. Jean cried out and twisted to avoid the steel swiping at him. His booted foot caught in a root, and he pitched sideways. The blade intended for his head flicked past his arm, slicing the linen shirt.

Jean rolled along the ground, over and over.

The redheaded man only laughed and ran for his horse. He mounted up and banged heels into his mount. Jean came up to a knee, watching him ride off across the meadow. Excitement was still a pounding tide in his blood. He wanted to go after the man—the black gelding could have caught the heavier animal in a hundred yards.

The sobbing in the hut made him hesitate. He climbed to his feet and walked to the door. The interior was dim, lighted only by errant shafts of sunlight peeping between wall chinks and through the thatchwork roof.

A naked woman was kneeling weeping above the body of the man who had been held captive by the bandits in the yard. She was young and fair, and her skin was very white below the neck. Long yellow hair made a curtain around the face of the dead man. A pool of blood lay under him, soaking into the dirt floor.

Jean watched her a moment, wondering what kind of man he had been to make a woman like this care for him so much. From what he could see of her body, mostly back and pale hips, she seemed very lovely.

"I'm sorry," he said softly.

She lifted her tear-stained face to stare at him. She had a beautiful face, with slant gray eyes and a ripe red mouth that reminded him uneasily of Marie Louvet. Her hand scrabbled in the rushes that served as her bed to lift torn brown wool and hold it in front of her heavy white breasts. She was quick to cover herself, but Jean nevertheless saw dark bruises on her upper arms and across her ribs.

"Burgundian bastards!" she whispered brokenly. "May *le bon Dieu* strike all of them dead!"

"Amen," he said and smiled crookedly.

Her eyes focused on him for the first time. "He was my

23

husband. We were married three months. Red Gui chased us out of Beaulieu so we settled here."

"Red Gui? The one who killed your husband?"

"A brigand of the worst kind. He gets his name not so much from the color of his hair as from the blood of the Armagnacs he spilled in Paris six or seven years ago, during the massacres."

"I remember. The Burgundians took me prisoner then."

Surprise transfixed her kneeling body. "And they didn't kill you?" Her glance moved over his leather jerkin, the frayed linen shirt under it, the taut brown breeches above his cavalier boots. With a toss of her head she said, "You don't look like an important person."

He laughed at her honesty. "I'm not important. I was—in those days. It's a long story."

"There'll be plenty of time for you to tell it to me," she informed him. "I'm coming with you. Now turn your head while I get into what's left of my dress." When she saw the hesitation on his face she asked dully, "Would you leave me here for Red Gui to find when he comes back?"

"I ride alone," he muttered. "I ride to kill three men. I don't know where they are."

"Burgundians?"

"Retainers of the dead Duke John. They serve his son Philip now, I'm told."

"Good. I'll help you kill them."

He stared at her, shrugged, then moved out into the forenoon sunlight. His eyes were caught and held by the two dead bodies in the yard. He supposed that this scene was being repeated, except as to small details, all over northern France from the Seine to the Channel. This was English territory now, its people helpless before the hordes of soldiers turned loose from the English and Burgundian armies and allowed to roam at will in robber bands across Picardy, Champagne and Normandy.

It was not an uncommon sight to come upon dead men swinging from tree limbs, nooses tight about their throats, or lying impaled on spears in their farmyards these days. All France groaned under the heel of the invader, from the Loire to the Strait of Dover. No man was safe in his home, be it rolling farmland or some twisting city alley. The English did not bother to check the bandits; in a sense they were their allies, for they kept the people in a servitude more frightening than any army of occupation could have achieved.

Life was hard enough for the serfs and peasants, even in time of peace. It was unbearable now. A woman could expect rape as a daily hazard from the leaderless bands of *routiers,* just as a man could expect death. The lucky ones might buy their liberty, but after a while the supply of deniers ran out, and without money the common people were helpless.

Pride was an ugly taste in Jean's mouth. He spat.

This was his land, this France. These people—the dead man in the hut and his blonde wife—were his people. On his own estate of Vaubernais, in the province of Dauphiné, the villeins were free men. So far to the south there were no brigands.

A footfall made him turn. The blonde woman stood in the doorway, a lighted torch in her hand. The brown wool tunic was patched and sewn, but her legs were bare above rawhide carbatines and her long hair still held bits of straw and rushes.

Slowly she walked around the little hut, touching the flaming torch to the dry thatch, finishing the task the bandits had begun and then abandoned for a better sport. When the hut was burning fiercely, she hurled the pitch-soaked stick through the doorway. She turned and looked at him out of red, swollen eyes.

"I'm ready now. Let's go kill those Burgundians."

CHAPTER TWO

WITH THE blonde woman riding one of the brigand's horses and Jean on the black gelding leading the spare, they moved along the dusty road toward Senlis. This was rolling farmland, with the river Oise to their right and the last traces of the forest world of Compiègne stretching away toward Soissons. From time to time Jean glanced at his companion, discovering a remoteness of spirit in her stare and in the lax manner with which she sat her saddle.

As if aware of his regard, she turned suddenly and smiled at him. "I ride with you without even knowing who you are. It speaks well for the determination in me."

"Determination?"

"To kill my enemies, who are also your enemies." Her gray eyes moved over his wide shoulders and lean hips. "You look like a fighting man. Are you?"

"I fought at Beauge four years ago when the English whipped us. And again at Verneuil."

"That was last year, wasn't it? And it was another English victory. Why do they beat us all the time? Are we all cowards?"

He smiled faintly. "Some of us are fools. Ever since Crécy the English longbows have been cutting us down. I think we need a new idea, a new kind of weapon. Nobody's come up with that new idea yet."

"So you're a soldier. You look like a nobleman."

His shoulders moved inside the leather jerkin. "In a way, I suppose I am. My father was a duke, my mother the wife of a wealthy noble. Obviously then, I was born out of wedlock."

His tone of voice dared her to make comment, but there was no emotion at all on her placid face. Bastardy was more common than not in her way of life. No one thought anything of it; indeed, most of her friends never knew whether they were legitimate or illegitimate, and, if they thought of it at all, it was with an utter lack of concern. Life itself was enough to give them worry these days. For a moment he studied her carefully, before deciding that she was unaware of his perturbation. Jean suppose he worried overmuch about his bastardy, yet the fact rankled in him like a sliver beneath the skin.

Out of that resentment he said, "I'd intended to be a cleric or priest and spend my days in a monastery. The Burgundians beat that idea out of me when they captured me in Paris during the Fourteen-eighteen Armagnac persecutions. They made me their prisoner. A year later I escaped, with the help of the jailer's wife."

"You don't have much trouble with women, do you?"

"I like women. I like everything about them, sometimes even their perverseness." He remembered Marie Louvet—he still refused to call her his wife—and sighed in melancholy fashion.

Her laughter rang out. "My name is Simone. What's yours?"

"Jean. The Bastard."

"You make it sound like a title."

"It's better than being ashamed of it."

She considered him steadily while swaying to the rhythmic walking of her horse. "You know, I think you like being a bastard. It gives you a feeling of being put upon, an excuse for failure, as it were."

He reached for her wrist so suddenly that she was dragged halfway out of her saddle before she knew what he was doing. The horses came to a stop, the gelding shaking its ringbits with up and down motions of its head. The blonde woman lay with a shoulder crushed to his chest, one foot completely out of the stirrup. If his arm released her, she would fall onto the road.

And yet she knew no fear. This young man was angry, but it was a controlled anger. He said to her blonde head, looking down at it, "I never fail. You understand? *Jean le Bâtard* never fails!"

"I was only testing you, *seigneur*."

"Don't call me *seigneur*."

"Jean, then."

"There's straw in your hair. We'll stop at the next brook and you can clean it."

He lifted her back into her saddle and smiled. As if the touch of her body had struck some psychic spark inside him, he looked at her with the eyes of a man who finds a beautiful woman before him. Simone preened herself, letting the brown wool outline her heavy breasts, the curves of her solid thighs. A lone woman needed a protector in these lawless times, and Simone knew only one way to acquire one.

They moved on for another hundred yards; then Jean asked, "Testing me for what?"

27

"To see if there's a fire inside your rib case. I think there is. I have an offer to make such a man."

"Go on."

"In the tiny village of Neufchâteau there lives an old soldier named Thibaud. He has an idea for a new weapon he calls a cannon."

Jean hooted. "A cannon? The Black Prince used cannon against Calais nearly a hundred years ago, when Edward the Third invaded the north countries!"

"I know nothing about that. All I know is that he claims it's new. It has something to do with the cannonball itself, I think."

He pondered that, riding through the dust of early afternoon. He would like to believe the blonde woman, but common sense told him there was no merit in the idea. A new type of cannonball? One made of wood or glass instead of iron? It would serve no purpose. The idea was ridiculous.

And yet—

Sometimes a man had to snatch at straws so that he might bring victory from despair, strengthening them with the fiber of his will and his own strength as straw itself is mixed with clay and sand to give bricks greater cohesion. And nowhere in all France, he thought, was there a man more despairing than himself.

"How far is this Neufchâteau?"

"A score of leagues away, near the River Meuse."

"This man could be dead by now."

Simone looked willful. "He may. I haven't seen him for five or six years. But if you mean what you say—that you're a soldier and need some fancy new weapon to fight Englishmen and Burgundians—I should think you'd want to make the trip."

"I also want to kill the men who murdered my father."

"Now there I cannot help you."

Jean grinned wolfishly. "Maybe you can, at that."

She asked questions, but he would say nothing until they reined in on the bank of a small stream that twisted through the ploughland country to meet the Oise near Creil. Beech trees grew all around, forming a little glade. Where the banks of the brook sloped downward, a wide plat of blue gentians bloomed in woodland splendor.

"We'll eat here from the food you put in the saddlebags," he told her, reaching up his arms to help her off the horse.

He watched her walk with swaying hips toward the brook, long hair flowing down her back. She knelt and bent her head, letting the water take the golden strands. Her hands moved in the stream, washing out the burrs and bits of straw. When she was done she put her head to one side, hands wringing the water from her thick hair, kneeling in graceful indolence and smiling up at him.

"There are cold turnips in the bag, and cheese with bread and some fruit," she told him. "Or do you want me to fetch it?"

Jean stirred himself, remembering his role of gentleman adventurer. It was hard to play at being two men, for he was so used to being waited on by servants he forgot that a commoner had no one to fetch and carry for him. With a grin he went and lifted down the saddlebags, and brought them to her.

Her yellow hair was spread fanlike across her back and shoulders. It glinted in the sunlight as if spun from faery gold, framing her slant gray eyes and ripe red mouth. Sitting beside her, he let her break the manchet loaf and pass half to him with a wedge of homemade cheese.

"If you're what you say you are," she murmured, "and your father was a duke, why are you dressed like an ordinary soldier?"

He saw that disbelief was strong in her. Impishness made him lift the leather *aumonière* at his belt, open it and shake out the *livres tournois* in a golden shower. Simone sat up straighter, crying out in awe. When he caught the signet ring set with the nettles of Orleans, she took it in her hand and regarded him steadily.

"You might have stolen it."

"I didn't. My father gave it to me."

"The duke?"

"Louis of Orleans."

She bent forward with laughter so infectious that he joined in her merriment. When she could talk, she wiped tears of

29

mirth from her cheeks with the back of a hand and said, "You aim high, in God's name! Louis of Orleans? Why—that makes you cousin to the Dauphin!"

"The Dauphin made me Seigneur of Vaubernais and one of his counselors. A little later he named me Grand Chamberlain of France."

"*Foul*" You're mad, utterly mad!" Her eyes went to the ring as she turned it over and over. "If you're all these things, why are you here?"

"To kill my father's murderers. I quarreled with Arthur de Richemont, who is Constable of France. I had my belly full of court life. I wanted to get away from it."

And from Marie Louvet who became your wife in name only, Jean? To escape the witchery of her dark eyes and red mouth, the mere sight of which always caused an agonizing pain to stab your heart?

He said thoughtfully, "In a way, I think I was looking for death. Perhaps I hoped one of the men who killed my father would kill me, too. None has, so far. Within the week I'll give another of them the chance."

"I almost believe you," she said, handing back the ring, lifting the leather pouch and filling it with the golden coins.

"Étienne Aymon lives in a small manor house near Montmirail, which is not so far from here we could not stop by on our way to Neufchâteau. He's one of the men who hacked my father to pieces on the Rue Vielle du Temple."

He looped the *aumonière* to his belt and stood, looking down at her. "Well? Are you coming with me?"

Simone held up her hands so he could raise her to her feet. Her eyes were somber. "You said I could help you, a while back. Now tell me how."

"I've reason to believe these murderers communicate with one another. They know I'm somewhere between Paris and Artois. They'll be expecting me, but they won't be expecting me to have a wife with me."

"Ah, you begin to make sense."

She pushed a sandaled foot into the stirrup and rose to the saddle, her brown woolen skirt riding back from a bare and shapely leg. Jean bent and kissed the smooth skin of her thigh.

Simone laughed and pushed him away. "What man kisses his wife's leg when he sees a bit of bared flesh?"

"A newlywed," he grinned.

Her eyebrows arched. "You think of everything, it seems."

Then she reined the heavy horse away from the brook and kicked it into a canter. Jean watched her for a long moment, lips pursed. This idea that had come to him so suddenly was not so poor in merit, at that. True, his wife would need more clothes than she wore at the moment to act out the part he had in mind, but his purse was heavy with *livres tournois*. Excitement began to build in his blood.

The common room of the Inn of the Gray Mule, which lay on the Montmirail road just beyond the town, was heavy with excitement in this early hour of the evening. A dozen young bloods from neighboring manor houses were crowding about the dice table, where Étienne Aymon was meeting a run of bad luck. Already a large pile of gold *ecus* lay before a swaggering young cockerel, whose laughter rang out with uninhibited delight. The rattle of the dice was loud in his cupped hand. Except for the patter of the barmaid's feet as she carried a tray of wine bottles across the rush-strewn floor, it was the only sound in the room.

"I win again!" the young man in the leather jerkin shouted, as the dice rolled to a stop.

"Devil take it," snarled Aymon.

"Mayhap the devil does take it, milord," whispered a slim, sly man at Aymon's elbow.

Jean le Bâtard reached across the gaming table. His hand closed down on the shirt front of the speaker and dragged him halfway across the tabletop. His dagger point pressed against the man's throat.

"We French burn scorcerers, *mon ami*," he whispered softly to the terrified man, who lay staring up at him with bulging eyes. "I wouldn't like to think some careless words of yours might bring me to the stake."

Aymon growled, "My Pinchon only joked."

"I spoke to Pinchon, milord. Let him answer for himself."

Pinchon nodded, sweat staining his pinched face. He could read death for him in the hard eyes and sun-browned face

31

above him. The others—the young ones from the manor houses—were just drunk enough to regard it as a good joke. He had seen evidences of the crude humor of the young bloods before now. His good friend Gilles Drouet had had to have a leg cut off because a group of nobles' sons had staked him out in an outer court during a snowstorm and then forgot about him.

He babbled, "I jested, good sir, as milord Étienne says. A jest, young lord. Only a matter to laugh about."

Jean grinned down at him mirthlessly. "Have you ever seen anybody burned alive, Pinchon?"

Pinchon shook his head back and forth.

"I have. A young woman accused of being a witch, in Dauphiné. It wasn't a pretty sight."

His hand yanked the man across the gaming table to fall at his feet. "I think we ought to give you a taste of the flames yourself to teach you proper manners."

The young bloods began to laugh and talk among themselves. Jean hoped they would not like the idea too much; he threatened only to rouse Étienne Aymon to the protection of his manservant. His quarrel was with the older man, not with the servant.

Aymon came forward, as Jean had intended. "Here now, no need to go to such lengths. No need at all. There's no harm done. My Pinchon spoke in jest. You heard him yourself."

"He accused me of serving the devil!" Jean rasped.

"Non, non!" Pinchon begged on his knees. "You misunderstood. It was only a figure of speech."

"Pah!" Jean snapped, thrusting the man away and reaching for the pile of golden *ecus* on the table. "Your master's a poor loser, Pinchon. You only spoke to placate him."

Étienne Aymon made a long face. "You've a sharp tongue there, young man. It might be necessary for you yourself to take a lesson in good manners."

The younger men shouted, scenting blood. Jean paused amid their cries and laughter, his hands over the gold coins. His dark eyes raked the older man as he said, "If you weren't old enough to be my father, I'd call you out for that, *seigneur.*"

32

Aymon grinned coldly. "I was killing men while you were in swaddling garments. I haven't forgotten the knack."

"With odds of seventeen to one in your favor, it takes no courage to hack a man to bloody bits."

Étienne Aymon paled and looked about him. Few men these days knew he was one of that band who'd cut down the Duke of Orleans outside the Hôtel Montagu in Paris, eighteen years before. Ever since this handsome upstart had crossed glances with him earlier in the evening, he had been aware of his strong dislike. He thought now that dislike might be too mild a term. What he read in that hard face was actual hatred. For a brief moment he wondered if he faced The Bastard himself, Jean de Valois, that headstrong son of Louis of Orleans who had adopted the task, so gossip went, of ridding the world of the men who had taken Burgundian gold to slay his father.

No, that thought was madness. This was no more than an ordinary soldier of fortune with a sharp tongue. He could not visualize the cousin of the Dauphin coming to a lonely tavern in Brie alone, without retainers, clad in plain leather and cavalier boots, with only a longsword at his side and a new bride waiting in an upstairs solar.

He said gruffly, "Come, now. We're all friends still, I trust. No need for lost tempers."

Jean smiled coldly. "A sensible about face. Lost tempers often result in lost blood."

The older man roared, "By God, young one! Don't force me to cut you down. You're on your honeymoon, you said. Go upstairs to your wife with your winnings and account yourself lucky."

Jean swept the last of the coins into the sack. Still on the gaming table was a silver brooch and a ring, which Aymon had lost on the final toss of the dice. Jean palmed them, swept them into the sack as well. He drew the tie strings and knotted them.

He turned on a heel and moved toward the outer hall, past one of the long tables still laden with overturned wine goblets and the dregs of a meal. He looked triumphant and pleased with himself, but inside he seethed with anger. Somewhere he had bungled, he knew. By now, Étienne Aymon should be standing out in the inn yard with him, naked swords in their hands. Instead the murderer was going home to his manor house while he went upstairs to Simone.

Eh, bien! He would make another try tomorrow.

"Stranger!"

The voice rang clear and loud across the common room. Jean turned in the doorway, not troubling to conceal his feelings. He did not know it, but there was an imperious manner to his Valois stance that was like a slap in the face to these country *seigneurs.*

Aymon growled, "I was about to ask you to share a last hanap of claret with me, but now I'm damned if I will." His face revealed the tortured thoughts that ran through him as his eyes assessed this hard-bitten stranger.

"It's just as well. I only drink with equals."

Ah, that did it! Aymon was halfway across the room now, taking great, pounding steps, hands outstretched to come to grips with his tormentor. Jean stepped sideways with the instincts of the swordsman and shoved the older man sideways into a table. For a moment Aymon hung there, gasping for breath, face flushed with rage.

"You'll pay, young one!" he roared when he could, straightening and waving an arm at Pinchon. "Outside in the yardway, with cold steel."

Jean bowed. "I'll fetch my blade at once."

He moved into the hall and up the worn wooden stairs, triumph making him tread lightly. Within the hour Étienne Aymon would join his comrades of that long-ago night in death by his hand. There would be two left then, two out of the original seventeen. Those he himself had not accounted for had died by this time, and lay in graves from Ponthieu to Navarre.

His hand thrust open the door to their bedroom. Simone was standing in one of the three kirtles he had bought for her at a mercer's stall in Soissons, head turned to study the drape of her long skirt in a hand mirror propped on a chest. Her thick yellow hair was piled carelessly atop her head. He paused to study her.

She laughed when she saw him and made a pirouette, the skirt flying above bare knees. "Am I not the lady of quality?

Oh, I've never had anything as wonderful as these clothes!"

She ran to him, caught him in her arms and kissed him gratefully. Under the blue velvet she wore nothing at all, not even the thin linen *camisa* which most highborn ladies adopted as an undergarment. The low neckline exposed the upper slopes of pallid breasts. Jean had not made love to her as yet. Vengeance was an exacting taskmaster, he was discovering.

"Aymon's challenged me," he told her. "It took a bit of doing, but we're meeting in the inn yard shortly. I've come for my sword."

Fright gleamed in her slanted eyes. "Suppose he kills you? I'll be left—no, that's selfish of me."

He removed the *aumonière* from his belt and pressed it into her fingers. "There's a fortune in *ecus* in this purse. I won more from Aymon at dice. It's all yours if what you fear comes true."

"I don't want your gold. I want you."

He kissed the corners of her mouth, then moved her aside so he could cross the room and lift the plain scabbard that housed his Missiglia blade. He frowned.

"There's always a chance those young men belowstairs may interfere if the swordplay grows too heated and I have Aymon on the run. If that happens, they may thirst for my blood as I thirst for Aymon's."

She waited, scarcely breathing. When he hesitated, she said, "Then we ought to be prepared to leave as soon as the duel begins." Her peasant common sense made him grin.

"You understand, *ma cherie*," he murmured.

Simone sighed and looked at her reflection in the little mirror. "I'll pack and be ready in the stables. *Peste!* I knew I'd never get a chance to enjoy these gowns."

She was slipping a white arm free of the downfalling kirtle as he paused in the doorway to stare. "You'll have plenty of time to play the lady on the road to Neufchâteau, I promise. For now, dress for a fast ride. I may be starting at shadows, but I'd rather be prepared than be caught napping. Have the horses saddled just inside the livery stable so I'll know where to find you in a hurry."

Her ripe white breasts hung naked above the fallen bodice

35

as she nodded. Simone caught the sudden longing in his eyes and smiled lazily. For the past two days, on the road to Montmirail, she'd begun to wonder about this young *seigneur;* most of the men she knew would have thrown her on her back in a roadside ditch long ago. She supposed noblemen did things differently than common folk, though.

Just the same, he might be a little more ambitious where she was concerned, she thought, watching the door close behind him. A woman liked to think she was desirable to a man, especially to such a man as *Jean le Bâtard.* Her hands pushed the dress down as she lifted a slim white leg from the pooling velvet. Almost without thought she turned her head to gaze at her reflection in the hand mirror. Simone giggled at what she saw.

Étienne Aymon and the others were waiting beneath the wooden sign carved in the shape of a mule and hung on creaking, rusted chains. Behind them the yardway stretched for fifty feet, opening onto the coach-house apron. It made a good place for a duel. As he advanced toward his opponent, Jean reflected that a lot of hot blood had been cooled on this narrow stretch of ground.

Aymon was scowling, waving his sword back and forth as Jean faced him. "First blood or death?" he wanted to know.

Jean said, "You name it, *seigneur.*"

"First blood, then. I'll be merciful to you."

There were no rules of nicety to govern swordplay between two enemies in this year of 1425. It was flail away with the steel until arms grew weary and one man faltered. The heavy shields that were carried into battle were rarely available at these tavern quarrels, and a style of swordplay was beginning that made the blade point and shield at the same time. In Saxony and Bohemia, guilds of swordsmen were already banding together to teach this new style of fence.

One of these Germans, a member of the Marcusbruder guild in Frankfort, had tutored The Bastard in his formative years. A bond had grown up between the old soldier and the lonely child, a bond which, begun in the castle courtyard at Angers with cold steel, had flowered into a firm friendship. For more than a dozen years old Rodolf had taught Jean as much as he knew about the longswords.

Now as he faced Étienne Aymon—as he had faced Guillaume the Fleming and François of Anjou—Jean once again blessed old Rodolf for his painstaking thoroughness. In his big brown hand the sword was more than an inanimate length of steel. It flashed in the lamplight with seeming life as it touched the blade of his opponent, disengaged and came flying in with a sidewise slash at the older man's unprotected flask.

Aymon managed to leap out of the way, but it was a near thing. Nervous sweat stood out of his forehead as he came stamping in, swinging his blade with overmuch gusto and little wisdom.

Jean caught the slicing blows, turned them aside with a twist of his strong wrist. He let Aymon expend his energy in a series of bull-like rushes before he took the attack, driving forward with a guile that made his darting blade seem a living thing as it parried and thrust and hurtled through the air in overhead molinellos.

The fear of death was clearly readable in Aymon's eyes now. He gave ground swiftly, betraying the fact that fright was a nausea in his belly. He yelled aloud in his fear, his face pale and wet, mouth twisted into a caricature of terror.

"Raimond! Arnaud! Peleria! Aid me for sweet Jesu's sake! He only plays with me. Pinchon was right. He's in league with Satan!"

Jean laughed harshly. "As you were yourself when you slew my father, *seigneur? Oui—Louis le duc!* Ah, you remember it, do you? I'm glad because—"

His sword was swinging down at a defenseless face when three of the young men who had been in the common room came bounding from the shadows, swords bared. Jean was forced to turn from the older man in midstroke to catch their flying blades and deflect them. He backed away slowly, parrying and disengaging, listening to Étienne Aymon pant as he leaned a shoulder against the inn wall. Fury was a fire in his middle.

The murderer had escaped him! In his terror he'd called out to his young hotbloods, urging them to take over his quarrel. Blind anger fueled Jean's arm. He cut and slashed until one of the three men facing him went down screaming in pain, his swordarm sliced to the bone.

The others drew back and stared at their kneeling friend. They had not counted on being hurt themselves. It was sheer sport to take up the Sieur Aymon's quarrel, sport to bring this stranger to his death in the inn yard. Now, however—

Jean whirled and leaped for Étienne Aymon in this moment of their bemusement. The older man saw him coming just in time to stop the sword slash, which would have cloven his head from his body. As it was, the edge cut deep into his shoulder.

Étienne Aymon screeched.

Jean was drawing back his blade for a deciding thrust when he heard the pound of boot heels. Half a dozen more of the young hotbloods were rounding the corner of the timbered inn, drawing steel as they ran.

"Until another time, *seigneur!*" Jean rasped.

He ran for his life, knowing that the slightest misstep or blunder would give his pursuers a chance to flesh their blades in his body. Pray God that Simone was packed and in the saddle. Pray God that his black gelding was eager to run!

He skidded on the yard pebbles, then raced for the open doorway of the inn livery stable. He saw Simone in a hooded *chaperon*, mounted on her gray—a fast mare he'd traded the two horses and a gold *tournois* for just outside the Abbey of Saint Madard in Soissons—and bringing the black gelding with her by the reins. Her face was flushed with excitement as she stared beyond him at the oncoming young men.

"Hurry, Jean!" she called. *"Vite!"*

He went up over the gelding's cruppers with both hands spread on its croup and hit the saddle with a jarring shock that ran up into his backbone. He banged a toe into the black's ribs.

Then Simone was a slim figure in her enveloping cloak half a pace ahead of him, bent low across the whipping mane of her fleet mare. They raced stirrup to stirrup out of the inn yard, swinging south on the winding road to Châlons. Jean blessed the foresight that had made him exchange those plow horses for the gray and the fate that had taught Simone, as a farm girl, to ride as well as himself.

38

They took the road at a driving gallop, dirt clumps flying up from under the thudding hoofs, the wind of their passage fluttering her cloak and cutting through his leather jerkin. His Missiglia sword lay in the inn yard, dropped in his feverish haste. Without it, he was defenseless.

Again he cursed those young hotbloods, under his breath but savagely, consigning them to hellfire for their efforts. To flee, like a terrified hare before the hounds, in front of Étienne Aymon and his Montmirail companions was a bitter mouthful for the proud Jean of Orleans. Twice he stood in the stirrups, turning to search the road behind him, both times seeing them hotfooting it after him, no more than a mile away.

His lips firmed. He must lose them! Without a blade he would be unable to defend himself or Simone. He knew enough of their kind to understand what would happen to Simone once they'd disposed of him. A sickness came into his middle at the thought. He'd grown fond of the blonde woman in the few days he had known her.

"Faster, faster," he called, and touched a prick-spur to the gelding.

Both animals responded by lengthening their strides. Now, when he looked back, it became harder and harder to see their pursuers. The mile became two, then three. By dawn and with luck, they might shake them completely.

The road curved through a little woods here. The overhanging branches were so thickly entwined they shut out the moon, the sky and its stars. Te Jean it appeared they were running through a Stygian blackness with neither beginning nor end.

And then the world erupted around them.

Men came leaping from underbrush and thickets, from behind tree boles and fallen logs, dirty clapperclaws in stinking furs and wolfskins and untanned hides, unkempt and ragged. Their hands caught at bridles and reins, pulling the mare and gelding to a halt. Greasy fingers yanked at Simone, bore her from the saddle to the ground. Jean went backward himself, flailing with fists and legs, striking hard again and again before sheer weight of numbers pinned his back to the ground.

"Rich pickin's!" howled a voice.

39

"Our luck be turned for fair!"

"The woman's mine!"

"No—mine!"

They might have fought like the beasts they had become had not Jean cried out, "Wait, you fools! Wait! Listen to me!"

A hand cuffed him hard alongside his jaw, but he shook his head to free his numbing wits and cried, "If you want gold—listen!"

The word was a magic incantation that threw a hush over them. A burly brute whose naked chest and back was sheathed in thick hair came crowding through the others, leering. Behind him he dragged a shivering Simone, trying to be modest in the few tatters the lusting fingers had left on her back.

"What's this talk of gold?"

Jean said, "I'm a runaway servant. The man I served is chasing us. I stole his mistress and his money. Here—see for yourselves!"

They let him go long enough for him to undo the tie strings of the purse in which he carried his dice winnings. His hand threw a score of the *ecus d'or* among the cutthroats. The men scrabbled in the dirt for the coins, but their hairy leader held his pig eyes tight on Jean, who had struggled to his feet and stood swaying among them.

The hairy man growled, *"Oui,* it's gold. There's more of it in the purse you carry."

"And even more coming along the road with Sieur Aymon!"

They cried out at that, turning to stare back along the forest road. Their leader grinned, showing blackened teeth.

"I can take your gold and their gold, no thanks to you," he said, yanking Simone to her knees before him. "I'll take your woman, too."

"I can help you get the gold with little effort," Jean said desperately, knowing the bitter taste of defeat. He watched the hairy man take a handful of Simone's loosened hair and turn her face upward. "You won't lose a man if you listen to me."

The bandit chieftain laughed harshly. "What do I care for these pigs' lives? Most of them have lived too long already."

40

The men were muttering behind him. Jean read their hate and fear of this brutish man who led them. He spoke to them, ignoring the hairy man. "Well? What do you say? Will you let this two-legged beast browbeat you for the rest of your lives? Or will you use what little wits the good God gave you to grow rich in a single hour with my help?"

The brute roared and leaped, a dagger gleaming in his closed fist, but Jean had been expecting this; he pivoted on a foot and caught the hairy arm, brought it over a shoulder and whirled. The hairy man flew through the air ten feet to land hard on his back with the wind knocked out of him.

The clapperclaws stared from their leader to this surprising newcomer. Some of them grinned in delight at what they had seen. A few scowled. But all of them showed the light of greed in their eyes.

Jean said, "Gold for all. Gold to buy you wine or a tavern wench! Eh? What about it?"

Simone had crept across the road to kneel beside Jean's legs. Jean smiled down at her, touched her head with his hand.

The outlaws looked from the woman to the man and then to their fallen chief. Indecision and doubt made them fidget from one foot to the other. Jean raised his hand.

"Listen! The Sieur Aymon comes at the gallop. Make up your minds. Is it my plan or not? Without yonder beast— his wits too addled to serve you now!—to command you, you're no better than animals before a plow. Well? Do you follow my plan?"

"*Oui!*" said an old man.

"*Oui.* Yes. Yes!" the others cried.

"Then back into the woods, and be ready to leap when I cry out, '*À Valois* for vengeance!' You understand?"

They melted in among the tree boles with the stealthiness of those whose lives depend upon their silence. Two of them dragged the hairy man between them. The road was empty. Simone rose to her feet, the tatters of her blue velvet kirtle hanging in shreds about her white hips and long legs.

"They are beasts!" she whispered to him fiercely. "Ride now—while we can!"

His laughter was soft but savage. "And forget Étienne Aymon, who rides to slay me as he slew my father?"

Her gray eyes were wide with shock. "Would you risk both our lives to satisfy your blood lust?"

"I would! Now this is what I want you to do . . ."

When the Sieur Étienne Aymon and his nine companions came thundering into view along the forest road, they saw their quarry dismounted—the man bent above the near fore hoof of the gray mare as if to fix its shoe, the woman crying out and pointing, turning to flee.

Sight of the man made Aymon stand in his stirrups and wave his sword. Sight of the woman caused his hot-blooded companions to forget everything but her long yellow hair and the tantalizing glimpses of white flesh that gleamed through her torn garments.

The knight was aiming a downward stroke with his blade when Jean whirled and leaped for the headstall of his mount, shouting, "À *Valois* for vengeance! À *Valois* for vengeance!"

The horse reared high. Men exploded from the forests on both sides of the road, daggers in their hands and hot greed in their eyes. The road became a confusion of shouts and stabbings. Riderless horses went plunging through the melee, one or two dragging the corpses of their recent masters along the ground.

The Sieur Aymon rasped curses but was unable to still the frightened dancings of his horse. The man clinging to the bridle was darting this way and that, avoiding the thrusts of his blade, reaching up powerful hands to clasp them on boot top and breeches, yanking sideways overbalancing him.

Étienne Aymon gave a loud cry as he felt the saddle slipping out from under him. He sought to ward off the wild-eyed stranger whom he was beginning to suspect was Asmodeus come up from hellfire to slay him. He screamed and struggled when those fingers wrapped about his throat.

"For your murderous lusts, *seigneur!*" a voice panted at him. "For your foul treachery! For your lack of manhood, which made you call for help in an affair of honor!"

Madness rode *Jean le Batard* in this moment of his revenge. His fingers sank deep into soft flesh. His powerful arms bore the full weight of his body down on his enemy.

Only when Étienne Aymon lay limp and lifeless under him did he roll free and kneel dazed and trembling in the bloody dirt.

Simone touched him with a hand.

"Jean—the hairy man!"

His glazed eyes rose to find the bandits motionless, the dead bodies of the young hotbloods stripped and bare at their feet. Their eyes touched their leader, who was advancing slowly with a bared sword in his hand.

Jean moved his eyes this way and that before he caught sight of the Sieur Aymon's fallen sword. His hand caught it up. The haft felt familiar; with a thrill of recognition he knew the Missiglia blade. At least Aymon had understood good steel when he saw it, he thought, and braced himself.

The hairy man charged, point ripping through the air to disembowel. Jean swung. Sparks flew as steel met steel. The bandit leader cursed, but Jean wasted no time in words. His arm completed its swing. Now his blade towered straight up into the air, a glittering length of death.

The brute screamed.

The steel sheared into his bare poll, splitting his skull with an overhand molinello. He crumpled and lay twitching in muscular spasms for several moments.

Jean stared at him, then looked around at the dumb faces of the riffraff. Awe and fear looked back at him from those brute features, together with an emotion that seemed very much out of place among such clapperclaws as these. After a moment Jean knew it for pride.

"You made us rich, *seigneur!*"

"*Oui!* You shall be our chief!"

"There's none can stand against us wi' you showing the way."

Simone was warm against his arm, pressing close. "They're telling you that you can give them their manhood back, Jean," she whispered. "Most of them used to be soldiers, I gather from what little I heard of their talk while you fought."

He snorted, "What need have I for leadership of such a pack? As well aspire to lead wolves."

When he would have moved toward the black gelding,

43

he found his way blocked. They were respectful but stubborn. Their hands stretched out, pleading. In their eyes he saw shame and guilt for sins without number, for murder, rape and torture.

"Lead us! Lead us!"

"We be your men. You won us in fair fight."

"Killed Pol, you did. You take his place!"

Half of them wore the rotting skins of beasts, the other half were clad in little more than their own hides, hairy and unwashed. They clasped crude weapons—a knotted club, a rusted scythe blade, a barnyard ax. And yet Jean fancied that he saw, deep in their eyes, a tiny flicker of pride, lost amid the years of murder and rapine, that said these were men, not animals.

In anger at himself he cursed softly. "What do you want of me?" he shouted, counting heads. There were more than forty of them, each man seemingly more ragged and less human than the next. Lead such as these to pillage and steal? He shuddered.

"I fought at Beauge," a man called out.

"And I at Verneuil!"

"This stump of wrist I came by at Agincourt ten years ago," yelled a third, waving a handless arm over his head.

A tall man, lean with starvation but with a twinkle in his eyes, slipped to the fore. "We all be soldiers, lord. When there was no more fighting, we went home and found our homes burned, our wives and children slain. There was none to care for us. We had to care for ourselves as best we could."

"And you stole and raped."

The thin man grinned wryly. "It was the only way we knew. When we went to till our lands, the English and Burgundians came and whipped us, driving us off."

"What do men call you?"

"Jean, lord. Jean of Lorraine."

The Bastard grunted and looked at Simone. Her hands were idly braiding a strand of thick yellow hair, but he saw pity in her face.

His voice raised above the mutterings. "All right, all right. I'll lead you if you want to be led. Where's your camp?"

44

"In the deep woods, lord, where none but us can go."

Jean shrugged and turned to Simone. "At least we can rest for the night in safety," he told her. "Tomorrow we'll worry about everything else."

His cupped hands made a rest for her foot as she swung up on the gray mare. The blue velvet kirtle she had donned so proudly in the bedchamber of the Inn of the Gray Mule hung in tatters from her shoulders. Jean could see one pale breast in its entirety and a smoothly rounded hip where a dagger had slashed the velvet.

"We left so suddenly I had no time to bring other clothes," she murmured, trying to pull the bodice together.

"I'm not complaining," he grinned, and slid his palm along her smooth thigh. She did not push his hand away but only laughed, softly and provocatively.

The brigands lead the way on silent feet, moving like shadows between the tree boles. Overhead the moon was a yellow fruit, glimpsed between tree branches. An aura of fantasy held Jean in its grip. He swayed to the movement of the gelding, staring at the bare heads and shoulders of the men who surrounded him, wondering a little at the fate that had brought him so far from his estates in Dauphiné to this lonely Brie forest. Just beyond the bobbing head of his mount rode a woman he had not know a week ago, a woman whom he had passed off as his wife, who did not resent the casual manner in which he stroked her naked thigh.

He wondered about Marie Louvet.

And if he would ever see her again.

CHAPTER THREE

JEAN CAME from the little wicker lean-to, stretching in the the early morning sunlight and breathing the crisp spring air. Much to his surprise, he had slept the sleep of the dead on the dirty grasses that had made up the bed of the former

45

bandit chieftain. Energy was alive in his veins. His cutthroats seemed not quite so filthy as they had in last night's moonlight as they moved now about the camp, gathering firewood and carrying water.

Someone had caught half a dozen hares and skinned them. They were boiling in a big iron cauldron above a campfire. To his amazement Jean found himself ravenously hungry.

A footfall swung him around.

Simone was emerging from the lean-to, her blue velvet gown neatly mended. She curtsied low at sight of him, then laughed roguishly.

"Did you think I would be on public display for the rest of my days? *Mais non!* I am a modest wife, my Jean." Her head tilted sideways, and a curious look touched her slanted eyes. "And married to a dull clod of a husband, if his conduct last night is any standard."

He grinned. "I thought you were tired."

She tossed her head. *"Pouf!* You spent your energy fighting. Why not admit it?"

Jean asked softly, "And you think I had none left to bed a bride, *hein?"*

She began to hum and braid her long yellow hair. He eyed her a moment, amusement warring with vexation in him. No man likes to have his virility insulted, and it seemed to The Bastard that this blonde woman was doing just that, though in a mild enough sort of way.

His hand clapped her soft rump. "Fetch me some rabbit stew and bread. We'll talk about our love life later on."

Her hips swung insolently as she moved across the cleared space. Jean called after her, "And tell the men to send me someone who knows the countryside hereabouts."

As he was wiping the last bit of moisture from a wooden platter, Jean of Orleans looked up to see a wizened old man leaning on a stick and looking askance at him. He waved an arm, beckoning the old man closer.

"Do you know the roads and towns closest to this forest?"

"Oui, lord."

"I have gold. I want to buy clothes and weapons for the men."

The gaffer shook his head. "It can't be done, lord."

46

Jean showed surprise. "Won't the merchants deal with us?"

"Oh, they'll deal fast enough—but they always take back what they sell. After we've paid their price, of course."

The Bastard sensed a wagging tongue held in tight leash. He patted a tree stump and told the gaffer to rest himself. Jean walked back and forth before he said, "I give you leave to speak, old one. Omit nothing."

The story was not new. Jean had heard versions of it since his twelfth year. The merchants of the town of Sezanne, which was a fairly large hamlet some ten miles to the west and close by the Saint Gond marshes, had hired a dozen soldiers, whom they employed as follows—when a purchase of goods was made, and where the buyer seemed unable to protect what he bought, the merchant who made the sale summoned the twelve, whom the brigands irreverently called the devil's apostles, and sent them riding posthaste after their customers. With many hard knocks, the twelve always took back such goods as had been recently purchased, restoring them to their former owner, the merchant who had made the sale.

"Thievery, pure and simple," snarled the old man. "They do name us rogues, but we're only simple folk, not sly and filled wi' trickery like the good burghers of Sezanne."

Jean laughed until the tears ran down his cheeks. Half the camp came and stood there, jaws agape, watching him.

"And business is good for these fine merchant fellows, I assume?"

The old man nodded gloomily. "They do get their price without losing their goods, half the time. Why shouldn't it be good?"

"Then let's change their luck, shall we?"

The gaffer looked glum. "Them devil's apostles be big men and strong. Not many of us can stand up to 'em."

"But if we cut their numbers in half? Six men, *hein?* Enough of you could hide in ambush to handle six of them, surely!"

"They always travel as twelve, lord."

"Not this time, they won't. Simone!"

Simone came running, to listen eagerly and then bite her lip to keep from laughing. The plan was simplicity itself. All it needed was for Simone to dress like a monied lady. She promised to clean her blue velvet kirtle until it sparkled.

An hour after midday, Simone entered Sezanne from the north, just as Jean, clad in the finest clothes that could be sorted out from among those from the young men who had followed the Sieur Aymon into the previous night's trap, entered the village from the south. One man rode with Jean, two with Simone.

They met once at the mercer's, where Simone was paying golden ecus for bolt after bolt of fine velvet and samite. Jean contented himself with purchasing strong hacquetons, which were worn by men-at-arms beneath coats of plate mail, but he, too, paid with gold.

Though he seemed to look anywhere but at the bobbing, smiling merchant, Jean was aware that excitement was running like wildfire through the tiny hamlet. He and Simone were buying with such lavish recklessness that the merchants' eyes rolled in their heads. Pack animals must be purchased to carry the swords and shields the armorer furnished, as well as the sacking that held the two score shirts of chain mail; a dozen clerks sweated to tie up the capes and jackets for which Simone had laid out a score of *livres tournois.*

Jean and Simone met again at the greengrocer's stall, where Jean bought Brie cheeses and assorted fruits and Simone ordered loaves of bread newly out of the ovens and more than two score capons and geese.

They bowed and smiled at one another, continuing on their way, fumbling at their purses for coin after coin. Jean must have a dozen pair of fine leather riding boots. Simone required hose and poulaines. When Jean asked for swords and battle-axes, Simone demanded daggers. It was as if each sought to outdo the other in the liberality of their buying.

Yet both were done with their shopping at almost the same moment. Jean swung into the saddle and, trailed by his servant—a rude, ignorant lout in the eyes of the draper and fuller —and four pack mules, headed south toward Troyes. Even as the gelding clip-clopped past the timbered overhang of the silversmiths' guild house, Simone was traveling northward in front of five pack mules, whose panniers and canisters were full to overflowing.

Jean rode along, content. As he paced along the single street that ran from one end of Sezanne to the other, he read indecision in the eyes of the staring merchants. Two small fortunes were slipping from their grasp. There would not be time enough to send the twelve after both customers. Jean laughed to himself, imagining the arguments which would be raging in Sezanne. The drapers and cloth merchants would want the woman followed. The armorer and farrier would insist the man be trailed.

The result was as he expected.

Five miles from Sezanne, half a dozen men leaped at him from ambush—he'd heard the pounding hoofs of their horses along the road which paralleled his own a short while back—crying out for him to surrender his recent purchases or be slain.

Jean rather imagined that these men had met with little resistance in the past. They were broad of shoulder but heavy in the beam, big and slow and somewhat ponderous. He felt he and his companion could handle them, given enough sword room, but he signaled to those other brigands who had followed them through underbrush and weeds, keeping always out of sight. These men leaped from cover as hounds slip their leashes at sight of the hare, bellowing their hate.

The cutthroats settled old scores in the road dirt that afternoon. Gnarled clubs and broken hoe handles bashed at noses and jaws. The attack was so sudden and so furious that the six devil's apostles had no room to swing daggers and swords. They went down, each of them with three ruffians hanging onto arms and legs.

They would have died if The Bastard had not pulled his men from their backs, buffeting with a hard hand when disobeyed.

"Let them up, you fools. They're worth gold to you, don't you understand that? Gold, I say! Let them up!"

His men gawked as if he'd suffered a sudden attack of the shaking sickness, but they rose nimbly enough when he began laying the flat of his blade across their shanks. The sheepish half dozen fidgeted in the dust as Jean walked around them, studying them closely.

49

A brigand touched his arm. "The fire arrow, lord. Jacquot informs us all has gone well with the others."

Jean swung into his saddle. "Time now to break out the mail shirts and the hacquetons. I want you to look as if you amounted to something, understand? You, Ned—men tell me you were a sergeant under my brother Charles of Orleans when he was made a prisoner at Agincourt. Act it!"

He waited in his high-peaked saddle, stifling the laughter rising past his lips; watching order come from chaos; seeing armed men appear where only ragged scarecrows stood before. Eager hands broke out what few swords and war hammers he had been able to buy in Sezanne, together with a dozen lances and, here and there, a few bows with arrow quivers.

Jean ran a critical eye over their uneven ranks. Every man had armed himself as best he could in that hurried snatching. Their hair was unkempt and their beards bred nits, but they had a look in their eyes he liked.

"All right, then. You'll do for the business before us. See you keep what you've taken and care for it. Lose what you have and it's the ducking stool for you. After the second offense, the lash. Understand?"

They grinned, remembering old scars from forgotten punishments, but they understood and respected him for the stand he took. He was giving them back a little of their pride by granting them a sense of responsibility.

They marched, not in unison but with ground-devouring strides that affected a rendezvous with the other half of their band two miles west of the town. Cries of jealousy rang out when the others saw what fine weapons and armor their mates were wearing. Jean had to go among them and cuff a few ears before they fell silent.

"Your tongues wag like young girls planning weddings," he scolded. "You know where we got the mail shirts, don't you? And the war hammers and bows?"

"In Sezanne!"

"From the merchants!"

Jean grinned down at them, quieting his gelding with pressing knees and a hand on its black neck. "Are there any more in town, do you think?"

They caught his meaning, and a roar went up. They would have fought with bare hands to get such weapons, but Jean of Orleans gave the post of honor to the best equipped and ordered them to obey Ned's commands under pain of death. "A ducking stool's all right for minor infractions, but a battle can be lost when a single man disobeys. I mean to have obedience. Is it understood?"

Their grinning faces were his answer.

As they moved in something like a marching step down the wide cobbled town street, doors slammed and shutters were hastily bolted. The population melted like snowflakes before a warming sun. Jean made a sign, and the twelve captured apostles formed a ragged line before him.

"Men of Sezanne, I come to bargain. I bring you more business. In me you see a lavish hand, ready to spend gold pieces as if they were no more than copper deniers."

An upper window swung open. A lean merchant leaned out, crying, "You're a trickster. You have no more gold."

Jean gestured at the twelve men before him. "These are my gold pieces. I trade them back to you—in exchange for hacquetons, mail shirts and weapons."

The lean man laughed in derision. "Keep them. We can always find more men with weak minds and strong backs."

Jean bowed slightly. "I accept the gift as evidence of your good will. In that event they are my servants. Ned!"

Ned ran with several men at his heels. In moments they were back, lengths of pitch-smeared sticks in their hands, blazing redly. They passed the torches out to the devil's apostles.

Fear was a quaver on the tongue of the merchant. "What would you, *seigneur?*"

"Burn your houses down around your ears, you miserable cheats!" Jean roared, standing in his stirrups. "When you're homeless we'll take what we want without a by-your-leave or whispered *merci.*"

A wail went up from behind the bolted shutters.

Jean leaned back against the high saddle cantle. "If you'd spare yourself the fire, come and bargain with me!"

The pitch torches hissed merrily in the spring air. Muttered words and laughter went up and down the line of men waiting in the street. Somewhere a shutter slammed, a door swung wide.

They came slowly, fearfully, edging sideways like crabs, ready to run at the first threat. Jean sat patiently, smiling faintly. He was enjoying himself immensely, and, for the first time in many years, a sense of pride in his nobility made him sit up straighter and look about him with the eye of a true *seigneur*.

When the merchants had grouped themselves about his horse, he said, "I'll be needing much armor, many weapons, and strong clothes in the near future. Treat me and my men well and our gold will flow into your coffers. Mistreat them and I'll burn Sezanne around your ears."

One or two of the townsmen nodded. They liked what they heard, but they were suspicious. They looked at Ned when The Bastard pointed him out, designating him as purchasing agent.

"One more thing," Jean murmured. "The question of damages."

"Damages, lord?"

"These servants of yours set upon me and my men. It shows a greediness of spirit that worries me. Best that we nip such greediness in its bud, before it becomes a habit. Mail shirts for all, weapons for all, hacquetons to wear under the mail. See to it."

They would have argued, but Ned brought the twelve among them, still carrying the torches, and singed beards and scorched houppelandes made the decision for their owners. Within the hour Sezanne was seeing the last of *le Bâtard* and congratulating itself upon having escaped so lightly. There were some brigands—like Henri d'Orly and Jean de Vergy—who would not have scrupled to have done what Jean only threatened.

As they paced along the forest road, Simone said, "You could have had our gold back. They were ready to give it to you, to spare them."

"Such an act would make me a bandit."

Her slant gray eyes regarded him soberly. "Oh? And what, in your pride, do you consider yourself?"

"A soldier. Or better, a French soldier."

52

He was a little surprised at his answer and wondered what impulse had made him give it. Simone only smiled as if to inner thoughts. . . .

For a week The Bastard hid himself and his men in the great forest of Brie, inspecting and assessing his cutthroats. A few were expert in the use of the long pike, and these he put to training the inexperienced among them. Two or three others knew the art of archery. These he drew aside and compelled them to practice, hour after hour.

He drove them during the lengthening spring days and into the dusk of twilight. They sweated and strained until they began to grumble openly. Jean considered this a good sign.

"Soldiers always grouse," he told Simone one evening when the campfires were burning down to red coals. "It's a kind of badge that shows when they're trained to fitness."

"They want to know what they're training for. I've been among them. I've listened to them."

He grinned and ran a hand down her back, finding her skin smooth and soft through the thin cotton tunic she wore about the camp. She sat very still under the stroking palm, aware that her loins were swimming in a pleasant lethargy and that her heavy breasts seemed bigger than she had ever known them to be.

Simone had wondered at this handsome nobleman. Not once in the days since they'd met over the dead body of her husband had he touched her flesh. Oh, he'd stared often enough—that night at the Inn of the Gray Mule, when her bodice had opened to expose her body to the navel, and once in a while in camp, when she stirred in a dreaming wakefulness on the grass cot, her skirt slipping up her thighs. But he showed no inclination to act on the fire that blazed at those moments in his eyes.

Sometimes she entertained odd thoughts about him. He was no man-lover, she knew. It was more a kind of waiting, a penance he imposed on his body, that made him hold back from the delights she was only too eager to share with him.

He said softly, "Soon now. Soon we will put all this fine training to good use."

"Are you speaking of yourself or of the men?"

53

"Of both, perhaps," he whispered, and took away his hand.

She glowered at him, not hiding her annoyance.

Two days later Ned rode into camp on the gray mare. He swung down from the saddle and came at once where The Bastard was standing at the archway butts marking scores.

"A supply train is three miles out of Baye, heading toward Châlons," the sergeant reported with a big grin. "Ten wagons heavy with armor and weapons, a following herd of mules and horses, trailed along by a merchants' cortege for protection."

Jean clapped the sergeant's shoulder.

"Pass the word, then. We break camp in moments. We'll attack just above Petit Morin, near the marshes."

The *routiers* scorned the dirt roads, knowing the forest pathways. They marched swiftly in single file. An hour past midday they were at their stations among the reeds, cold and wet but safely hidden from the most curious eyes.

The supply train was escorted by a score of men-at-arms. The bandits who preyed on town merchants and farm folk always fled at sight of armed troops, so no more than twenty were ever needed for escort service through the ploughlands of Brie and Champagne. Seven of those men fell at the first two arrow volleys. The others stood only long enough for five more to die under the thrusting pikes. The remaining eight bolted for Esternay and safety.

The wagoners ran also. Only the merchants remained to defend their wares, and these were unused to arms and the ways of warfare. Three of them died before Jean could ride to their protection, ordering his men back and away.

"Fools!" he shouted. "Have you never heard of ransom?"

They knew the word well, these ragamuffin soldiers. It was their custom to capture a rich chandler or cloth seller when they could and threaten to hang him until he bought his life with gold and silver. Ransom? Oh, they knew the word, and they savored it on their tongues like a *doucette* tart. They roared their understanding and began herding the tradesmen before them.

The loot was almost unbelievable.

54

Half a score of leather sacks contained *ecus d'or*. Two small coffers bearing the crest of the House of Barbarini were heavy with Venetian ducats. Tiny chests held necklaces and bracelets, earrings and rings, each bit of jewelry studded with balas rubies or Egyptian emeralds, amethysts or rubies. Spice castors from the Maghrib in North Africa, bound for the Flemish towns of Bruges and Ghent, *appliqué* work in gold and silver, splendid chalices and goblets. Sicilian brocades, fine cloths of Tartarus, all found their way onto the clearing before the lean-to where The Bastard sat his tree stump like a throne.

He distributed the wealth with a casual hand, tossing a priceless sable pilche about Simone's shoulders, insisting that each man accept a *capa*, which was a woolen mantle fitted with a hood, as well as the shields and daggers, maces and crossbows which had been on the pack mules.

When they were done there was armor and clothing left over for new recruits. "And new recruits will come," Jean prophesied to Simone as he watched her bundling herself to her ears in the great fur coat. "Word of our haul will run throughout Brie and Champagne and even down into Lorraine within the next few weeks. Leaderless men will come seeking a chieftain. Bands of roving brigands will tire of starving and will come here to be fed."

"And you will feed them," she murmured.

"Gladly, if they become part of my band."

Her gray eyes considered him. "For what end? To grow rich, as well you might with this beginning? Or to kill Burgundians as you and I started out to do?"

"To loot for the sake of looting would make me no more than a bandit. To loot in warfare is to distress the enemy."

She smoothed the fur with a soft palm. "You play with words to make excuses."

"I have no need of excuses."

"Every man has such a need. On what he makes excuses for, we read his character."

Jean laughed at her for a farmyard philosopher and told her to get ready to go. "We're due in Sezanne by sundown. I've ordered a tavern table to be set with wines and cheeses, veal pies, capons roasted on a spit, pastry and tarts. With the golden wine of Champagne ready to our hands."

Her mouth was open. When she saw his sly grin, she closed it with a scowl. "I'm not at all sure I want to go," she said haughtily.

"Then stay. There'll be tavern maids to rumple."

She turned at that and ran for the lean-to, yanking off the pilche. Jean studied the slim white legs which her flying skirts revealed almost to mid-thigh. This past fortnight had been something of an experiment to The Bastard. Out of a spirit of perverseness—or, remembering the Lady Alix d'Anquetonville, might it have been a guilty conscience?—he wanted no part of Simone until he had proved something to himself.

He was a military man. Ever since he'd given up the idea of tonsuring his hair and adopting the black habit of the Benedictines, his eyes had been turned toward martial affairs. And, as his thoughtful gaze looked upon French chivalry and French soldiers, he found dissatisfaction strong within him. At Beauge and again at Verneuil he had seen French soldiers flee in panic when the English merely cried, "Hurrah, hurrah!" His shame had given way to pity, after a while, that men could sink so low in their own esteem as to flee like defenseless mice before a shouted word.

As he turned from the campfire and moved between the piled bolts of Arras tapestry and wooden casks filled with oil of Valencia for sale in Flanders and England, *le Bâtard* told himself that what he did here in Brie was in the nature of a great test. He must prove to himself that Frenchmen were as good, if not better, fighters than Englishmen. Somewhere he had to find a measure which would afford him the answer he sought. He hoped to find it here with these cutthroats.

Ned came to his feet at sight of him, saluting.

"Twenty men, your best horsemen," Jean said, "will go with me. I don't expect trouble but, if there is any, give me men who won't panic before cold steel." He smiled grimly. "My trip to Sezanne is supposed to be a holiday. I won't insist on men who can hold their wine, but it would be a help."

"I'll go with you myself, lord."

"No. You'll stay in command in my absence. Find another to take your place."

"Jean, then. The Lorrainer."

The Bastard frowned. "The tall, very thin man who spoke with me the first night after I slew Pol?"

"A good man. His weapon is a cannon but—*tonneres de Dieu!*—what bandit ever used a cannon to rob?"

Jean nodded and resumed his walk, thinking of Thibaud, the old artilleryman from Neufchâteau who had a strange new weapon, according to Simone. Well, he'd go see Thibaud one of these days—but not now, not now.

A stir of noise at the edge of camp drew him. Half a dozen ragged men were shepherded toward the late afternoon campfires. They had a hangdog look about them, and The Bastard could count their ribs at a glance, but they were men. And he needed men.

"Want to join up they do, lord," an archer told him.

"We have no man to follow," one said.

"They do say in Sezanne you be the son of Satan, but we don't believe that."

"Even if you were, we'd serve wi' you for food and clothing," another added, jerking a thumb at the neatly equipped soldiers moving about the camp at their chores.

"Feed them," nodded Jean. "Feed all who came seeking service with us. They don't share in the loot we've taken already outside food and shelter. They'll earn their keep in future ventures."

Everyone looked satisfied with the arrangement. The newcomers saw hope for the future, the oldsters recognized the fact that they were not to be robbed. The more hands, the more weapons to be swung; and the more weapons they could muster, the greater would be the loot they could capture. Even clapperclaws such as these knew that much.

For Jean it was another beginning.

Candles and oil lamps made a yellow brightness in the early dusk of Sezanne as Jean swung down from his saddle and moved with Simone, swathed in her sable pilche, toward the oaken doorway of the Royal Crown Tavern. In one of the captured packs she had found a flagon of Arabic perfume and had sprinkled it liberally over the thin linen *camisa* and kirtle of bright red samite that rustled to her every stride. Her yellow hair was done up in a coronet and thrust under a high hennin, whose double veil floated behind her to her knees.

She looked very much the great lady, Jean admitted.

She carried herself well as the door swung open and they moved into the wide common room, where a number of long tables had been set, flanked with dining benches. Half the town stood here in the long room, bowing slightly as they entered. Simone smiled a path toward a table which had been placed before the great fireplace. Jean followed after her, nodding to Albert Sielieu, who owned the Mercer's Hall, to Raudolf Conte the brewster, to Anaulf Thedier the fuller, to many others thronging the tavern.

"Word travels fast when a man becomes a success," he murmured to Simone as she sat beside him on the wooden bench, the fire before them and their backs to the other diners.

"I marvel at its speed. Surely less than five hours have elapsed since we attacked the supply wagons."

"Oh, I sent a rider into town to spread the tidings. I as good as ordered the tradespeople to be here tonight." He smiled at her expression and leaned to whisper in her ear, which, as was fashionable, lay pink and exposed beneath her hennin and upbound hair. "We have more loot than we know what to do with, surely?"

"Tapestries from Arras, fine plate armor from Tours, Neapolitan linen, which is rumored the best in the world. Murano glass and much more."

"We shall sell it to the merchants."

Simone looked dubious. "What need has Sezanne and its farms of such worldly riches, even supposing they could buy them?"

"Goose! None whatever. But Brabant and Bavaria, Swabia and Franconia lie not so far to the east but that a merchants' cortege could reach them easily."

Her laughter flattered him. "You have the instincts of a thief! At another time you might have been a robber baron."

Jean sampled the jussel, a dish comprised of bread and

58

eggs mixed with herbs and broth. He said, "When we're done with the lamb, I've bidden ten of the richest to join us over berry tarts and wine." His eye touched the low-cut bodice that bared the upper slopes of her white breasts. "Distract them as we speak, Simone."

She made a little bow, which allowed the bodice to gape. "In such manner, my lord Jean?" What she saw in his eyes made her flush and touch her lips with the tip of her tongue.

They feasted on capon bakemeats and custards, roast chicken and sweet tarts. There were spiced apples and pears, and flagons filled with white Moselle and the red claret of Burgundy. Small platters heaped with ginger, columbine and paste puffs tempted the appetite when it flagged.

With the honey cakes and Champagne wine, a number of the merchants, sedate in furred houppelandes and ornate capuchins, seated themselves on the opposite bench with their backs to the hearth. Several of them chose the faldstools that serving maids brought at the run.

Jean signaled a red-headed woman to pour wine for their goblets. After they had sipped, he said, "Tomorrow five of you will be permitted to enter our camp for the purpose of assessing the price of certain furs and bolts of satin and velvet that have come into our possession."

Simone leaned forward, reaching for a tart. Jean watched the eyes turn from him toward the rounded flesh revealed in her low bodice. He said gently, "There remain certain terms of purchase to be understood, but I think in the main we can be agreed on the price you'll pay me for these goods.

"I'm no merchant. I seek no profit. I'll sell you the goods for a third their normal cost. You can resell them to Swabia and Brabant for more than triple what you pay me."

A few of the mercers asked questions, seeking to know the types of furs, their state of preservation, the quality of woven goods, the guild marks on the bolts of cloth. Jean answered from a sheet of parchment that had been prepared under the watchful eyes of Ned the sergeant.

Seeing their interest, he thrust the parchment at them and busied himself with a flagon of Rhine wine. It needed no sorcerer such as Merlin to understand the greed in their eyes as they weighed the lists of kirtles and jupons, reliquaries, jeweled goblets and necklaces. Each man stood to double his worldly wealth at the prices *le Bâtard* offered.

An older man, evidently chosen as their spokesman, nodded slowly as he folded the parchment over and returned it to Jean of Orleans. "A more than fair offer, if the goods prove as represented. It's true we take a risk in shipping them—"

"No more than normal. The English and Burgundians will be searching all Brie within the week. Before two days are gone you can be well on your way to the Rhine castles."

The leathery face of the old merchant broke into a faint smile. "You make it sound easy to hoodwink the beefeaters."

"Only because they aren't expecting it. Almost a century of subservience won't have prepared them for rebellion." Bitterness lay on his tongue. "Few Frenchmen would dare make a profit from goods stolen out from under English noses. I came hoping to find courage."

His eyes ran around the little circle of hard faces. "I believe I've found it," he said quietly, making it into a compliment.

The old man flushed. "Courage—or greed, milord?"

Jean grinned honestly. "Who cares so long as English purses suffer? If a man has nothing else to serve, he serves his own best interests. It's not how much you profit that concerns me but how much England loses."

A younger draper looked curious. "Are you so much the altruist?"

"I have selfish interests, too. We're all a pack of greedy-guts, it seems." He sighed. "Better that than white-livered cowards. *Hein?*"

They laughed politely with him, but respect was in their eyes. One by one they took leave of him and his lady, leaving them alone at table with only each other for company.

The red-headed serving woman came with a candelabrum in her hand to light their way out into the hall and up a wide stair to the upper rooms. Simone walked with faintly swinging hips, a curious smile on her mouth. Outwardly she was all serenity; inwardly she knew cold fright. She had never been to bed with a nobleman. Until this night the only man in her life had been simple Pierre, her husband. Now Pierre was dead, and the half brother of the King of

60

France was a tread behind her heels. She wondered if a nobleman made love differently than a common man.

At the bedroom door Jean took the copper candelabrum from the serving maid. Once inside, his fingers slid home the bolt. Then he carried the candles and went around the little chamber, touching the flames to the tapers and oil boats hung from the wall. The room was provided with a tall pole with a large number of spikes protruding from it. These spikes he fitted with candles, a candle to each spike; they thrust out at an angle, filling the room with radiance.

Simone watched him with wide eyes. *"Morbleu!* The room blazes like the sun. Are you expecting an attack?"

"Only by Eros," he smiled. When she looked blank he added, "The god of love. Eros scorns the darkness, which is for clods in these matters."

An eyebrow arched at him suspiciously. "You regard yourself as an expert, *hein?"*

Jean made a little bow. "As knowing as Ovid himself."

She eyed him warily, moving to the window, throwing open the casements to the late spring night. Instantly he was beside her, an arm about her middle, drawing her against him. His other hand went to the lacings of her bodice, releasing the bow. Her white breasts tumbled forward into the loosened samite.

"I need no maid to undo me," she whispered.

His mouth was fire along her soft throat. "Even the humblest maid has a tirewoman on her wedding night. This is our wedding might, *ma belle Simone.* All Sezanne regards us as *mari et espouse.* Good. We shall not prove them mistaken."

His fingers had been as busy as his tongue, Simone found. Her bodice gaped now, the laces half out of their eyelets, the thin stuff of her *camisa* little more than white mist before her bosom.

"Ma foi, how you stare!" she whispered.

She tried to cover herself but found her wrists caught and held at her sides while he looked his fill, saying softly, "So then, these are the mounds of love with which you have teased and tempted me ever since we met."

She gasped in angry dismay. "Tease and tempt? I? You? *Tonneres de Dieu!* If you think—"

His head bent, and she cried out softly in shock at the touch of his lips. Not even Pierre had done such a thing! Her hands lifted to push him away; instead her fingers closed convulsively above his head and held him to her, and she began to breathe quickly and harshly.

"What are you doing to me?" she whispered, rolling her head from side to side.

"Proving how right you were to tease and tempt. Venus herself has no such charms as these."

"Do you really like them?"

"Let me show you how much."

She whirled away from him after a moment, the thin *camisa* split to her waist, she took only two steps before she was dragged back into his arms.

"Your skirt now, *ma petite.*"

"The lights. First the lights, dear Jean."

"What? Are you knock-kneed? Bowlegged?"

"Of course not!"

"Bien. Then I'll judge your legs' loveliness with my eyes. Quickly, now. The skirt. Here, I'll help—"

"Ohhhh!" she cried, feeling the samite kirtle slip from her waist, slide down her thighs and past her knees. Now only thin linen veiled her nakedness from his gaze.

"The *camisa,* too. It's torn anyway, so—there!"

She wore only white leather brodequins now, and for once Simone wished her thick yellow hair was not coiffed quite so cunningly under her hennin but hung free and heavy, so that she could hide her milky flesh behind it. And yet Jean was looking at her nudity, not with the eyes of a man like Red Gui, but rather with the eyes of someone to whom she was very dear. Instead of animal lust she discovered awed pleasure.

Her body straightened. Pride returned to her face. "I am not so bad, *hein?* For a farm woman I—"

His hand made a motion. "Walk around, *ma belle.* Oh, go on. Modesty's all very well in a sweetheart, but in a wife it's out of place."

Simone sniffed, but she obeyed, moving to the lead-backed

standing-mirror to unfasten her hennin and veil, releasing the golden spill of her long hair. Well she knew that his gaze was fastened on her body, on the long slim legs, the curving hips and gently rounded buttocks; for an instant shame made her cheeks red, and the color spread down into her throat. Then her shame changed back to pride, pride that she was so perfectly formed and so beautiful, pride that her loveliness might so intrigue a nobleman.

Out of pride was born impishness. She swung about, using her blond hair as a veil to cover her white flesh. "Do I please my lord?"

"Very much," he murmured, striding forward.

Then she was pressed against him, her lips catching his kisses, her thighs and hips receiving the fevered touches of his palms. Swaying, they moved toward the low bedstead. Jean swung her high, fell with her onto the coverlets.

Simone clung to him. "My life, you are my life," she cried brokenly. "You are everything to me. Without you I would die!" Her voice made a broken sound as his grip on her became even tighter. . . .

Much later, when the candles were guttering and dying, Simone came out of a deep slumber, turning to rise on an elbow and stare down at this young nobleman who had become so much a part of her life. Her hand went to his forehead and smoothed back the tawny hair.

"*Je t'adore, mon cher,*" she murmured softly. "You called me wife, and wife I shall be to you from now on. This Marie Louvet whom you married—pah! She shall be nothing to you, beside me. I want you for my very own, and I'll have you!"

Her murmuring voice and her caressing fingers woke Jean to the moment. Drowsily, his arm encircled her bare waist and tugged her over against him. "What are you saying, golden one?"

"I was telling you how much I love you."

"Tell me more."

And so she whispered and stroked him while the pallid moonlight crept across the rush-strewn floor.

CHAPTER FOUR

THEY COULD HEAR the scream of a frightened woman as they paced their horses along the narrow forest pathway. Jean rose in the stirrups, straining to see the camp, which lay ahead. There were no women in the outlaw encampment. Simone rode behind him, one knee hooked over the bow of her saddle, a dreaming smile on her red mouth.

Jean lifted an arm. The dozen men-at-arms who had gone into Sezanne with him two days before came forward at a gallop, trailing him along the narrow dirt road, loosing weapons as they rode.

A gigantic roar of mirth lifted skyward beyond the last few oaks and chestnuts that hid the camp from Jean's eyes. Doubt made him slow his pace and restore his longsword to its scabbard. Laughing men were in no danger. At the very edge of the clearing he drew rein and stared.

His men had been busy. Pack mules and horses stood in a rope corral; piles of goods, with ironbound chests and panniers, made a small mound close beside them. His gaze brushed over these; it was the little group in the middle of the camp that drew and held his attention.

A fat merchant, his furred houppelande hanging in tatters from his shoulders, stood with a noose about his neck. A weeping woman knelt before him, clinging to his knees. A little beyond them, half a dozen men were crowding about a naked woman seated on top of a huge chest. From inside the chest came muffled shouts and thumpings.

Jean toed the gelding forward.

At sight of him, the men drew back in confusion. He leaned on the pommel of his saddle as he looked from one outlaw to another.

"We amuse ourselves, it seems," he said conversationally.

A one-eyed man cried out, "We intend to make them pay a ransom, lord. These men—him wi' a noose about his

64

throat and him who's locked inside the chest—are rich turncoats who serve the Duke of Burgundy."

"And these are methods you use to ransom them?"

"Aye! Tried and true they be. Free men like us use them everywhere in France. Put a husband in a chest and his wife atop it. Either he pays or he listens to the fun we have with his female. The other we string up a few times—just enough to let him choke and kick a bit—until he agrees to send for his moneybags."

"Let them go," Jean said, swinging down from the saddle.

The one-eyed man would have protested, but he saw how dark and forbidding the face of this young noble had become, and so he sighed and shrugged and made a motion with his hand. The naked woman came running to fall on her knees, catching Jean's hand and covering it with kisses.

"May the good God have you in His power, whoever you are. Yvonne de Chicault will keep you in her prayers."

"De Chicault? That name isn't Burgundian."

"I'm from Guyenne, on my way to a wedding."

Jean nodded and, lifting off his cloak, threw it about the woman. She flushed, meeting his eyes, then laughed. *"Merci. It's little enough to be stared at after what I almost went through."*

Out of casual curiosity Jean asked, "This wedding, now. Where's it taking place?"

"In Champagne where Count Philip de Basoches weds Marie Louvet at his castle on the Marne some miles below Reims."

Jean felt the world turn over beneath his mailed feet. "You said—Marie Louvet? Or did I misunderstand?"

The woman glanced at him curiously. "She's the widow of The Bastard, Jean de Valois, son of Duke Louis." The tip of her tongue touched her lips. "Do you know her?"

Jean made a slight bow. "Even a scapegrace son can have his memories. I saw her once in Valenciennes, just before her marriage to The Bastard. Now, you'll pardon my persistence, but—isn't she still married to him?"

Yvonne de Chicault made an airy gesture. "Oh, he's dead. Rode out of his estates in Dauphiné a year ago and hasn't been heard from since. Somebody brought his wife a signed parchment attesting to the fact that he was slain over a wine tun during a street brawl in Cahors. The writing paved the way for Philip."

"Ah yes. Basoches. A hothead, if I remem— if gossip speaks truth. I seem to have seen him, too, before now."

There was a coldness in Jean that reflected itself in his glinting eyes and hard, bronzed face. The woman drew away from him a step but continued to eye his good looks with a calculated coquetry. Her eyes seemed to say if *he* wanted to put her on that chest . . .

"We were bringing them wedding gifts," she murmured, studying him more closely, drawing the heavy cloak about her nudity, "when your outlaws attacked. Those others are the Sieur and Lady de Braux who travel with my husband and me."

Jean said lightly, "The gifts shall be restored."

Despite much grumbling among the outlaws, the chests and panniers were loaded back onto the pack mules and the wedding guests sent on their way. As the dust of the road to Châlons swallowed the little caravan, the grumblings burst into outright shouts of anger.

"God eat your tongues!" Jean snarled, whirling on the rebels. "Would you take five silver deniers for twenty golden *ecus?* Let the lesser go that we may take the greater! I mean to get the gifts back—together with the rest—but in my own good time."

His men fell silent, overwhelmed both by his anger and by the vision of even greater riches he was showing them. Elbows nudged ribs, and heads nodded knowingly. Their Jean was no fool. Already he had made each man wealthy beyond his dreams. Now he offered them a prospect of still more gold for their moneybags.

"Aye, lord."

"We be your men."

"Lead us is all we ask."

That night Simone crept into his arms as he lay on his tent pallet, clad only in her shift. "You're going for her, aren't you? For your real wife, the woman you love."

His hand stroked her back through the thin linen. "I go

66

to save her soul from sin. Would you have her commit bigamy?"

Her mouth captured his lips as she urged herself upon him. "Where you're concerned—yes, I would. Let hellfire have Marie as long as I have you."

"You have me," he assured her, and in the dark hours after midnight proved his devotion until Simone fell asleep with her anxiety allayed. Twice she woke to find him sleeping on her breast, twice she drew him even closer, smiling tenderly, holding him like a baby.

The Castle of Basoches stood on a high hill overlooking a land filled with vineyards and fruit trees. Below its sheer battlements the Marne flowed in quiet majesty toward Paris and the sea. From its dozen towers and a score of smaller turrets flew the black pennon of Arnais as well as the golden lions of England and Burgundy. The tiny town nestling along the eastern wall of the castle was hung with flowers and bits of gaily colored cloth.

The countryside was in a fever of excitement. Half northern France was gathering for the *fête*. There would be much feasting and all the dancing anyone could wish. Criminals would be pardoned. Strolling players would perform in the castle courtyard, then in the village streets. Wine barrels were set up in the squares and hot food dispersed to any who asked it.

It was a simple matter for The Bastard to bring his two hundred men into the village. More than fifty went as musicians who would play for the street dancing and whatever coins they might collect. Another fifty were garbed as laborers, in from the fields for a rare holiday. Some wandered by twos and threes among the wayfarers crowding the roads to the country fairs in this early summer of the year. Some posed as merchants, some as tinkers, some even as monks from some distant abbey.

Jean himself took a room in one of the village's two hotels, the Inn of the Hanging Lamp. Its wooden sign was carved to represent an oil boat, with the common brush, the symbol of the public house, hung beneath it. He had brought with him a dozen of his best fighters, and hired almost a quarter of the big sleeping room, which was fitted out with truckle beds so closely placed together that there was barely room to walk between them.

Inquiry told him there would be a series of dances in the afternoon and a feast under lanterns at night. It was during this evening supper that the wedding would take place in the great hall of the castle. Jean made his plans, then sent his dozen retainers through the streets of the little town to spread the word among his men.

For the remainder of the day, more and more retainers of Count Philip were seen standing by the wine barrels and the vats of hardier metheglin, swilling drink for drink with common laborers, with down-at-heels soldiers in search of employment, even with tinkers and ploughmen. Oddly enough, these travelers produced good silver pieces with which to pay for the wine and the metheglin. Few noticed, as they wandered off singing ribald ballads, that only the retainers of the count seemed any the worse for the liquor they had imbibed.

Nor did anyone see these servants of Count Philip lying bound and gagged, stripped of the fine raiment that bore the black stag of Basoches, deep within a glade of the nearby forest.

The viols and lutes made sweet music from the great hall dais as Philip de Basoches sampled a berry tart in the privacy of his upper solar. His castellan fussed about his eating sweets with the ceremony just minutes away, insisting that a bowl of water be brought so that Count Philip might wash pastry and jelly from his fingers.

"You spoil me, good Jacques," the count grumbled.

His castellan said nothing, only shaking his head against an inner perturbation of spirit. "I mislike the signs, lord. Less than an hour ago Old Therese cast the bones to divine your fortune. It was not good, she said. Some evil may befall before this day is out."

Philip roared with laughter. He was a big, dark man with the suns of many campaigns against the French coating his heavy face and big hands with deep bronze. "Old Therese and her bones! It's time she was retired to the corner of a hearth."

"It was Therese who found the cows when they wandered off, Therese who foretold your wound at Verneuil."

"Guesswork only. Why didn't she foresee that Marie Louvet would consent to wed me, *hein?* And that my English cousins would fall over themselves to give me rich gifts? Bah! Therese is a fraud, and lucky I don't have her burned at the stake as all witches ought to be."

The Lord of Arnais took another tart and swallowed it whole, washing it down with a beaker of red claret. He brushed his hands on the towel the castellan proffered. "Damn the delay. Where's Bishop Guillaume?"

"Moments ago he crossed the drawbridge, lord, with many of your men, who were dancing in the village."

The music changed tune, became livelier. The castellan held up a hand, tilting his graying head. "The bishop ascends the dais. I instructed Mace to play me a warning. It's time to get below. Your bride will be descending the tower stair."

Duke Philip nodded, shrugged his wide shoulders and took up the sack of gold coins which would be thrown over his head and the head of his bride at the solemnization of their nuptials. He would hand it to a page as he entered the hall. Right now it made a gentle weight in his big hand, reminding the duke of the more pleasant weight of his bride's breasts as he would caress them this night.

Marie Louvet shook out the long skirt of her white velvet gown. Impatience to have the ceremony over and done with made her nervous. The mirrors in her solar already had told her how lovely she was, with the white velvet clinging to her full bosom and slim waist, loosening as it fell away below her hips. Under the wimple, her dark eyes and full red mouth were pert with youth.

Three maidservants moved about her like hovering birds until she stamped a slippered foot. "Leave be, leave be. I look as well as I care to look this evening. God knows Count Philip thinks me pretty enough for his purposes."

She frowned, thinking of Philip.

A traitor to France, of course; everyone knew that, since

69

he fought so much beside the English lions. Yet he was vastly rich in lands and vineyards, orchards and fields of grain, with many chests of captured gold belowstairs in the castle cellars. As his wife, Marie would be one of the most important women in the kingdom. She made a wry face, remembering her other husband, that bastard boy whose tormented face still haunted her dreams.

"I was a selfish little fool in those days," she muttered, listening to the music swell into a *galliard*. "I was never a wife to Jean. Perhaps I'd be a happier woman today if I had been."

A virgin still, at close to twenty years of age, at a time when girls married at fourteen. Not an old maid, though, thanks to Jean. Her cheeks flushed as she wondered what Count Philip would say when he discovered her intact body. Secretly she dreaded this coming night in the huge Basoches bedstead. If she loved Philip, it would have made all the difference in the world.

"First Jean, now Philip," she murmured.

She wondered if she were capable of love.

The Lord of Arnais would be no boy-husband on his bridal night. He would demand his rights, would take her as he might a particularly attractive kitchen maid. She could not put him off with insults as she had put off *le Bâtard*. Very well, she would let him have his will of her and in time be delivered of a child to him. Other women put up with such a lot in life; the smart ones let their lords carry on behind their backs with the serving maids; it was enough for them that they had the title and the lands and the riches. The servants could have the man.

And yet, for all her irony, Marie Louvet yearned for love. An inner voice told her she was shaped to be worshiped by a man, given beauty to tempt and tease and then satisfy some handsome noble. When the minstrels stroked their viols before the fireplace on a long winter's night, she would listen with chin on hand, eyes dreaming of such a love. He had no face, no body; it was sufficient in her mind that he have a name. To herself, she called him Parsifal.

Parsifal, Parsifal—do you exist? she wondered. Somewhere

in this whole wide world is there such a man to make my fancies come to life?

Her tirewoman was making frantic signals with a hand. Marie smiled and bent, lifting the hem of her long skirt, and began to descend the tower stair. Once wedded, now to be married a second time, having given her heart to a dream lover; was there ever such a fool as she?

Jean of Orleans stood amid the wedding guests and watched his wife move with stately stride toward the dais where Bishop Guillaume waited beside Count Philip. There was no emotion in him other than a faint sense of excitement. His men were lurking in the shadows. Less than thirty of the Basoches retainers were here to stand against them if it should come to a fight.

Now, as Marie came opposite him, his eyes widened. He had forgotten how lovely she was! Her face was pert under her wimple, saucy and lovely, with staring brown eyes and a sweet red mouth. Ah, and her figure—how well she had developed in these years of his absence! The childish bosom had been replaced by fine full breasts that rode gently up and down beneath the white velvet bodice.

"No wonder Philip wants her," he muttered.

"Eh?" asked an old man, cupping an ear.

Jean only shrugged and tugged his swordbelt about in front so the haft would be ready to his hand. Soon now the bishop would make his challenge. He must be prepared to answer it, be prepared also to cut a swathe to freedom if he must.

Even expecting it, he was a little surprised when the sonorous voice called, "Be there any here who know of reason why these twain should not be joined in holy wedlock, let him speak now or—"

"I speak!" Jean cried.

All heads turned in his direction. It was a little like a dream with the kneeling man and woman on the *prie-dieus* at the dais swinging about, Count Philip rising to his feet as if he thought himself at some disadvantage while kneeling. Marie was staring with wide, troubled eyes—even now she did not know him, he realized—as she pressed a hand tight

71

against her heart. The bishop goggled at him over their heads.

"What's this? What's this?" the churchman cried. "You know a reason why Duke Philip may not marry this woman?"

"The best reason in the world, your grace. Her husband still lives."

Marie cried out at that, and now she rose and stood beside Philip de Basoches, staring down at him. Men and women in furred cote-hardies and kirtles drew away from this madman risen in their midst. They left him exposed to all eyes, a tall and stalwart man in Orleannaise green with the golden nettles worked into its weave. He seemed a little out of place, for his bearing was that of the soldier, and he stood amid fat merchants and lean tradesmen.

"A lie!" Philip shouted furiously. "Take that man prisoner."

No one moved, and Jean thought, My men have done their work well. The realization gave him new confidence. He took three steps forward.

"Let Marie herself say who I am. Come, my love."

Philip roared, "Henri! Jules! Disarm this man!"

Jean laughed harshly. "Too late, Lord Philip."

His men were moving out of the shadows and through the hall, turned outlaw in this moment of their triumph, stripping rings and necklaces from the wrists and throats of the ladies, jerking bulging *aumonières* from their husbands' girdles. An urge to shout out his gigantic mirth rose in *le Bâtard*. Surely no *messe des fous* could be merrier than this wedding!

Jean called to Marie once more. "Come, my sweet. Look again on the face of the boy—grown now to manhood— whom you taunted with his bastardy."

His wife seemed to shrink within the white velvet. Philip must have heard her sudden groan, for he swung on her, put an arm about her middle.

Jean was beside them suddenly, like a demon summoned up by the spells of a sorcerer. His hand caught the count, whirling him around so fiercely that he lost his balance and staggered, plunging headlong from the dais. As angrily, Jean caught the bride by an arm and thrust her ahead of him between the staring merchants.

72

"If you're this anxious for a bedding, *ma cherie*, I'll oblige you before the sun next rises!"

"How hateful!" she cried.

"Hateful, is it? More hateful than running into Philip's bed on the trumped-up evidence of a lying bit of parchment? Who paid the author to perjure himself? You? Or the count?"

She shrank away, face white before his anger. Then Jean found his attention caught and held by the raging Basoches, who came at him with dagger naked in his fist. Jean crouched, yanking out his sword; there was no time to draw it fully before the count was on him, glittering blade making an upward stab at his middle. Jean knocked the long blade aside with the tip of his scabbard and, putting out a foot, tripped the furious Philip.

As the count went sprawling, The Bastard freed his blade and touched its point to Philip's throat.

"Easy now, milord duke," he said softly. "A wrong move on your part and you'll slit your throat without my so much as moving a finger. Ah, that's better."

"Who are you?"

"Why, I thought it was plain enough. I'm Jean. The Bastard. Marie's my wife. And I have two hundred men-at-arms within your castle walls. At the moment, most of them are stuffing your wedding gifts into leather sacks, since you won't be needing them and since you are, after all, an enemy of France."

"You devil!" Basoches roared. "You byblow out of hell!"

Jean forced himself to calmness. "You'll govern your tongue, milord duke—or I'll slit it down the middle for you. My wife can name me bastard, as she has. But none other may. You understand?"

Duke Philip read the fury in those glinting eyes and fell silent. The long blade whose point was pricking his neck was as steady as his castle walls. He shuddered with frustrated rage, but he was motionless. And, after a gasping sigh, he fell silent.

Half a dozen of the outlaws had barred the great oaken doors, penning wedding guests and churchmen in the great hall. Now, as Jean brought his wife forward, those gates swung wide, permitting them to move down the stone steps into the courtyard, cleared of visitors by staves and cudgels.

Jean boosted a protesting Marie into a saddle so that she straddled it like a man. "I—I can't ride like this! Shame alone would—"

"Bother shame!" he rasped. "Safety's more important. I'll bring Philip a little way with us for protection, but I can't hold him prisoner forever in his own land. So we must ride and ride fast. Now—be off!"

His hand caught the rump of her gray palfrey, sent it at a gallop across the courtyard and out onto the cobbled road that led past the village toward Sezanne. A dozen of his outlaws rode at her heels.

Jean waited as the Lord of Arnais was dragged from his castle hall, shouting protests, and tossed across the saddle of a big white stallion. Walking toward his prisoner, Jean said, "Ride quietly, milord duke, if you want to ride a living man. I'm in no mood to play at pacifier."

For the second time within minutes the nobleman choked on his wrath, sitting straighter in the saddle, clasping the reins with only a sullen face to show his inner ferment. A day will come, Bastard, he thought viciously, when you will think back to this afternoon with regret and horror at the part you played. I swear it on the bones of Saint Denis! He toed his horse into a gallop as he followed the gray gelding beneath the raised portcullis.

They galloped until the moon rode high in the night sky. At times Jean let his cortege go on without him and sat motionless by the side of the road, listening with keen ears for the sound of pursuit. Only the night wind sighing through the heavy branches of the oak trees answered his vigil. After a little wait he would put heels to horse and overtake his companions.

Where a white milestone glowed silver with moonlight at the fork in the road, he left Duke Philip on foot. "The longer to get home, the longer to reflect on the treachery in your heart." Jean grinned.

"Remember this day, Bastard! Remember it when my time to strike has come!" Philip told him.

The Bastard pretended surprise. "*Foi!* I saved your soul

from Hell today, milord! Isn't there any gratitude in your bones?" His laughter was a goad thrust into Philip de Basoches as *le Bâtard* rode on his way with his wife and men trailing after him. Not until the cool wind blew that laughter out of existence amid the forest copses did Philip allow his muscles to relax.

He was so filled with rage he almost wept.

Simone came to the front of the tent and watched as Jean stood beside a gray palfrey, lifting his arms to a ripely rounded woman in a white velvet gown, catching her beneath the armpits, swinging her easily to the ground. They make a handsome pair, she thought, watching Marie Louvet turn and approach the campfires, walking a stride ahead of her husband.

Hatred crystallized as a thin red mist before her eyes, and Simone unconsciously lifted a hand and brushed it across her lashes. Slowly she drew back into the shadows, waiting while several outlaws came at a run to break out a coned tent from the loot kept in a storage shed and set it up.

Marie sat on a flat stone, a small and lonely figure.

Simone drew a deep breath. It was time now to get a better look at this mistress fancy-airs, to discover for herself what it was about her that caused the pain deep in Jean's eyes whenever he spoke of her. She came sauntering forward, hips rolling, long yellow hair spilling over her shoulders—she had bathed in the clear waters of the Marne less than an hour before and had donned a thin tunic for the occasion—well aware that her skirt was just short enough to show her knees and handsome calves.

As if she knew by animal instinct that a danger of sorts threatened, Marie turned on her stone seat. Her eyes went over the farm woman slowly, studying her earthy loveliness, missing neither the shapeliness of those white legs nor the thrusting fullness of her breasts. In turn, she felt herself picked apart by gray eyes that seemed to lift her bodily, pull her apart for a careful inspection, then put her back together again and drop her.

Without breaking stride Simone moved on until she stood close beside her lover, a hand resting casually on his shoulder. Jean said, "You'll keep her safe from the men."

Simone said softly, "You've been gone a week. Kiss me."

He leaned forward and kissed her soft mouth. Grinning, he whispered so that only she could hear, "Was that for her benefit or mine?"

She tried to pout, but laughed instead. "She watches you as a hawk the baby rabbit. For a woman who's as indifferent as you claim her to be, she evinces a peculiar interest in everything you do."

"She hasn't said a word since I dragged her out of the great hall at Basoches."

"It isn't a woman's tongue that speaks the truth but her eyes. When I look into them, they tell me she loves you."

The Bastard roared laughter and slapped Simone on a rounded buttock. "Get off with you, wench. Go start my supper. I'm hungry as a bear. And forget this nonsense about love. She hates me, and there's an end to it."

The blonde woman rubbed her stinging buttock thoughtfully as she walked past the flat stone. Marie Louvet was staring off into the distance very studiedly, almost as if she were blind to anything closer than the grape vineyards of Champagne. Simone sniffed and tossed her head. The noblewoman didn't fool *her* one bit. She hadn't missed the byplay between Jean and herself; now she knew they were on an intimate footing, that Simone did his cooking and that when he was away from her for a little while, he kissed her on his return. *Bien!* She would be able to add one and one, that dark beauty in the bridal gown!

She would understand that when he needed comforting, *Jean le Bâtard* came into her arms. The knowledge gave Simone a warm feeling.

Jean smiled to himself, turning to stare at the two women. They resembled strange cats walking humpbacked around each other, not knowing whether to fight or flee. He himself was a bit of fish between them to be fought over.

His shrug was disdainful. "I tell myself fairy tales," he muttered. "Marie would not fight over me. She does not want a bastard for a husband." He tried to look into her eyes, but she was too far away.

A shout roused him from his reverie.

76

A thickset redhead was moving toward him, clad in the skins of wolf and bear, a throwing spear in one hand, a longsword dangling at his hip. Behind him came a score of ragged fellows bearing an assortment of weapons.

Jean of Lorraine was running to intercept the newcomers.

The Bastard waited, positive that Red Gui did not recognize him. When the outlaw came to a halt and stood leaning on his spear, Jean saw the close-set eyes widen, the mouth fall open.

"Grâce à Dieu! You!"

Red Gui looked around him. By this time, half the camp had formed a ring about the strangers. Terror gripped the redhead, but he dissembled its grip behind a wide smile. "I've come to offer myself and my men to your service. I—I didn't know it was you doing the raiding around here or maybe I wouldn't have come."

"Thanks for your honesty. Thanks also for the lesson you teach. If such as you can walk uninvited into our camp, my sentries are asleep. Each one will have cause to remember you, Gui. Ten lashes on the back. Now be off about your business."

Red Gui lifted his spear and moved away. He took a dozen steps before he halted and snarled at the men who had come into camp with him. "You others! Come along."

One of the ragged men held out a hand to Jean. "We be clapperclaws and thieves, lord—but once we were honest peasants."

"With neat little huts to call our homes."

"The English and Burgundians changed all that."

They saw a chance to regain their lost manhood in him, Jean knew. He ought to send the twenty on their way, but, if he did, he was dooming them sooner or later to a hangman's noose.

"Stay then," he told them.

Red Gui rasped a curse and lifted his spear as if he might throw it. A dozen bows went up in the instant of his hesitation, arrows pulled far back. If he moved a single muscle to threaten The Bastard, he was a dead man. He spat and, lowering the spear, moved off into the forest with a catlike tread.

"You have an ability to rouse hate in some men," a voice

murmured at his elbow. "Philip de Basoches. Now this ragged outlaw."

His wife stood beside him, brooding silently. When she saw the surprise in his face, she smiled gently. "I was a foolish girl those years ago, Jean. If I ask you to let me stay with you as those men just asked—how would you answer me?"

"Those men need me," he told her hoarsely.

"I think I need you even more."

His eyes narrowed. "I'm still a bastard, you know."

"More than that, you're a man."

"And your husband."

Her eyelids flickered. "And my husband."

He grew aware that Simone was standing by the cooking fires, shading her eyes from the setting sun with an upflung hand, watching them. Seeing her reminded him that he had set out with this woman to find a weapon that might help France against the English invaders. The thought came to him that he had allowed himself to be turned aside from his original plan long enough.

His eyes touched Marie. "I ride to Neufchâteau in the morning. I'll have to leave you behind. I'll appoint half a dozen men as your bodyguard. They will always be with you, in teams of two, right around the clock."

The thought that anything might happen to this woman beside him stabbed pain through his chest. He said gruffly to hide his feelings, "Come along now and meet them."

At the campfire he found Simone wiping sweat from her forehead with a corner of her skirt. "We ride at dawn tomorrow to find your precious cannonmaker. After we eat you'd better get some sleep."

"I'll sleep when and where you sleep."

Her eyes were calm as they regarded him, but he caught a touch of her panic and felt a sudden flash of tenderness. His smile was gentle as he put a hand on her shoulder and squeezed. It was his way of telling her that she had nothing to fear from Marie Louvet.

The province of Lorraine was a land of gently rolling hills and long, wide stretches of farmland and vineyards. From the crowns of the wooded hills across which his hundred lances traveled at a steady jog, Jean could see the distant forests of Moselle and, this side of those firs and cedars, the little farms that dotted the countryside.

It was a world at peace, with afternoon sunlight throwing black shadows from wicket-gate and treetop. The metallic jangling of plate mail and ringbits, the steady creak of saddle leather and quilted hacquetons, struck an odd, jarring note even in his ears.

As he rode, Jean brooded.

The trouble in which France now found herself had begun close to ninety years ago at the sea battle of Sluys. Edward I of England, resenting the fact that, because of his ownership of French lands in Aquitaine and Guyenne, he owed tribute monies to King John of France, chose war instead of payment. Crécy had followed, with the Black Prince—then only fifteen years of age—standing firm against the frantic charges of the French chivalry.

After Crécy there was Poitiers, with the Black Prince grown older and more cunning with the years, fighting overwhelming odds to wrest total victory close by the woods of Saint Pierre. For a little while—after the Black Prince and Edward I had died—France fought back behind the banners of its own great hero, Bertrand du Guesclin, to achieve some measure of its former glory.

But Du Guesclin, being mortal, must die; at his death England surged again to victory, and now for many years the beefeaters had ridden up and down northern France like the masters they were of Brittany, Normandy, Ponthieu and Picardy.

All men were mortal. Only war did not die.

An anger blossomed in The Bastard that made him touch spurs to the gelding and send it careening down the road toward Neufchâteau at a headlong gallop. An order flew on the wind as his lances came pounding after him.

It was in this bitterness of spirit that he saw the dust cloud moving between a row of poplars and a small tributary of the Meuse. Reining in, he leaned his weight against the high wooden cantle. Simone came up beside him, her palfrey dancing nervously.

"There's something wrong," she told him.

"Wrong?"

"Those are cattle being driven at too fast a pace."

"I can see that for myself."

She smiled gently. "You remind me I'm a farmwoman, used to these things. No farmer in his sane mind would run his beef like that."

"Thieves, you mean. Cattle thieves in need of a lesson."

His waving arm brought his lances over the grasslands at his back. The last time he had cut across fields in this fashion it had been to rescue the blonde woman who rode at his elbow, laughing a little in her excitement. And the thieves —ragged, unclean fellows, outlaws all—were no better than Red Gui and his companions, he saw as he came closer.

They turned and fled at sight of so much armed might. Jean followed the slowest laggard, using the flat of his blade across the man's poll, tumbling him from the saddle. When a bucket of water brought the man around, he grumbled out that he and his companions had made a raid on Domremy, a little village in the Meuse valley close to the borders of Champagne and Lorraine.

"A few miles from Neufchâteau," said one of the troopers familiar with the territory. "Maybe ten or twelve."

"We'll turn farmers for the nonce, then. God knows the people of Domremy have suffered enough because of the English and their brigands without the necessity of starving to death."

A large crowd of peasants—there were a few wealthy landowners on horses among them—came out of Neufchâteau to meet them, armed with pitchforks and cedar clubs. When they learned it was not the outlaws returned to loot and ravish, their delight knew no bounds. They caught Jean and his men, pummeling them, clasping their heads between workhardened hands and kissing their cheeks.

Those who had gone out from the little village in hate and fear came back singing and shouting gleefully. Jean learned that Neufchâteau was normally not so thickly populated; more than half Domremy was here, seeking refuge from Sieur Henri d'Orly, a Burgundian knight who raided in Lorraine upon occasion. It was during his raid that an outlaw band had seized the opportunity to do a little looting on its own.

"A bad time to be alive, sire," an older farmer told Jean as he dismounted close by the watering trough of the village inn.

"Still, better alive than dead."

With Simone at his side, he moved toward a timbered inn whose high gables towered above the dusty street, whose tiny, shuttered windows seemed like grotesque eyes peering forth at the tiny shops across the way. A young girl standing beside the wooden steps was staring at him out of wide, dark eyes. Thick black hair fell to her shoulders. She was a plain girl in a coarse red woolen skirt, but there was an air about her that made him glance twice at her. He guessed her age as fifteen.

The old farmer caught the direction of his glance.

"A girl from Domremy, sire. Her name is D'Arc. Jeanne d'Arc, I think it is. Her family fled here for protection from D'Orly. Jeanne helps *la Rousse*—the red-headed wife of Jean de Valdaires who owns the inn—in her chores."

The girl turned and watched the Bastard until he moved through the inn doorway. Her eyes were soft and strangely glowing.

CHAPTER FIVE

THIBAUD THE ARTILLERYMAN was an octogenarian, but he walked with a little skip to his steps and talked with a tongue that stayed young with exercise. His shanks, revealed in baggy brown breeches, were thin to the point of emaciation, but his shoulders were wide and he had a deep chest. In his little stone cottage by the banks of the Meuse, he poured red wine of the Kronenberg vineyards into three earthenware beakers, two of which he handed to his visitors.

"*Montjoie Saint-Denis,*" he said softly and with reverence —for that was the French battle cry—and lifted his goblet.

Jean echoed his voice and swallowed.

As he set down the empty mug, his glance roamed the room, moving from whitewashed walls across the crude bedstead to the butter churn and wooden settle before the fireplace, on to an empty cradle on thickset rockers and a stool beside the spindle. The house was neat and clean. He had liked the old man at first sight. Now his liking ripened into respect.

"You fought at Agincourt?" Jean asked.

The old man cackled. *"Oui,* and before that at Navarre under Bertrand du Guesclin and again at Montiel. I carried a pike behind Du Guesclin, too, when he marched into Languedoc against the Duke of Anjou."

"And your interest in cannons?"

"—began when I saw a stone ball fall among the pikemen where I marched. Everyone around me turned and ran. I was too stupified to move. Inside my head a voice was saying, 'Thibaud, here is a weapon that can ruin any army ever assembled.' "

The gaffer shook his head and poured more wine. "I must have run, all right, though I don't remember it. At least I'm here now, and most of my fellows lie rotting in the woods of Tramecourt. I asked around about these round tubes that did such deadly work with so much noise. And I learned a little.

"The powder that makes them work from the other end of the world, in China. A man named Marco Polo brought it back with him from his travels. Powder and ball and a tube big enough to hold them, that's a cannon." He swallowed and smacked his lips with relish. "Keeps me going, this claret. I can go without food for a day but not without my wine.

"Well, now. Back to cannons. Clumsy things, most of them, mounted on wooden stands, made of wood with iron bands around 'em. Sometimes there's a wooden shield—a mantelet—on hinges to protect the cannoneers. But you know all that, I guess. You must've seen them work."

"I did at Beauge and again at Verneuil. I never thought much of them, to be truthful. English longbows, now—"

The old man slapped the wooden tabletop with a big

hand, making the earthenware beakers dance. *"Tiens!* To hellfire with your English yew bows! Cannon is the weapon. Here, look—"

Thibaud moved across the room to kneel and lift the cover of a big chest. His hands fumbled a moment, then brought out a heavy tin cube. There was no top to it, and as Jean stared down he saw that it was filled with bits and chunks of metal. He shook his head.

"It hasn't the weight of a ball. What good is it?"

The gaffer grinned gleefully. "What good is it? I'll show you, young sir."

Jean and Simone followed the old man out onto the grassy slope of a riverbank where a shed had been built, eight feet high and twenty feet long. A cooling summer breeze had sprung up to wash away the heat of August. Across the river a bed of water lilies made a green carpet. It was a perfect day, Jean thought, a day on which to enjoy the world and not to consider ways and means of killing.

He sighed as Thibaud unfastened a chain and swung open a wide door. A cannon stood inside the shed, mounted on big wooden wheels, its carriage and stock freshly scrubbed and polished. The old man patted the iron barrel as he walked around the gun.

"Come, young sir. Look your fill of her."

The Bastard was no novice in the arts of war. He understood what it was he saw. "Wheels to make it mobile. With a team of horses, it can be dragged into battle at any point a commander thinks best."

Thibaud nodded. "True, true. A traveling soldier down on his luck told me about those wheels—he'd seen them in Bohemia during the rebellion of John Ziska, with the cannons mounted on wagons. I cut and shaped this carriage, whittling out a model in wood before I built it."

Excitement touched *le Bâtard.* "Its range? Man, how far can this thing shoot?"

"Farther than a longbow."

The old man turned away and went to a dark corner of the shed where half a score of tin canisters were stored. He bent and lifted one, and the sag of his shoulders as he did so attested to the fact that it was filled with chunks of scrap metal.

Jean watched as the gaffer loaded his weapon, poured the black gunpowder, struck iron on flint and ignited his tinder. With the tiny flame he set fire to a waxed paper.

"My lord, if those water lilies in the Meuse were English bowmen, think now what might happen to them."

The water lilies were a long bowshot away. From this distance, the men who worked the cannon would stand in comparative safety. Jean nodded and saw Thibaud lower taper to touchhole. There was a flash, a deafening detonation.

The cannon bucked against the braces behind its wheels.

And six hundred yards away the water lilies erupted in shreds of leaves and stems. Water geysered upward. If a company of English bowmen had stood there, they would be lying broken and bleeding on the ground.

"Jesu," whispered The Bastard.

Thibaud eyed him with head tilted to one side. "Eh? You see what my old eyes see each time I fire my iron beauty?"

"*La petite mort!* The little death for all Englishmen!"

Thibaud nodded. "*Bien!* And freedom for all France." He said it with hope on his tongue tip.

Jean took two of the canisters in a length of sacking, together with the model of the wheeled cannon, which he strapped to his saddle pommel. From his *aumonière* he drew out a small bag of golden *ecus*.

The old man shook his head. "I want no payment. I do this for France. When beasts like D'Orly and Jean de Vergy can run free to loot and rape, then France needs all the help it can get. Take the cannisters and the model as my contribution to her cause."

The Bastard smiled. "I'll do that gladly but I'll also leave the gold. Look on it as a retainer, not as a reward. Spend your time with your cannon. Learn all you can, make notes and forward them to me. The gold will make you independent of everything else."

The artilleryman considered that, scratching his stubbled chin. At last he sighed and nodded. "I'll take it. You make me understand I'm not selling my cannon but merely taking service under the *oriflamme*. It's like going to war, in a way."

"I wish I could take you with me."

The old man cackled. "I'd come if it weren't for my legs. I can't march any more. The juice is all gone out of them."

"Everywhere your cannon goes, you go, old one."

"That's a good thought. I'll cherish it when I'm alone."

He stood before his cottage door and watched until Jean and Simone were tiny dots on the old Roman road that curved around the forest of Bois Chenu. He was seeing not the departure of a man and a woman but the birth of a lifelong dream. All his life Thibaud had fought the invaders. Now he was old. Soon he would die.

His cannon would not die. When he was rotting in the ground they would go on fighting in his name. In a way it was a kind of immortality.

Red Gui lay on his belly and drank from the cold waters of the little stream. Then he rolled over onto his back and stared up at the darkening sky. It would be night in an hour, and night was a good time for killing. His hand touched the dagger at his belt. His fingers closed on the haft and he drew the blade halfway out of its scabbard.

His dream was always the same—to find and kill The Bastard, to drive the cold steel deep into his chest so that his blood would spurt forth and he would choke out his life on the ground before the feet of the man who held the dagger. For the past month, *le Bâtard* had not been in his camp. Only this morning he had returned, he and his hundred lances and his blonde doxy.

This night, then, he would die.

It was the waiting for darkness that annoyed Gui most. For the past month he had been patient enough. Yet now—with his dream so close to fevered reality—he found impatience like a tapeworm eating away inside him. He took out the dagger and tested its point for sharpness. He polished the blade on the sleeve of his jerkin until it gleamed red where the rays of the dying sun caught it.

He tossed stones into the water. He broke off a grass stem and chewed it. He sang a little rondelet under his breath.

Finally darkness lay upon the land.

Red Gui rose to his feet, filled with vitality, with fervor. The bastard son of Duke Louis of Orleans did not know it, but death was walking toward him. He strode away from the little brook and up a ridge to its crown, then down the far slope. Red Gui began to hum, increasing the length of his steps. There was still a long way to go, and he had to gauge his arrival at the exact moment when the sentries were being changed.

There was always confusion at that moment. His eyes had watched that confusion, noting it, turning it over and over in his mind so that he might use it to best advantage.

The bulk of a stone fence fell behind him as he crossed a meadow. In the distance he could see the black stones of a ruined monastery that once had been a Roman building. Overhead the moon was rising higher.

He was much closer to the monastery now, so close he could see the reflection of moonlight on—no, hold on! That was no moonlight but a candle flame, flickering back and forth before the wind.

"A candle flame in those old ruins?" he wondered.

Red Gui was not a brilliant man, but he was sly in the manner of a wild animal. Where there was mystery there was often villainy, and he was a man used to most forms of evil. Sometimes there was even a chance of profit. He forgot revenge for greed and began to creep closer and closer to the fallen stones of the sacristan's cell.

His tread was that of a cat as he moved through the ruins. What he had thought to be one candle flame was many, all about the cloister yard. Curiosity was fully alive in him now. Who gathered here where only the birds and the squirrels ever came? And why at night and in such secrecy? There was light, but there was no sound.

He touched a coping stone, and his fingers tightened as he stepped closer. Moonlight beat down into the courtyard, adding its brilliance to the candles. Red Gui frowned. A score of men and women were congregated here, shrouded in black cloaks, whispering among themselves. Many of the candles had been placed about what looked like a stone chest, which stood in the middle of the yard. Red Gui scowled in puzzlement.

A sound made him shrink against the stones, not daring to breathe. It was repeated again, and now he knew it for the rustle of clothing. He turned his head and saw a woman not ten feet away, lifting her kirtle over her head so that her *camisa* rode upward to the middle of her firm white thighs. Then she stooped and, grasping the hem of the *camisa*, drew that upward past her pallid hips to bare her jutting breasts and shoulders. The thin linen garment drifted from her fingers as she dropped it on the fallen kirtle.

For a moment Red Gui could not breathe. He knew her, now. It was that blonde farm woman, Simone. The blood pounded in his head. He licked his lips, and his gaze ran over her nudity as she bent, lifted a black cloak and threw it about her shoulders.

Draped only in the cloak, she walked toward the inner cloister. The lurking man watched her, wondering. What in the name of the Christus had he stumbled on? Why were the men and women gathered here? Were they also naked under their mantles? He crowded close against the stones of the old cell, staring.

Simone walked toward the stone altar. When she reached it she let the *capa* fall away and stood like a silver statue in the moonlight.

A man hurried toward her, his voice hoarse with excitement. "Everything has been arranged. It is time for you to mount the altar. Lie on your back. The celebrant will be with you shortly."

Simone stretched out on the stone, feeling it cold on her back and buttocks, and stared upward toward the full moon. There was no shame in her, only a dire hunger to win the love of Jean of Orleans for herself alone. Discreet inquiries had made her aware of a defrocked priest who, for sufficient gold pieces, would conduct a Black Mass upon her naked flesh. Gold had been exchanged, a night set for the rite. There would be worshipers on hand—always there were some rebels to whom a *messe noire* would be an attraction— ready to add their voices to the chanting, their bodies to the orgy.

The touch of metal on her belly startled her.

The defrocked priest was resting a chalice on her flesh.

87

His eyes were hungry, avid of her nakedness. When the paten followed, his fingers stroked her and he smiled.

Simone closed her eyes convulsively.

The sonorous Latin phrases dripped from his loose lips as he chanted. Behind him the voices of the others made rhythmic response. The six consecrated candles on either side of the stone altar burned. She could feel their warmth as she lay there, shivering.

The uplifted arms made a V above her as the stolen Host was elevated. She had been given enough hints to know what would happen now, so she threw an arm across her eyes as if to blot out these enormities from her consciousness. It was not Simone the farm woman who lay before the excommunicate, permitting this defilement of Host and human body, but a stranger.

She moaned when his fingertips brought the Host down.

The others were chanting softly, and she knew they were staring at her and at the priest, eagerly savoring this evil intimacy. Their eyes were hungry, she knew without seeing, and their breaths choked in their throats.

The priest bent above her.

Simone gave a soft, liquid cry at the instant of contact.

The excommunicate rose and the Black Mass went on, but now there was a change in the attendants. No longer was it curiosity that gripped them, but lust—and Simone could understand the spell that this rite had held over the downtrodden through the centuries since Christ had died upon the cross. Oppressed both by royalty and nobility, the serfs and peasants turned in any direction they could for easement from their daily pains. Asmodeus alone held out hope, and to him they turned in their need.

A knife flashed. An animal—Simone had seen a young lamb tied to a sapling earlier—bleated. A golden cup caught running blood. Sacrifice had been made.

"*Sathanus magnus*, hear our cry! Hear the plea of this woman famished for love of mortal man, *Jean le Bâtard*, son of Louis, Duke of Orleans. Direct his eyes to her in love and lust, O great Beelzebub, Prince of Eternal Darkness. Give him to her as her own. Consecrate this potion which, once given, may never be used again. Hear us, Lord of Evil. Hear us!"

Simone felt coldness touch her flesh and opened her eyes. A glass vial of colorless liquid rested on her abdomen.

Her eyes closed slowly as she shuddered.

In the shadows of the ruined cell, Red Gui stood frozen with mingled horror and delight. Now at last he knew the nature of the deed he witnessed, finally understood why Simone must be naked. His eyes gloated on her nudity even as he shivered in dread of a celestial thunderbolt. Superstition was rife all over his world, and the outlaw shared the beliefs common to his fellows.

Men and animals he could fight, with sword and club, even hands and teeth if need be; Satan was another matter. How could a man fight a devil? Satan had the power of an evil god. His works were on every hand—the Black Death of close to a century before, the great famines that struck every now and again, the crippling illnesses that bent bones and bodies into grotesque caricatures of humanity. These and more were all the works of Asmodeus. A man might be brave, but he had no way of fighting sorcery.

And so Red Gui paused between desire and departure.

It was time now for the mass bacchanal. He saw a woman scream and stand, tearing her clothes away with savage hands, then fling herself into the open arms of a young man. A couple beside them were locked in a kiss; even as the outlaw watched they fell to the ground, shivering convulsively. The others, too, were hurrying to join them. He saw breasts bared to the candle flames, and slim white legs and curving thighs.

Red Gui would have liked to stay, but he was too afraid. It was rumored that Satan himself came to these revels. He had no wish to see the cloven-hoofed one face to face.

Regretfully he turned away, remembering The Bastard.

Simone had known shame and fear this night. Never before had a man looked with such eyes upon her unclad body, except for her husband and the man she loved. This defrocked priest hovering over her—bright pig eyes gleaming above an unkempt beard and loose red lips—was an unclean spirit in her eyes. The touch of his hands made her quiver in revulsion. The breath from his mouth was foul and oddly lecherous. No, no. If she had it to do over, she would never again consent to this sacrilege.

She heard the revelers only distantly, as if they were in another world. The *messe noire* was over and done. The vial with the colorless love potion was tight in her fist. And she lay naked upon the desecrated altar.

"Come, milady," the defrocked priest whispered. "Let us pay tribute to Sathanus."

Simone made a gesture of disgust and rolled off the altar, bending to lift and throw the heavy *capa* about her white shoulders. The priest was grinning at her, pulling her to him and slipping a hand under the cloak.

"If you have so much love for this bastard, you'll have a little to spare for an honest rogue."

"Judas!" she hissed, and pulled free.

She ran to her clothes, not pausing to don them but gathering them into her hands for a later moment. She ran on slippered feet through the bramble bushes, between stands of oak and beech trees, ignoring the branches slapping against her arms and face.

She was intent only on reaching the outlaw camp and safety, her hand a frozen vise on the love philter.

Jean of Orleans was restless. Twice this night he had attempted to soothe his spirits by plucking at the strings of a *gigue*, a long instrument in the shape of a figure eight, that had been taken from a Burgundian cortege three days before. And twice he had thrown the *gigue* from him to stare across the clearing at the blazing fires, brooding.

Simone was nowhere around. Marie Louvet had laced herself in her little tent. He thought of strolling down to the sheds where Jean of Lorraine was supervising the making of the cannon carriages, but he had spent the past two days watching the carpenters at work; he was sick of the sight of them.

Movement to one side of the tent caused him to swing about. Marie had unlaced the tie strings, was standing at her tent opening, gazing at the stars. He stared a moment at her loveliness. Her rich black hair was undone and hung down as far as her hips. She wore a thin shift, under which he could see the flesh tints of her body. A velvet mantle was draped about her shoulders.

As he approached her, she looked at him calmly, betraying no surprise. "My lord is restless," she murmured. "I heard you playing a *galliard*."

"Only out of boredom."

"Simone has failed in her duties, then." She smiled.

He frowned. "Simone? What duties has she?"

"To keep you amused, rested, content with life."

She spoke without animus, and, though he hunted for sarcasm, he found none. Nevertheless he said bitterly, "If she does so, it's because I have no wife to care for me."

Ah, that touched the cold lump of ice she had for a heart! Her gasp was almost angry, yet Jean knew that could not be. As she lifted her face into the moonlight toward him, her dark eyes seemed enormous.

"My lord jests. I seem to recall the Bishop of Avignon standing before us and a Provençal choir singing—"

"It takes more than Latin words and songs for marriage."

"What does it take, Jean?"

"Marriage needs a man and woman in love—so much in love they cannot bear to be apart, so much in love that the sun rises only to show them the face of their beloved and sets only that they may enjoy one another's kisses beneath the light of the moon."

Her smile was wistful. "No one ever told me this."

The Bastard scowled blackly. His hands opened and closed at his sides. "You mock me!"

She glanced at him curiously. "No. I only weep for what might have been between us. You see, I was so young—I'd read so much of love and *chivalry* that my poor head reeled from dreams of some knight cantering up on a white war horse to carry me off for his very own—that I couldn't truly appreciate you as a husband.

"You were not at all the knight of my daydreams. You were a boy, a few years older than I, but still a boy—unused to fine words with which to sweep a girl off her feet, unused to wearing armor, to being another Roland."

91

"I was a bastard."

Her hand touched his arm a moment, and Jean of Orleans was surprised to find that, where her fingers lay, a kind of wildfire was growing, leaping throughout his body. If her mere touch could cause this, what might not the feel of her naked body do to him?

Marie shook her head, smiling faintly. "It was not your bastardy that bothered me so much. It was only an excuse. It wasn't your fault you were not my dream lover. A part of me realized that. Another part—call it my womanly unreasonableness if you will—blamed you for not being everything I wanted in a man." Her shoulders shrugged. "Now that I am older and, I trust, more sensible, I recognize the fact that life and dreams can never be one and the same."

Hope leaped in his chest, a dazzling potpourri of excitement. All his life he had loved this woman, this dark temptress with the thick black hair and molten eyes and a ripe red fruit for a mouth. She was no longer the bride who had railed at him. She was a girl grown to womanhood.

"Ah, but they can," he told her. "A man and woman can make their dream, mold life itself to fit it."

Her hands touched the embroidered edges of the velvet mantle, ran up and down the cloth-of-gold stitching which so cunningly held the nettles of Orleans. "I think my whole trouble was that you never wooed me."

Her eyes lifted and let him see the depth of her hunger for romance. "Every woman likes to be won with fair words, to be made to feel she is a woman and so needed and desired by a man that without her he is nothing. You never spoke such words to me, Jean. I resented it. You let the Duchess Yolande select me as your bride. Never once did you tell me you loved me."

"It was understood," he said slowly. "We were young. Valentina Visconti had sheltered me, practically raised me from childhood. I only obeyed her."

"Yes, I know. Perhaps that's what I objected to. You married me out of obedience and not desire."

His hand caught her arm and whirled her, brought her up against him as he stepped inside the tent. The flaps fell into place, hid them from all eyes as his arms caught her up and

92

crushed her softness to his body. His mouth devoured her lips. For one wild, pulsing moment he felt her lips yield and open. Against his body her soft loins were a gentle cradle as her breasts pressed against his chest.

She was scented, panting womanhood in his arms. No dream of her had ever given him this mad ecstacy, this delirious pleasure. His heart sang in delight as his hands slipped under the velvet *capa* and along the thinly covered hips.

Then the soft mouth he was caressing tore itself free. A palm came up to slap hard against his cheek. Panting and flushed, Marie Louvet tore loose from his arms.

"Am I your farm woman to be treated so?"

"God in heaven! You said—"

"I want to be wooed, not ravished!"

His harsh laughter rose into the tent, filling it with bitterness. "Marie! Marie! Are you still a child? Don't you know what love is between a man and woman? Or was Philip of Basoches as laggard a lover as I seem to be, where you're concerned?"

"You dare say that?" she whispered.

She would have struck again but his hand clamped her wrist and held her still. Above her proud face he smiled bitterly. "I dare. Aye! I dare say also that you are no true woman! You're a weaver of childish dreams, afraid to face reality. I want no part of you."

His arm hurled her from him so hard that she stumbled and fell on the hard dirt of the tent floor. He left her there, crumpled amid her linen and velvets, staring at him with dismay and anguish etched on her lovely features.

In rage and fury The Bastard swept back to his own tent. A hand that trembled in anger tore open the tent flap. Clenched fingers balled into a fist that was lifted and shaken in bitter disillusion.

Almost at his thigh boots, a coverlet of rich Lille cloth lifted into the air. Jean saw a dagger and an arm in a torn brown sleeve thrust from the heavy robe, the dagger aimed for his chest.

A man less shaken by emotion might have taken that length of steel full in his heart. The Bastard was so beside

93

himself with virulence, however, that he saw only a chance to relieve his pent-up fervors.

His upraised arm swung like a club. It hit the wrist of the dagger hand, numbing it with the force of the blow, dislodging the dagger so that it flew through the air. Jean thrust both hands at the man hidden in the coverlet. His powerful fingers closed down like clamps. He swung the man off his feet, this way and that. He drove his clenched fist where the face was hidden, again and again.

It was not often that The Bastard gave way to such a paroxysm of fury. Nor was it the hidden assassin he struck so often with a big fist, viciously and in the need to hurt and maim. He was striking at his wife, at Marie and all the lost years of their youth.

They could have been so happy!

When the man fell and lay unmoving on the ground, Jean bent, lifted him and hurled him outside the tent. Then he swept away the coverlet.

Red Gui had been battered to insensibility by that mad onslaught. His nose was broken—it lay split and bloody above a torn gash of mouth—and his eyes were blackly swollen. The Bastard stared down at him, then threw back his head and laughed harshly.

Men were moving toward him from all sides. They stared from Jean to the red-headed man in fright and awe.

"Lash him!" roared Jean. "Tie him to a tree bole and lash him fifty times. Then pin a parchment above him which is to read, 'Thus does France treat its assassins!' "

Marie had come to the front of her tent, staring.

Simone was in the shadows, breathing fitfully. Deliberately, knowing his wife was watching, Jean crossed to her and put an affectionate arm about her shoulders.

"I missed you, Simone. I find myself lost when you aren't around. I don't like to be so dependent on a woman, but, since I must be—never leave me for so long again."

Simone flashed Marie a triumphant smile. Her fingers held the vial against her heart. Now—this night—was the time to pour the philter into his wine. Now—as his hand slid up and down her back, patting her affectionately—she would fill his goblet with claret and aphrodisiac alike. Then he would belong to her alone, and the glances he had cast at Marie during this last week would be a thing of the past.

"I only went a little distance to say a prayer for you, milord," she told him, letting his hand on her hip urge her toward their tent.

"Devote yourself to me in the future," he smiled.

At the tent opening he bent and kissed her soft throat. Simone accepted his caress with backflung head, smiling lazily, letting her blood stir to life, knowing Marie Louvet stood with a hand clenched on her tent flap, eyes wide with jealousy. It might be that she did not need the love potion, Simone told herself. The Bastard seemed aflame for her this night. Yet she would take no chances.

While his back was turned, inside the tent, she emptied the philter into a silver tankard and filled it up with wine. Then she turned and brought it across the hard dirt floor to him, offering the goblet with both hands, holding it while he sipped so that his own hands could begin her disrobement.

First he loosed the strings of her cape, then the clasps of her pale blue kirtle, thrusting it down to her hips. His fingers explored the thinness of the sendal *camisa*. The wine and the love potion and the touch of fingertips roused a demon in his body.

Yet, even while his fevers demanded that he satisfy himself with this blonde woman, The Bastard continued to dally. He took the goblet from her so that he might drain its contents even as she set about removing his own garments.

"Come back here," he cried hoarsely when she went to extinguish the oil lamps. "Let them blaze until morning. Let me see your beauty, drink its fill with my eyes."

"Lord Jean, you speak too loudly. Your wife—"

"Let her hear, if she will. Let her listen to the way a man may love a woman! Are you ashamed?"

"Say, rather, I'm proud you love me."

"*Bien!* Then come and listen to me praise your charms, one by one, slowly and with kisses and caresses. Let me love you as a woman should be loved!"

There was a madness working in him, Simone knew. She wondered if it were the effect of the love potion. But, madness or sanity, she did not care. All she knew was the touch of his mouth on her flesh, the tenderness of his hands as he drew her toward him.

If he wanted Marie Louvet to learn how much he loved his farm woman, then let her listen! His wife would know once and for all that The Bastard belonged to Simone alone and that she would not share him.

They stood in the middle of the tent, kissing and stroking one another. Simone grew pleasantly flushed at his words and the fire of his kisses. It seemed that he was branding her for his very own—as craftsmen in precious metalware indented their reliquaries and chalices with the guild stamp—that his every caress was a mark burned into her flesh for all eternity.

As they toppled onto a heap of piled cushions, she cried out thickly, knowing Marie would hear and understand the pleasure he was bringing her. She wanted to scream out her triumph but found her lips caught by mouth of her lover, her words silenced in the wild flood of animal passion.

And even as the burning lips of the farm woman crushed against his, Jean realized with uncanny insight that he was using Simone as he had used Red Gui—as an outlet for the fury and the fevers that Marie Louvet had roused in him this night. Aye, he loved the blonde woman! Aye, he meant each word he spoke! But there was no ecstacy in his soul, where it counted most.

Book Two: *The Warrior*

CHAPTER SIX

MONTARGIS was a small city that lay fifty miles northeast of Orleans, astride the road to Paris. It commanded the approaches to that city and to the provinces of Touraine and Anjou. On every side it was surrounded with thick forests of oak and birch, with occasional copses of beech and hornbeam. In ancient times it had been a fortified city. Now it was famed only for its Church of the Madeleine.

Grouped at a little distance from the city walls stood the massive *trebuchets* and catapults of the English army. Behind them were rows of tents, wet now and bedraggled from the recent rains, with limp pennons attempting to flutter in the slight breeze. A group of men had detached themselves from the tents and were pushing and heaving at a long, low shed that held a battering ram.

An indentation at the base of the wall closest to the ram showed where it had been pecking for the past few days. A tiny pile of rubble lay across this section of the moat, which had been filled in with felled trees and wagonloads of dirt and refuse to make a path for the ram.

Two men sat their high-peaked saddles, out of sight of the English camp, on the crown of a ridge more than a mile from the city itself. They wore plate armor covered over

97

from hip to shoulder with velvet jupons. On the green jupon worn by Jean of Orleans, golden nettles were embroidered. On the other, quartered on fields of blue and black, lay the peacocks and vine stocks of Vignoles.

"Well?" asked The Bastard impatiently. "Why wait?"

The other man grinned wickedly. Étienne de Vignoles, Marquis of Vignoles in Gascony, was one of the foremost soldiers of France. A tall man with huge shoulders, he was known affectionately as La Hire. His popularity with the common folk was exceeded only by his power with lance and sword. He beat a mailed fist on a thick thigh.

"Why wait, he asks! Why wait—when Frenchmen have not defeated Englishmen in battle for more than thirty years! Why wait—knowing those beefeaters' yew bows can cut our lances to shreds!"

Jean laughed and said, "I brought you cannon, Étienne. Forged in the furnaces of Troyes, mounted on carriages built to my own specifications. With cannon, we can destroy anything."

"Not English bowmen."

"Aye, even those. I know it here!" His hand struck his velvet-covered cuirass above his heart. "I have been gone almost a year, searching for a weapon with which to fight the *godons*. Now—for love of *le bon Dieu!*—give me a chance to use it!"

La Hire gloomed at him. "If Montargis falls, Orleans falls!"

"I know the risk. Give me the opportunity."

"Why bother to ask me? You command here as well as I. Take your cannon and your men. Attack."

The Bastard laughed harshly. "By methods such as these our fathers lost France. Divide our command—and fail! Unite—and win." His voice almost pleaded, so intent was he on his argument. "Together, Étienne! Not La Hire for glory, nor *le Bâtard*, but together—for the glory of France!"

La Hire grunted. He was thickset and in his late thirties. Gray hair mingled with black on his large head, but his eyes were young and his smile was as youthful as his eyes. He asked slowly, "What's your plan?"

"A diversionary attack in force with lances and men-at-

98

arms to draw them away from the city. When we have them lined up for battle—*voilà!* Then we introduce our cannon to the beefeaters."

"Your artillerymen won't get near enough to use them. English arrows will pick them off, one by one."

"I'll scatter the bowmen with my cannon."

The older man widened his eyes. "You talk madness. How can a few round balls break the longbows? No, no. I can't believe it."

"If I fail, Montargis falls. As does Orleans. I risk more than you, milord. I risk my city, my people. Well? What's your answer?"

The wind whipped at their close-cropped heads, bared to the morning sunlight. Their huge helms lay thonged to their saddlehorns. La Hire stared across the little valley toward the city. Even from this distance he could see the white dust that told where the ram was beginning its deadly work. He sighed and nodded.

"Unless we do something, Montargis will fall anyhow. I like your plan as well as any. No risk, no gain. I just hope these cannon of yours will do half what you boast they will."

Jean laughed lightheartedly. "A wager, milord. My war horse against that Savoyard dagger your wear at your belt."

The Gascon chuckled. "The horse is worth a thousand daggers. You must be sure of yourself. Even so, I'll wager—mayhap to teach you not to bet on losing ventures."

They touched mailed toes to their mounts and galloped side by side down the ridge and toward the forest road that had hidden their approach. Beyond the forest was their own encampment, where a thousand men, under the peacocks of Vignoles, lay with the three hundred men and score of cannon The Bastard had brought from Brie.

Fair hair and dark hair, they rode between the standards into camp. Men paused from their polishings of weapons to shout greetings and to exchange jests, for these men were popular with their followers. As The Bastard had fought at Verneuil and at Beauge, so La Hire had swung his sword at Agincourt and Beauge. Gossip was all over the camp because of the twenty shed-enclosed cannon that had come along the Villeneuve road with Jean of Orleans. They were cannon sent from heaven and blessed by the warrior-saint Martin, rumor had it. A few agnostics claimed they had been forged in hell. In heaven or in hell, they would be accepted could they defeat the hated English.

They dismounted before the commanders' tent. La Hire walked with a limp, suffered when a tree had crashed on his leg before the battle of Mons-en-Vimeu, but his hand rested on Jean's shoulder in good-fellowship rather than for support.

"Your blonde wench watches from your tent," he said to Jean. "She never lets you out of her sight, does she?"

The Bastard chuckled. "I found her in Picardy two years ago. She's brought me luck. And she gave me the cannon."

"What of your wife?"

"I sent Marie on to Chinon. What use is a wife who slaps when you kiss her? But enough talk of women. Send for your esquire. I want to see the maps of Montargis and pick as flat a meadow as I can for the battle."

Jean hurled a hundred lances at a corner of the English camp that afternoon, following it up with a rain of crossbow quarrels. There was little damage done on either side— only an unlucky Englishman was killed when a spent quarrel caught him in the eye—but the attack served notice on the Earl of Salisbury, who commanded the foreign forces, that his seige of Montargis was not to be continued without a fight.

Scouts reported to Jean and to La Hire that the English were readying themselves for combat on the morrow. Their campfires were lighted. There was the sound of sledges on lance point and sword tip, and the supply wagons were trundling along the dirt roads at all hours of the night.

"Good," nodded Jean. "Salisbury takes the bait."

La Hire grunted sourly. "By that you mean he hastens to destroy us. I don't like it. I don't like it at all. To put our dependence on those pieces of iron with holes in them—devil's work, all of them!—is to deny the strength *le bon Dieu* put in our hands and arms."

The Bastard smiled grimly. He was at his ease in an X-chair in their big tent, munching lazily at a tray of Burgundy grapes, wearing scarlet velvet jupon and hose of scarlet and green. He looked the figure of a citified dandy—a foppish gallant rather than a general—with close-cropped yellow hair and a neatly shaven face, stained a deep bronze by the summer sun.

"Étienne, you worry too much."

"*Tonneres bleu!* You don't worry at all."

"I find no need of it. My plans are made."

"And you're satisfied with them?"

Jean lifted a heavy bunch of grapes and studied it. "I hate the English. I hate them almost as much as I hate the men who slew my father. If it were not for those beefeaters, my father might still be alive, since the Duke of Burgundy was their ally. Yes, my good La Hire, I am satisfied with my plans."

His fist caught the tabletop. His eyes blazed with inner fury, which, until this moment, he had kept hidden. "I'm satisfied because those plans mean victory. The first victory in over thirty years! Think what that will mean to France."

La Hire scowled sceptically. He had seen these young hot-heads before, just before the battle. Always they were confident of victory. He himself was a realist. He knew the French would be defeated, but he planned to salvage something from the campaign. There was a red-headed barmaid at the Inn of the Three Roads. Twice now he had promised to send for her and fill her hands with golden deniers.

Tonight would be as good a time as any.

Étienne de Vignoles was a good man, as good men went in his day. Yet he believed that a man was entitled to recreation, especially when he went off to war, which was almost all the time for La Hire.

And so the tavern wench came to his tent, had her palms filled with coins and herself with a surfeit of love. She lay naked amid the rumpled coverlets of the crude tent bed, letting La Hire amuse himself as he would with her pallid flesh, her eyes half closed in drowsy languor. Through the tent-flap slit she could see the redness of the rising sun. The night was now almost gone, and yet she had not slept. Nor had the nobleman.

"Jean is a madman," he whispered, kissing the tip of a

101

heavy breast. "A sadly befuddled person. He thinks we can beat the English."

"Mmmm," mumbled the girl, who was exhausted.

"He conceives that cannon can replace people."

The girl snored. La Hire smiled and whispered, "I'll stop by at the inn later, *ma cherie*. On my way from the battlefield, while I'm running from the beefeaters."

Lord Salisbury ordered out his pikes and longbows as English pikes and longbows had been ordered into battle formation since the days of Edward I. First the pikes and then the bows, with the lances forming a reserve. Such tactics had worked twelve years ago at Agincourt, eighty years before at Crécy. What had worked then would still work, against these Frenchmen. Some men would call the Earl a conservative. He liked to think of himself as a military expert.

"Expert because he knows we can't whip such strategy," La Hire grumbled into his closed visor, letting his war horse dance off its energy, cursing his exuberance of the night before. "Nor can we."

Le Bâtard had gone to sleep early, with Simone still fussing with his cushions. He was light-hearted as a boy, and his laughter rang out again and again, much to the exasperation of La Hire, who was feeling his sleepless night.

"Watch, *mon ami*. Watch and marvel!" Jean made answer.

With tongue-in-cheek gravity, The Bastard ordered out his lances, as other French commanders had done since the days of King Philippe IV. Only a few saw him lean across the tall horn of his saddle and give orders to an esquire.

In response to those orders the twenty covered cannon, which had trundled in his supply train all the way from the Brie forests, began to move. Each cannon was drawn by four horses, so they made good time across the flat meadowland. Slowly they approached the French lances and merged with their formation.

The waiting English paid no heed to this score of sheds advancing on them. It may be doubted that they noticed them at all. Pikemen were digging in their butts to repel horsemen who might slip through the arrow hail. Archers were

102

thrusting long shafts into the ground in a circle about them, for easy reaching. These men were veterans; they had faced French lances before; they were ready to kill once again.

Only La Hire noticed that the French battle line moved almost within arrow range without breaking into a charge. A spirit of friendship moved him to give advice. "Order your charge now, Jean. Or your men cannot muster enough speed to break the English pike line, assuming they ever reach it."

"No, not yet."

The Bastard lifted a mailed hand. Sunlight glinted on its scales, and in answer to that flash of light a trumpet brayed. The French lances opened a score of lanes through which the cannon sheds bumped and trundled.

Now the cannons were within arrow flight of the English. The horses were unhooked, and trotted to a safe distance. The shed doors opened. Twenty cannon muzzles stared across the meadow at the waiting pikes and bowmen.

An archer from the fen country, who had faced French cannon before, said with a laugh, "The Armagnacs have gone mad! What damage can they hope to do with those things? They're too close to harm us—and too far away to kill our officers."

The soldiers all around him laughed.

Men ran to the cannons with lighted tapers, held them to the touchholes. They poised like that an instant before the gunpowder flashed. The cannons roared and bucked. Twenty sheets of flame ran out of the muzzles toward the English.

There was a hiss of sound in the air, and, where the hiss went, there went red death. Pikemen and bowmen fell as if poleaxed. There were no cannonballs, only this hiss of sound and the frightful wounds of the dead and dying as they fell. A wail of terror rose from English throats.

Sir Thomas Morton rode down from the high ridge where Salisbury commanded. "Close ranks, close ranks!" he shouted. "If the French lances charge now, we're done for."

Obediently those veterans from Lincolnshire, Sussex, Westmorland and the Cinque Ports country stepped forward, straight into the metal teeth of a second cannonade. Men

103

went down, some silently, some screaming in agony. Sir Thomas Morton fell with his horse at that first blast.

Another knight rode down with orders.

For half an hour the English stood up to that steady pounding before their courage failed; by this time they had learned that instead of cannonballs the French were firing little chunks of metal, and they milled in confusion. Pikes mingled with bows, and half a dozen mounted knights came with flailing swords to attempt to restore a semblance of order.

The Bastard lifted his arm. "Now, Étienne!" he shouted. "Now is the time for the charge!" His arm fell, and four hundred Frenchmen in heavy armor drove spurs into their caparisoned horses and pounded across the meadow.

Lances lowered. Each lance was tipped with a foot of solid steel, and those steel points drove through armor and quilted hacquetons into quivering flesh beneath. Swords and maces came free, lifting and falling as the lances pushed their first onslaught to the point of carnage.

Étienne de Vignoles stared with bulging eyes. His mouth was open inside his helmet. To see better, he lifted the visor as if in disbelief.

"Sweet Jesu on the Cross," he breathed. "It cannot be. It is a miracle! Never have I seen such a thing in all my days." The thought came to him that he might be seeing history made.

The Bastard clouted his armor plate with a mailed glove. "I told you, *hein?* I predicted what my cannon might do to these beefeaters. You would not believe me."

La Hire looked at him as if he were a wizard.

That night in an upper room of the Inn of the Three Roads, Étienne de Vignoles marveled even more at the French victory. The red-headed barmaid was serving him claret in a leather jack while he lolled at his ease on the bed.

"It makes The Bastard out a hero, of course," he told her. *"Ma foi,* what a hero! To engineer the first French victory since Du Guesclin's time? His name will be on every lip—his name and his cannon."

He sipped the claret with relish. "I wonder if he serves

the devil? Could that be it, *ma petite?* Has *le Bâtard* sold his soul? He isn't saint enough to get any help from heaven."

His arm hooked the girl about her waist and tumbled her onto the coverlets beside him. When she squealed with laughter, he kissed her. "He'll have to go to Chinon where the Dauphin holds his court, naturally. They'll want to make a big fuss over him. It's like having a hero in the family. After all, the king's his half brother, according to the gossip."

La Hire slipped a palm beneath the wool skirt, discovering the softness of the tavern woman's thigh. "And the English? What will they think about the day's doings, do you suppose? They'll try and get Jean excommunicated, of course. The beefeaters won't believe his cannon is a new kind of weapon. They'll swear he serves Satan, being too proud to admit somebody might have thought of a way to overcome their longbows."

When she caught his hand and held it, he laughed down at her. "All right, all right. You need more wine, I can see that. And you're still tired from last night. I am, myself. It's a good thing I didn't have to do much fighting today other than brain a dozen fleeing Englishmen with my axe. The cannon did all the work for us."

His hand stabbed for the wine jack. "The Dauphin will have a *fête* to celebrate. We'll all be there, Jean and I, his farm woman and his wife. It ought to be an interesting time, *hein?* A hero to his country, a nothing to his wife. It's amusing, isn't it?"

The tavern woman wriggled closer to the big, hairy bull of a man. "You talk too much, *cheri.* Kiss me."

"In good time, in good time. Oh! Well—if you feel that strongly about it— Here, move a little so I—that's better. You women of Touraine think up the damnedest positions! Easy, curse it! I'm still thinking about those cannons!"

The Bastard rode into Chinon at the head of an army decked with flowers and scraps of gaily colored cloth. He rode alone—La Hire was asleep in a two-wheeled cart—and he made the most of his opportunity. His golden head was bared to the late summer wind above a green mantle thick with golden nettles. Against that background his armor shone

105

like silver in the early morning sunlight. His longsword clanked gently to every rhythmic stride of his horse.

He was young Mars, and Chinon accepted him as such.

The Dauphin waited on a garden balcony of the Palais, an ugly young man with a receding chin and an over-prominent nose. His legs were spindly and faintly twisted, the result of a childhood ailment. His homeliness was made more evident by the good looks of his courtiers and their ladies, his personal poverty more apparent by the costliness of their cote-hardies and the patchwork on his own.

Jean went to a knee before him, bending his head.

"It is I who should kneel to you," the Dauphin said wryly. "My advisers tell me you've won a great victory and, because of this, my throne is a little more secure. I thank you, cousin."

"Thank my cannon, sire. All I did was place them before the English."

"You saw opportunity. That takes genius, of sorts. At any rate, know that we are grateful. The palace—all Chinon, for that matter—is yours. Now rise and walk with me a little way in the gardens."

Jean towered a head above his future king. In his armor and rich cloak he was an odd contrast to the man rumor named his half brother. The Dauphin was poorer than any man in his retinue. His clothes were patched; short months ago he'd had to borrow money to put poulaines on his feet. Such poverty amid the wealth of his nobles reflected itself in his humility.

"Do you think we will ever be free of them?"

"Montargis was a victory, sire. It takes many victories to win a war. When that war has gone on for a hundred years, who knows how many victories must be won?"

"I'll never live to see France free."

"Ah, there I must differ with you. Montargis was only a victory, but it was also a beginning."

The Dauphin brightened. "Do you really think so? If I could but adopt your courage, Jean. Always you see things in a roseate light. My eyes must be blind to gay colors."

They stood before a marble bench that bordered a stone fountain. The splashing of the waters made a soft backdrop to their conversation. The Bastard said, "France needs an ideal, Charles. An ideal in which to put its hope and trust. You might be that ideal."

The Dauphin laughed harshly. "I'm too ugly to be anything so revered. You, now—the army would follow you."

"The army, yes. France needs more than an army. It needs something the people can believe in so they'll be lifted out of their misery."

"You ask for miracles."

"La Hire said something like that a few days ago when he saw what my cannon could do. I'll pray you get your miracle as he got his."

Charles thrust out his thick lower lip. "There's been talk of a holy girl from Lorraine, someone named Jeanne. She may be this ideal we need."

"I'd like to think so."

"Speaking of girls, your wife is still in Chinon."

Jean looked surprised. "Marie? Now what particular bee is buzzing in her bonnet?"

The Dauphin smiled gently. "I understand she seeks her husband. She seems to have fallen in love with you, according to the story she tells. You saved her from Basoches. In doing so you played Lancelot to her Guinevere, with Basoches in the role of Modred."

The Bastard was not amused. "Say rather, Troilus to Cressida."

"Cressida betrayed Troilus in the end."

"You catch my meaning, sire."

The Dauphin rose from the bench to put a hand on his cousin's arm. "Jean, Jean, don't be so proud. Go to her. See what she wants. Unbend a little, even if you have to take off that armor that so becomes you. I fancy that to win Marie's love, you might do more than that."

"If I could so much as hope, I'd doff everything."

"In time you may yet do that."

They laughed together and continued their stroll.

Gaily colored pennons flew atop the challenge poles, announcing that the finest knights in France were gathered here on the Field of the Thousand Roses to do honor to the

Dauphin and the signal victory of Montargis. Already the judges had arrived in the old castle of the Plantagenets, passing through the great gates followed by the armor bearers and the townsfolk, who were out to make holiday at such an event. The inns and taverns of the town were hung with the boards and banners of the competing knights. The lists and viewing stands were in readiness.

In the great gallery, the courtiers and their ladies were gathered to review the helms, those massive helmets decorated with carved beasts and embroidered mantlings, which would be worn by the competing nobles. Poles slanted outward from the cloth counters on which the helmets were displayed, bannered by the devices of the jousting knights.

In rich houppelandes of samite and velvet the ladies of the court walked with their lords, commenting on one helmet or another, wondering if a complaint would be made against any knight entered in the tourney so that the four judges might disqualify him. More than one pair of eyes was slanted at Marie Louvet, who walked alone amid the throng, head held high, green velvet kirtle swishing to her stride. She wore only one ornament, a life-size nettle of gold hung on a chain about her throat.

"She pines for The Bastard," some said.

"Aye! See the nettle of Orleans nestled on her bosom."

"Jean busies himself with the farm girl."

"A beauty, that one. And note the way she dresses!"

Simone was at the elbow of *le Bâtard*, resplendent in cloth of gold gown with the high cone of a veiled hennin atop her blonde tresses. The golden motif repeated itself in her hose and slippers. It was admitted by all that she was the most beautiful woman there. In her fashion she might be copying that other famous beauty, *le dame d'or*, mistress to the Duke of Burgundy. A pity she was not of noble blood, men murmured; then she would be certain to be named queen of the tourney.

Simone herself aspired to no such honor. It was enough that envy gleamed in the eyes of other women, desire in the eyes of her knight. By being beautiful, she did honor to Jean of Orleans; for her, this was enough.

When she saw Marie Louvet alone before the great helm of The Bastard, Simone went to stand beside her.

"A pity he can wear only one favor," she murmured, "and that he has already chosen a length of golden cloth torn from my kirtle."

Marie flushed. "I've no right to expect him to wear anything of mine," she murmured. "I was never really his wife."

Simone pursed her lips and looked shrewd. "Jean tells me the same thing, but my eyes have seen the way you two stare at one another—when you fancy no one can see you—and sometimes Jean dreams at night and cries out your name."

The smaller woman opened her eyes wide. "He does? Even when he sleeps with you?"

The farm woman went red and tightened her lips angrily. "I'm honest with you. I love Jean. I sold my soul to win him. I'll do even more to hold him. I just wanted you to know."

Marie shook her head. "You could have saved your breath. To me *le Bâtard* is still a bastard. I wish you well of him." She made as if to pass by the blonde girl, but Simone put a hand to her wrist and held her.

"Perhaps the stag visor would interest you more than the nettled one. Basoches made his peace with the Dauphin, and has been invited to take part in the tourney."

"Philip? Here in Chinon?"

"If you hurry, he might agree to wear your favor."

Marie looked grim. "Orleans green against cloth of gold?"

Simone shrugged and let her hand fall away. Marie moved away with a firm step but hesitated when her eyes fell on the stag device of Basoches. Simone saw her hand reach out and move over the tilting helm, as if in caress. Slyly she turned and glanced back at the farm woman.

There was a bold challenge in her stare.

The tourney was to be conducted according to the rules laid down by Geoffroi de Preuilly 'over three hundred years ago. There was to be a *grande mêlée* in which fifty knights on either side were to do battle in the name of the Dauphin and the Duke of Alençon. The knights fighting for the Dauphin —The Bastard was among these—wore a mantling bordered with lilies on their helms. The others carried a scarf embroidered with the Alençon arms. They stood now facing one another across the gaily colored ropes, horses dancing restlessly, saddle leather creaking faintly, armor beginning to get hot under the bright September sun.

A voice roared, "Sever the ropes!"

A dagger sliced downward, cutting swiftly.

As one man the combatants surged forward. Swords clanged and maces thudded home on upraised shields. In the *grande mêlée*, it was side against side, but the victories of each man were kept by the judges, working with a number of assistants, and one man eventually would be declared champion.

The stands cried out with one voice as Hectoire de Rochemont unseated the old Count of Foix with a wild swing of a battle-ax. La Hire bore down two men at once with a sidewise sweep of his longsword. The Bastard fought carefully but steadily, with little flamboyance in his manner of wielding sword and shield; old soldiers watching him were seen to nod and say that in such fashion was Du Guesclin wont to fight, and, as all the French world knew, there was no greater fighting man than Bertrand du Guesclin.

For the honor of the Duke of Alençon, a dark knight from Brittany—Giles de Raiz—struck many savage and heavy blows. He was followed closely by the young Lord of Arnais, Philip de Basoches. Stirrup to stirrup they ranged the field, smiting hard and often, and where they fought, only riderless horses were left to oppose them.

The sun rose higher into the sky, and now the heat was a torment inside the heavy armor. Men fainted from exhaustion on every side. The fifty became thirty, then ten, then five, on each side.

When Gaston du Caumont clashed from his saddle before the mace of Giles de Raiz, La Hire rode fast to meet the man from Brittany. Jean of Orleans found himself opposed by two men at once, Basoches and a knight from Provence. At that moment the fifth and last man of the force of the Dauphin was unseating his opponent with a backhand swing of his mace. Free, this knight rode to engage Basoches while The Bastard fought the Provençal.

Jean was near exhaustion himself. Sweat ran in rivulets from his forehead and armpits. The world reeled and swayed through his visor slits. One moment he would see the sable shield of his opponent, the next he would be staring at the stands, wondering whether his last sword swing had unseated his opponent. Then a crested helmet would appear, and Jean would lift shield, raise sword and jab spurs to his mount to ride to the attack.

His sword edge clanged home on a shield rim. He struck again, and yet again, hard, jarring blows that shook his arm to its socket. On the third blow his blade bit into the crested helmet. The Provençal swayed wildly.

Le Bâtard rasped, "A nettle for victory!"

His horse hit the other horse with its shoulder just as his blade was in mid-swing. Rather than risk a disqualification, Jean jabbed in his spurs and rode past his opponent without striking. A burst of applause for his gallantry rang like hollow thunder—and as meaningless to him in his fevered state—inside his helm. Reining in, he turned to see the other knight swinging about.

Spurs jabbed. They rode upon each other with swords raised and threatening. As they came within striking distance, both swords fell as one. The Provençal hit the edge of The Bastard's shield. Jean felt his own blade drive home on a pauldron, the curving plate that protected the shoulder.

The Provençal went out of the saddle and hit the ground hard. He lay, unmoving, while The Bastard rode to the end of the lists.

Jean lifted his visor and gulped in air. Nausea churned in his belly. He would have given much to be able to squirm out of this heavy armor, to dive naked in some woodland pool and forget that both Giles de Raiz and Philip de Basoches were waiting to be unseated. He shook his head, fighting the sickness. Then pride forced the sickness out of his body.

He turned back to the field, saw that La Hire and Giles de Raiz were walking together toward the stands; they had unseated each other, he guessed, with simultaneous blows. Only one horseman for the Duke of Alençon was left to stand against him—Philip of Basoches. Even as he stared, the knight from Arnais put spurs to his mount and came thundering toward him.

Jean closed his visor and rammed in his spurs.

And then, so suddenly that he could not know what had happened, Philip de Basoches was gone. To Jean it seemed the very earth had opened and swallowed him. A roar from the onlookers let The Bastard know there had been an accident. He reined in and lifted his visor.

Arnais lay on the ground, writhing back and forth in pain. His horse was whinnying shrilly. A page ran by shouting, "He fell when his horse slipped on a bit of bloody ground. His leg may be broken."

His own esquire came running, his wide face split with a grin. "You are champion, sire! Tonight at the feasting, you shall receive the prize!"

"Get me to my tent, for the love of God—and swiftly. All my insides are coming up at once!"

His armor was half off when the nausea come.

Jean walked alone through the long gallery to the upper solars that had been assigned to him as his rooms during his stay at Chinon. Weakness made him stagger a little, and twice he paused to seat himself on a marble bench, but he felt his strength coming back and knew a good sleep would work a miracle with him. He had given his esquire Rolf orders to fetch wine and bread, with some meat and fruit. He would eat first, then sleep.

The solar was quiet as he entered and closed the heavy oak door behind him. He began disrobing as he crossed the rush-strewn floor to the massive ambry that held his garments, tossing his richly decorated hucque onto an X-chair and his paltock across the huge bedstead.

He was naked when a sound from a recessed windowsill swung him about. Marie Louvet stood before the casement, framed by the setting sun, staring at him with wide eyes.

After his first astonishment had passed, he growled, "Had you told me your intention of paying me a visit, I'd have been dressed more appropriately."

Her hand made a hesitant gesture, as if to hinder him from reaching for a linen braies with which to cover himself. A

112

flush lay on her cheeks, and her eyes were bright with an emotion Jean could not name.

"I'm your wife," she said softly. "A wife may look at her husband if she so desires."

"A true wife, yes," he nodded.

"Would you rather Simone awaited you than I?"

"You speak foolishness."

"It was her favor you wore into the lists today. The favor of a common woman. Was it to make a mockery of me?"

"I had no other lady," he said simply.

She glanced down at her hands, which were clasping and unclasping nervously. In her kirtle of tight green velvet, which bared smooth white shoulders and the upper swells of firm breasts, she was very beautiful. The thought came to Jean that he was alone in a bedchamber with his wife for the first time in nine long years.

"There's a tub of water before the fireplace," she murmured. "And a tray of food. I took the food from Rolf when he brought it. The tub was my own idea." Her eyes lifted and went over his nakedness frankly and without shame. "Your doxy offered me Philip de Basoches this morning before the tourney. She said he might wear my scarf, as you wore her golden cloth."

"He bore an empty helm. I saw that much before he fell."

"If my husband will not wear my favors, no man shall." Then more brightly she said, "Come, into the water. Wash yourself. Rest and be comfortable. I'll serve you with my own hands."

He looked at her a long moment before he turned and went toward the big stone hearth and the wooden tub sitting before it. Warm water filled the tub to the brim; there were rushes thrown about to catch its spill as Jean stepped into it.

When he was lathering himself his wife came and sat on a stool to watch him soberly. After enduring her gaze for several minutes, he put down the chunk of mutton-fat soap and said irritably, "Must you stare so at me?"

Marie smiled roguishly. "I've never seen a man at his ablutions. I find the sight most interesting."

"Look your fill then," he growled, and rose to dry him-

113

self. Before he was done with his task Marie was at his elbow with a goblet of claret. He took the goblet in exchange for the towel, and as he sipped he grew aware that his wife was drying him very gently, almost tenderly.

"You're a strange woman," he told her.

"Am I, Jean?"

"You claim to be a virgin, yet you handle me so shamelessly one might think you a strumpet out of the Halles quarter of Paris."

"Are you objecting to the way I handle you?"

"No, no. Of course not."

The Bastard was not as weak as he imagined, nor was he as indifferent to the presence of his wife as he liked to suppose. More than once she brushed him with her fingertips, more than once he felt the fragile touch of her breath upon his flesh. Such treatment was more than a man could stand without responding.

The towel was rubbing down his thighs as she crouched on one knee before him. "You're a very strong man, Jean. So strong I—I'm not at all sure I should be—doing this with you."

She raised her eyes so she could stare at him boldly.

Jean said softly, "Fetch me more wine."

While she was gone to the corner of the solar where a table stood, The Bastard sank onto the velvet cushion of an X-chair. He was pleased and confused by this woman, his wife. According to his thoughts on her, she should be fleeing from him as the stag flees before the hunter. Instead she was closeted alone with him, playing the wanton as well as any Petit-Pont trull.

When she returned with the wine, he caught her by a wrist and drew her to her knees beside him, holding the goblet so that she might drink, stroking the thick black hair that was coifed so cunningly beneath a silver caul.

"I find my disbelief warring with my desire," he told her softly. "A part of me rejoices in your presence. Another part is filled with suspicion and curiosity."

Her red mouth smiled. "In which camp shall you plant your banner, my lord? In that of disbelief? Or in that of desire?"

114

"Don't mock me, Marie," he said harshly.

Her eyebrows arched. "Mock you? *Ma foi*—I only seek to win your love." When he would have drawn back she pressed against his thigh, looking into his eyes with something like hunger in her own.

"*Oui*—your love! Your love which I threw away nine years ago at Avignon. In the forest camp of Brie I asked you to woo me. Instead you ran to your farm woman. *Voilà!* I knew then that I must do more than sit like a statue for your coming. *Hein?* Is that true, *mon desir?*"

His hand caught the low collar of her kirtle to hold her still when she would have risen. Marie smiled langorously, both hands spread on his leg, pushing herself away. The green velvet tore, together with the thin linen *guimpe* beneath, giving him a tantalizing glimpse of a full white breast before she could cover herself.

"If I am grudging where you prove generous, forgive me," she whispered. "I'm not used to sharing my nudity with anyone."

She rose and walked away from the X-chair where he sat crouched, devouring her with his stare. Before a standing-mirror of Murano glass from Venice, she began to remove the crispin that bound her hair. There was such a casual air about her that The Bastard was deceived. She did not seem the stranger any longer but a wife of long standing, pinning the torn opening of her kirtle, black head bent slightly, lips pursed in concentration on what she did. In a moment, he told himself, she will begin to remove her garments and go to bed with me.

Excitement leaped in him at the thought. For so long a time that it seemed forever he had yearned to make this woman his wife in fact as well as name. She came to him in his dreams, a succubus to steal his senses with lewd posturings or a laughing sprite with merriment in her eyes, dancing about him and teasing until he had to laugh in sheer joy of being with her. Yet these were only dreams.

He rose to his feet and moved silently over the rushes to stand behind her. The pin had caught now; the torn green velvet hid the pallid breast. Jean put his hands on her shoulders and drew her back against him.

115

"Undo the pin, Marie," he said hoarsely. "Remove the kirtle and your *camisa*. Let me see you as a man should see his wife, in the full loveliness of her body."

Her lips twitched. "If I were your wife I'd be happy to expose myself to you, my lord. I'd run naked around the room and taunt you until you came after me and caught me and bent me to your will."

"You are my wife!"

"Only by reason of a few Latin words."

"And what else is there, in God's name?"

"A courtship. A wooing of a woman by a man. Oh, I know—it doesn't seem important to you. I don't imagine you've ever wooed anybody in all your life. What did you do with the farm woman? How did you get her to tumble with you?"

"I saved her from a rogue named Red Gui. She became my traveling companion to Montmirail and Sezanne. In Sezanne she posed as my wife."

Her eyes were stormy, staring into the mirror. "I trust she made a more loving wife than I?"

"She was honest about it, if that's what you mean. She wanted me. I wanted her. There was no talk of wooing or courtship between us."

"You were no better than two animals, then."

"Why yes, if it pleases you to think so. But sometimes it's a relief to be an animal and not a man. Unthinking. Living only in the impulse of brute passion. Without cares or worry."

She twisted free of his hands and crossed the room, walking slowly with head bent. She came to a stop near a *prie-dieu* and idly turned the pages of the psalter that rested there.

"This morning at the showing of the helms I swore I'd win you from her. She was so boldly confident you belonged to her that I grew angry. I intended to come here and do whatever you wanted—to let myself be an animal, too."

Her upraised hand held him motionless when he would have come to her. "I hoped with those tactics to win you away from her. Now I see I was wrong."

"Wrong?" he echoed numbly.

116

A tight smile twisted her mouth. "We are more than brutes, you and I, or so I like to think. There can be something more than animal love between us." Her hands made a wide gesture. "Oh, call me foolish! Say I'm only uttering the words of a terrified virgin if you want. And yet—"

Jean felt his eyes opening wide. This woman was putting into words the thoughts that had been his for so very long a time. Now her hands were not enough to restrain him. He leaped for her, caught her up with fingers widespread on her hips, held her in the air.

"Oui, ma petite belle! It is so. There is something finer for us, *hein?* Something big—like the love the poets and the *jongleurs* speak of! The love Yseult and Tristram had, or Héloïse and Abélard."

Marie Louvet was very much a woman. Held high in his strong hands, staring down into his bright, upturned face, she felt the magic of his words and body causing a change in her. Her breasts swelled full and hard. There was a melting warmth in her loins. This was her man, she knew now with full certainty—her lover, her Parsifal.

As if he sensed the change in her, Jean lowered her to her feet. He whispered, "Ah, now you know? Now it touches you here—" his finger caressed her breast—"and here. *Hein?"*

"Yes, yes. I've been so silly! Such a stupid little idiot! Oh, Jean—how could you still have any love for me?"

She made such an appealing picture to him that he gave a cry and fell to his knees before her. His arms embraced her legs and drew her close so that he might bury his face against the softness of her belly. In an agony of spirit he whispered, "How could I still love you? How could I not love you, my dearest? Can you understand that? All my life—ever since the first time I saw you with the Duchess Yolande of Anjou when you were only ten years old—I've been in love with you."

"Really?" she whispered, her eyes brimming.

"You carried a little lute hung with yellow ribbons and wore a gown of red samite. Your hair hung below your shoulders."

"It is longer than that now. It hangs—" she laughed softly

117

and murmured, "If you'll free my legs, dear one, I'll show you just how far it does fall on me."

"Dear one," he repeated. "You called me dear one!"

He was rising, still clasping her in his arms, so that when she replied their mouths were very close together. "You are my dear one, Jean. You have always been dear to me, but I was so young and so foolish with daydreams that I never knew it. I was a very naughty girl. I should be punished."

"Only with kisses," he murmured, and caught her mouth with his lips. His arms held her tightly and, after a long, delirious moment when his senses swam around him, Jean grew aware that she was responding with a fervor equal to his own.

Her fingers were spread on his shoulders, digging in convulsively. Untutored, she thrust herself against him, letting him know her softness and her need.

"Oh, dear heart, dear heart," she whispered, quivering uncontrollably. "I've never known such a feeling as this, never before. I can neither see nor hear, and everywhere I turn there is only you to touch and hold and kiss. You are become my world, my Jean. My entire world, my darling."

His kisses roved her throat, down into the valley between her firm young breasts, and now Marie clung to him with only one hand while the other tore at her kirtle, baring herself to his mouth, moaning as she felt the touch of lips and tongue on flesh.

"This must be paradise for—oh, I have heard the *jongleurs* sing and the poets recite their verses about—yet I never knew—never conceived there could be such a— Jean, you drive me mad! I can stand no more! I vow I—"

His lips silenced her even as his hands explored among her falling garments. Then he drew her close and held her, whispering all the while.

"Ah, *mon Dieu!* What am I doing to you? My love for you is stronger than the lust of the animal. *Oui!* So much stronger that I must torture myself—and you—and push you from the room."

"Jean, Jean," she whispered, burying her flushed face against his chest. "Oh, was there ever such a man?"

118

He laughed a little in mockery at himself. "I hope not, for the world would be a sorry place if everyone were like me. No, no. I'm a very human being, my darling. But I'm also very much in love with you.

"There's something spiritual about this feeling I have, Marie. As if—well, as if bedding you is not enough. Between us there must be something more than lust. You understand?"

She pressed to him. "I've known it all along."

"Then you'd better go, *ma petite*. It is very hard to be spiritual with you in my arms and me without so much as a poky-sleeve to cover myself."

"You will woo me? As a lover ought?"

"With sweet words and songs, with gifts and kisses."

She sighed, "You'll make me very happy, Jean."

"Not half so happy as you'll make me when you tell me I've won your heart at last."

She wrinkled her nose impishly. "To punish you for not teaching me sooner how very much I love you, I shall be a hard taskmistress."

His hands framed her flushed face, lifting it so his mouth could close on her lips. For a long moment they swayed together, lost to everything but one another, until a discreet knock sounded on the oaken door.

Marie pushed herself away, laughing breathlessly, deviltry in her feverish eyes. "That was a near thing, my darling. A few moments more and there wouldn't have been any need for courtship."

He grinned. "I must reward Rolf in your name, then." He reached for his hucque and threw it about his shoulders as he walked with her to the door.

The esquire gaped at Marie, then at Jean. As if waking from a dream he shook himself, saying, "The feasting will begin very shortly, my lord. Already the *jongleurs* are tuning their instruments and the serving men are bringing in the water that the guests may wash their hands."

Marie touched a fingertip to her lips and placed it against Jean's mouth. "Until the feasting then, my love."

Rolf gaped, his jaw fallen, as she walked down the gallery. Only when his master clapped him across his shoulder blades did he rouse from his surprise.

119

"Well?" roared The Bastard. "Can't a man entertain his own wife in a bedroom without shocking you to the nines?"

Jean had never been so happy.

CHAPTER SEVEN

THE PRIZE for the tourney was a great silver helm, crested with a golden griffin and hung with a blue mantling. It glittered in the candle flames as if with inner life, the focus of all eyes. The words *sans peur avec honneur* had been scrolled above the visor. A worthy prize for such a tourney. A worthy prize, too, for such a champion.

For The Bastard was clad all in white this evening, his short cote-hardie of white velvet, his hose of white wool. A golden chain about his throat, from which hung a roundel carved in relief to represent a courtier and his lady, was his only touch of color.

As men stared at the great silver helm, so they also stared at this man who had been its winner. He sat—not with his *dame d'or* but with his wife. He laughed—not thickly and drunkenly, but with quiet enjoyment. He drank—always after lifting his goblet to Marie Louvet and whispering a toast to her. He danced—and always with the dark-haired beauty in the maroon kirtle.

"People are staring, Jean," she whispered once as he bent to caress her palm with his lips.

"People are jealous. Of your beauty, of my luck."

"The *jongleurs* are coming to sing of love."

"What do those poor clods know of love?"

He rose to his feet, handsome and powerful in his white cote-hardie, his close-cropped blonde hair above the sun-bronzed face giving him the look of a mountain hawk, and beckoned to a *trouvère* from Languedoc. At The Bastard's words the man grinned and handed over his lute. Jean touched the strings a moment before taking his place among the *jongleurs*.

They drew back to give him room. Jean laughed and strummed a chord with a careless hand. The company in the great hall grew silent.

"Je chante d'amour!" he cried. "Neither of the love of the priest for his God nor the child for the mother, not of the wife for the son and the husband for the daughter, but of the love of a man for a maid."

He was possessed of a fine voice, and he had learned the uses of a lute many years ago. He sang, improvising as was the custom among the *jongleurs* at times—but always was his song a *chanson,* a song of love—and always he sang the praises of his wife.

Like Tallefier before him he was both warrior and minstrel. There was no embarrassment in him; in his day men proved devotion to their lady by some such ostentatious show. His eyes were for Marie alone. He saw her sitting rapt, eyes shining tenderly. He saw the rounds of her white shoulders, bared above the low-cut collar of the kirtle, and the upper swells of her firm white breasts. Of these, too, he sang, as well as of her eyes and her lips and her flowing black hair.

When he was done, the hall shook with applause.

Jean tossed the lute to the grinning *jongleur* and added a handful of silver coins. He took his place beside Marie and felt her hand reach out and clasp his own. She pressed his fingers tenderly for a long moment while her eyes glowed with happiness. For Jean, this was reward enough.

When the Duchess of Alençon stood and summoned him forward, it was anticlimactic. While she praised his bravery and his skill in the lists, he scarcely listened. Even when a page came and handed him the prize, he merely touched it fleetingly with a hand.

When the page brought the helm to the table and placed it before Marie, he roused himself, but it was only her soft words, her hands stroking the great silver helm, that meant anything to him.

"The man's bewitched," grunted the sour Count of Foix.

"In a way that does credit to his wife," snapped his countess.

Already the tongues were at work with their eternal gossip. According to the rules of the Love Courts, a man could not be in love with his wife. He must devote himself to other women while other men whispered their devotions to his mate.

"Is she his wife?" asked a duchess.

"Not from what I've heard. They have never lived together. It might make a difference. What do you say, Gautier?"

Gautier did not know, and neither did anyone else. Jean and Marie were seen to walk the long stone gallery together that night and kiss one another in the shadows. A page swore they parted at her door. She went in, and he stayed outside whispering to her and then went away to his own room.

"The man's mad," said young and handsome John of Alençon. "Imagine sleeping neither with Simone nor Marie when he might have either—or possibly both—for the asking."

They rode on picnics in the woods bordering the Vienne river with a pack mule fitted out with hampers, containing such delights to the palate as *doucettes,* bakemeats and apples, spiced cakes and jellies. Always they returned to the *palais* when the shadows were long and dark on the ground, and always were the hampers untouched.

"They live on love," murmured a young girl dreamily.

"I tell you they only hug and kiss!"

"Are you trying to tell me she's a virgin?"

"I had it from my maid through her maid. It seems he is to woo her for a little while and then—you understand?"

"I wonder how that would work with my husband?"

"Darling, you aren't Marie Louvet. Of course your Nicolet isn't Jean of Orleans, either."

They were observed walking the high walls of the town, hand in hand, and strolling lazily on a sunny morning throught the Street of the Clothsellers. Twice a page interrupted them while Marie, locked in the crook of Jean's arm, sat in an inglenook reading to him from a psalter.

Their love was a scandal at first.

After a while it became a source of secret pride.

In the tiny Inn of the Gray Cowl, Philip de Basoches lay

122

propped on cushions on a fireside settle, his black scowl made more bitter by the tales his esquire whispered in his ears of the happiness of the lovers. Again and again his fist hammered at the carved wooden arm on which he propped his elbow.

"Devil take The Bastard! My bad luck was his good luck. While I lay abed, he seduced the woman I love." It did not matter to the Lord of Arnais that Marie and Jean of Orleans were man and wife. He wanted the woman for his own, so his twisted mind made excuses.

One night, when his obscene curses became particularly violent, a red-headed man detached himself from the men crowding about a wine tun and knuckled a brow to him. This effort at politeness amused Basoches.

The man was an out-and-out rogue, with an evil leer to his thin mouth and hate in his tiny eyes. His jerkin was ragged, and his hairy legs were bare between patched boots and torn hose. A sword hung by a chain at his belt, where a flat leather purse spoke of depleted fortunes.

"Well?" Philip growled. "What's on your mind, red one?"

Red Gui grinned, showing blackened teeth. "You spoke a name, lord—the name of the man I hate most in this world, the man I've sworn to kill somehow, somewhere. If you hate The Bastard as I do, I'm your man."

He had trailed Jean of Orleans from the forests of Brie into Lorraine, down to Montargis where he had witnessed the battle from a high ridge, flat on his belly. From Montargis to Chinon was close to a hundred and thirty miles, but Red Gui had walked them, letting the dust of the victorious army add to his dull fury.

Philip signaled his squire for a jack of cheap wine and presented it to the red-headed Gui, saying, "Tell me your story. Omit nothing. If I like what you say, you'll be my man."

The Lord of Arnais listened quietly, nodding occasionally. When Red Gui was done Philip tossed him a velvet *aumonière* packed tight with silver *ecus*. "You'll do for what I have in mind. Here's proof of my sincerity. Now then, this is what I want—some way to strike at Jean. You understand? I don't

123

care how or when or where. The man has a chink in his armor. I want to learn what it is."

"Men say he loves his wife, milord." To Red Gui that seemed suspicious in and of itself.

Philip laughed coldly. "Am I to run a dagger between her breasts, then? And have myself named murderer? No. No. There's another way. There must be. Your job's to find it."

"If there's a way, I will."

September ran into October, and the foliage of the trees beside the Vienne changed color. Now the woods were filled with brilliant crimsons and tawny golds as the lovers walked their horses along the forest pathways. There was a chill in the air, too, which gave excuse sometimes for Jean to slip an arm about Marie's waist and draw her close against him.

"For warmth," he always told her, but his adventuring hand was discovering the firmness of a breast through velvet or the curve of a hip beneath a caressing palm.

And when his hand had stroked enough, Marie turned and offered her parted lips, whispering, "Please, please, my dear one! Kiss me and then—oh, hurry! We must gallop to our *sollière*, where we can be alone!"

And yet, as if to punish him for the long empty years when they had been apart, she would not yield to his pleas nor enter his bedchamber at nights. The Bastard continued to woo her like a schoolboy, and he bore her teasings cheerfully enough because eventually they had to end.

Even the Dauphin commented wryly on their newly born love. "If I didn't know better, I'd say a sorcerer had whispered a spell over you."

"The only spells that work their magic on me are the ones Marie carries on her person, dear cousin." Jean laughed. "I am in Paradise. I wish it would never end."

"Paradise is eternal. Happiness isn't," Charles answered.

As if to prove the words of the Dauphin true, the English struck at the city of Orleans in the middle of October. They came twenty-five hundred strong, with hand guns and brass cannon called fowlers, under the command of the Earl of Salisbury, a veteran array with a huge supply train filled

124

with siege engines. The surrender of Orleans could be expected hourly, and, when Orleans fell, so also would fall Touraine, Anjou, Aunis and the rest of southern France. The Hundred Years' War would be over at last, with the English the final victors.

Marie Louvet sat stiff and frozen as she watched her husband being armored, fright whitening her cheeks. "Must you go? Has Charles no others soldiers he can send? We've been together for such a short time. And I've been so greedy, so selfish!"

Rolf was tying the arming points of his cuirass as Jean smiled at her. "For shame, my love. Would you forget Montargis and my cannon so soon? When we get those long barrels inside the walls of Orleans, they'll hold off the English, you can be sure. As for your selfishness, you'll make it up with your generosity another day."

Despite his apparent confidence, The Bastard was worried. Cannon were of more use besieging a city than in its defense. There would be no orderly rows of English bowmen to cut down as there had been in the battle outside Montargis. At Orleans it would be cut and stab, and devil take the hindmost.

His face showed none of this concern as he strode across the solar floor, bending to press his lips to Marie's wan cheek. "Come, now. We must make a show of bravery, no matter how much we weep inside ourselves."

She shook her head and bit her lips. "I've been such a fool, such a fool, to have stayed away from you so long." Her laughter was bitterly brave. "If I were an old married woman instead of a bride—for that's what I am, in reality—I suppose I'd be glad to get rid of you so I could climb between the sheets with a handsome page."

His hand clapped her buttock. "A bride you'll always be. And what's this talk of handsome pages? Must I put you into a chastity belt?"

She laughed a little, with something of real amusement in her eyes. "No need for that. You're the only man I want. Only—try and get it over with, Jean. I'll pray for your success."

They walked down the spiral staircase hand in hand.

125

From a darkened corner of the gallery, Simone watched them go. She stood with her back pressed to the cold stone wall, eyes wide and staring. Not since their arrival in Chinon had Jean come to sleep with her. It was as if that morning before the helms, when she had taunted Marie Louvet, had put a curse on her.

The wife had accepted the challenge of the mistress and had won the love of her husband for herself. It was that simple, yet the farm woman was not one to admit an easy defeat. Because of her high rank, Marie must remain at Chinon or go south to their estates in Dauphiné. Simone herself could follow Jean to Orleans, like any camp follower.

She would have walked to Hell for The Bastard. Orleans was not nearly so far. She would take rooms at an inn and send Jean an invitation to come and visit her. It would be her chance then to show what she might do to win back his love. In a way, love was like a war, filled with attacks and alarums, sieges and surrenders.

Her hips swayed languidly as she moved toward the staircase. Jean would be under twin attacks when he arrived in Orleans. Though she hoped he might resist the English assault, she was equally hopeful he would succumb to the French.

The siege of Orleans began October 17th, 1428.

Before the end of the week The Bastard was in the city, in command of its defenses. He found the English occupying the forts of the Tourelles, Saint-Loup, De Saint Pouair, Des Douze Pierres, and others that all but encompassed the city, leaving open only a road along the river by which to come and go. Yet life inside the high walls was not so intolerable. There was a goodly supply of food on hand, and firewood against the coming winter. Small parties of riders could travel out of the city or enter it as they would.

In one sense, this news delighted Jean; in another, it depressed him, for there was no real desire in either merchant or housewife, beggar or cleric, to raise the siege. The longer the English stayed, the higher went the cost of a tavern meal or a night's lodging, the more expensive became a bolt of Amiens cloth from which to make a kirtle. Purses waxed fat among the tradespeople—and they formed the majority of the city dwellers.

"The trouble is, they aren't Frenchmen any longer," he told his esquire. "They're just hucksters."

"What can be more important than the pocketbook?"

Jean gloomed out the biform window of his apartments in the palace. "An idea, Rolf. An idea strong enough to lift them out of themselves, to make them remember they were created to serve God, not mammon."

"You want a miracle," his esquire chuckled.

Five days after he took up residence at the *palais*, a perfumed letter was placed in his hands. He knew that perfume. It needed only a glance at the writing itself to let him know that Simone had taken up quarters at the Tavern of the Three Crosses.

The Bastard went to see her at once.

He found her in the dishabille of a linen *guimpe*, the many candle flames revealing the shapeliness of her thighs and hips beneath the thin folds. She was dining on roast capon and a crocket loaf, with fruit and Burgundy wine. A wave of a hand invited him to join her.

Jean contented himself with a small goblet of wine. "You know I've been reconciled with Marie. You were in Chinon for the tourney and afterward."

"Your wife is on her way to Dauphiné right now. I am in Orleans, where you are."

He smiled with gentle irony. "You tell me I'm a man and that, sooner or later, when the cares of defense grow too much for me, I'll need comforting."

"Am I so very wrong?"

Her eyes were steady over the rim of her goblet. Under the wrapper she wore nothing, only brodequins on her feet. The thick yellow hair through which he had delighted to run his fingers was in calculated disarray. A few locks tumbled across her shoulders and down her back, while some others were yet pinned up, giving her a raffish appearance.

"Not so wrong, no. Except that I'm in love with my wife and want you to know it. What there was between us—" His shrug made an end to all her high hopes.

127

Simone ran a fingertip up and down her thigh. "I will wait. I am very good at waiting. When you find yourself so hard-pressed you don't know which way to turn, I'll be here in this room. Ready for you at any hour of the day or night."

Jean knew a touch of shame. "You're too fine to play the part of camp strumpet. Go back to Picardy. You have monies enough to buy a fine farm."

She shook her head. Her eyes were never more smoky, never more filled with devil fires. They whispered mutely to The Bastard, saying, "I want only you. No other man will do, nor do I seek any other role but that of mistress to my love." They made Jean uncomfortable. As soon as he finished a second goblet of wine, he took his leave. He told himself that Simone would grow tired of her role and would soon leave the city.

In a little while, he forgot her.

Autumn became winter and then spring, and the siege went on with sporadic attacks by the English, vigorous defenses by the soldiers under The Bastard. A dozen times Jean tried to rouse his men and the men of the city into mounting an offensive designed to sweep the enemy from their forts. As always, his persuasions failed.

The Duke of Orleans, Charles de Valois—half brother to Jean but of legitimate birth—was a prisoner in England, to which he had been carried after he had been taken at the battle of Agincourt. He was content to write his poems and hold his little court in London Town. The Bastard sometimes suspected that Charles had infected his people with his own laziness.

Then one morning in April, 1429 a dusty rider came stamping into the great hall where Jean sat at breakfast. He bore strange tidings, which he told eagerly, after washing down the dust of a dozen country roads with two goblets of wine.

"A girl named Jeanne has come out of Domremy claiming to be sent by God. She claims to have heard voices and seen visions and that she's going to lift the siege here. She went to Vaucouleurs and talked Baudricourt into sponsoring her by sending her to the Dauphin.

"In Chinon she picked Charles out of a number of his

nobles. She told him that he's destined to be crowned king at Reims."

Jean sat up straighter. "Did she, now?"

The rider nodded. "Some men say she is a witch, others that she is truly sent by God. Me, I don't know what to believe."

"Fool! If you love France, you'll believe in her. She's the miracle I need! A figurehead—an idea strong enough to move men's minds from their purse strings to the state of their souls' salvation! From Domremy, you say? I was in Domremy not so long ago. I must know more about this Jeanne."

The Bastard dispatched two men to Chinon to speak with her, to form their opinions of The Maid and to report back to him.

Things had not gone so well in Orleans of late. The burghers were feeling the pinch of warfare, now, and had begun to complain bitterly. A constant harassment wore thin the line of defenders, and Jean had sent to the Dauphin for reinforcements.

On the next to last day of January, Saint-Sévere de Boussac and La Hire, smarting under the lack of knightly action, hurled their lances at a concentration of English pikes and archers only to be cut down and slaughtered. Saint-Sévere, foreseeing possible disaster, withdrew his forces, much to the disgust of the firebrand La Hire.

In February La Hire could not be put off any longer. He itched to fight, and, though The Bastard technically commanded at Orleans, he was only too well aware that his knights might march themselves and their retainers out of the city unless he turned them loose occasionally.

And so La Hire rode to intercept a supply train under the English knight, Sir John Falstolf. The Count of Clermont, who commanded the reinforcements marching from Blois to Orleans, countermanded the attack. A chance to strike a surprise blow was gone. Falstolf was given an opportunity to set up his pikes and archers so that when the French assault was finally launched it was confused and uncertain. In the middle of the fighting the Count of Clermont came up with his four thousand men; but he was so angry, because La Hire had failed to wait for him to join in the attack, he turned aside and went on to Orleans without fighting.

The Bastard raged in vain against this stupidity. "I call it stupidity rather than cowardice, my lord Clermont, because I have served with you in other campaigns. God grant me strength! Will ever you men agree to serve one commander instead of each one making his own decisions and going forward like bulls in heat?"

When his two messengers to Jeanne returned to Orleans, The Bastard let himself dream a little of what a maiden from Domremy might do for all France, as he listened to their words.

"She has cut her hair à la soldât so it looks like a skullcap on her otherwise shaven skull. She wears a military cape and men's garments, and high riding boots. Men say she's a virgin and that she will do what she says, free Orleans and France of the English."

The other messenger said earnestly, "She has an air of sanctity about her, not the withdrawn holiness of a hermit but the zealous piety of a crusader. She's plain enough, no beauty, but is very firm and determined. And she believes in these voices she claims to have heard."

The Bastard felt good and rubbed his hands together. "So long as she makes the people believe in her, I care not what her own beliefs might be." He sent the two messengers to report to the people of the city while he busied himself in making an inventory of men and equipment.

Jeanne came to Orleans in the latter part of April, clad all in armor, with pansière in front and garde-reins behind, her cuirass covered with white velvet. She rode with her black hair cropped close to her skull as the messengers had described, and as she rode she stared about her with what some men called arrogance. The Bastard was to call it the curiosity of one in whose hands the fate of France might well rest.

They met on a little wharf that jutted out into the Loire, The Bastard all in armor, as was Jeanne. As he stepped ashore from the boat in which he had come to meet her, Jean thought back to Domremy and to an intense young

woman who had stood outside the inn of Mme. Valdaires and
stared at him with wide, limpid eyes. Mother of God! Could
this be that same girl? But yes—the haunting eyes, the black
hair, the plain looks, all were the same!

Jeanne seemed as surprised as he. Her first words to him
were, "Are *you* The Bastard of Orleans?"

She put out her hand, and he gripped it as if she were a
man. She was direct and sincere. There was no nonsense
about her. He said, "Yes, I am. And I'm glad for your
arrival."

She was put out that she had come by the river way and
not along the opposite bank where Talbot—who had suc-
ceeded to the English command on the death of the Earl
of Salisbury—and the beefeaters lay entrenched. Jean let
her scold him, studying her all the while. The men had been
right. There was an air of energetic holiness about her. She
had the zeal and the spirit that France needed. His messengers had reported that she had also the quality of person-
ality that could make men forget self and serve the state
wholeheartedly. Some of that inner spirit came through to
him as she spoke so angrily.

He could have silenced her. His was the authority, here in
Orleans. But he let her speak, knowing others were watching
and listening. Jeanne d'Arc was something more than human.
She was the chosen of the Lord. This, all Frenchmen must
believe. Jean knew it instinctively. Whether she were saint
or devil, it was imperative to believe her another Michael
come to do battle with Sathanus.

In all his future dealings with her, The Bastard was to
adopt this submissive, serious attitude. To him she was in
truth a miracle—the figurehead behind which France might
win her liberty—and so she must appear to all men.

The supply train went on into Orleans by barges along the
Loire. Joan herself remained overnight in the Manor of
Reuilly. The Bastard wanted her entry into Orleans to be
the forerunner of a victory parade. For that she must be
fresh and rested. He sent a courier to Jacques le Prestre,
Seneschal of Orleans, to receive her with all due honors on
the morrow.

Next day, as he paced behind The Maid on her entry into

131

the city, Jean told himself that she might have come in answer to his own prayers. All along he had known that this Jeanne d'Arc was what France needed to join all men against the common enemy, to unite Guyenne and Gascony, Aunis and Languedoc. The cheers and shouted pleasantries with which the people greeted her were echoed in his heart.

Nor had he any reason to change his mind in the days that followed. Jeanne d'Arc was not easy to get along with, convinced as she was of the sanctity of her mission and impatient with anyone who might retard its fulfillment, but Jean adopted an attitude that let him cajole his knights while at the same time placating the impatience of the Maid. Now that he had his miracle, he intended to nurse it to full flower.

On May 4th, Joan unfurled her standard at the Burgundy Gate when a sortie of hotheads began to attack the Saint-Loup fort, strongest of all the English bastions. In answer to her ringing voice and armored figure, the French surged forward in a massive, irresistible wave. Toward the hour of vespers the fortress fell, and The Bastard knew that the flower of The Maid was blossoming at last.

She was everywhere in the city—at the wall walks, where a bowman fired a message in her own handwriting to the English war captains, or weeping softly when the harsh voices of the enemy called her "the Armagnac whore," or simply walking in the cobbled streets with a crowd about her. In battle conference she was haughty and impatient; such captains as La Hire and Saint-Sévere took affront at her blunt words; but always The Bastard was there to soothe injured feelings and restore the feeling of good fellowship.

And The Bastard was rewarded.

One by one the English forts fell, Saint-Jean le Blanc and then the Tourelles. Jeanne herself was wounded during the struggle over the Tourelles, but, while her wound was being treated with meat fats and olive oil, a fireboat was sent against the fort. Its licking flames brought the towering rafters down in crimson destruction.

On the following day, a Sunday and the Feast of Saint Michael, the English formed into two companies and marched away from Orleans along the road to Meung. La Hire rode after them to attack their rear guard and capture a quantity of siege engines and bombards, armor and metalware.

In nine days Jeanne d'Arc had raised the siege of Orleans.

All men were agreed that it was a miracle.

Only The Bastard heard himself whisper, *"My* miracle!"

Jean of Orleans was restless. He strode the rush-strewn floor of the palace solar that was his bedchamber, only faintly aware of the sounds of revelry rising from the streets and from the outer bailey. The *Te Deum* had been sung in the Cathedral of Saint Croix. The Maid was asleep in her bed at the house of Jacques Boucher. His captains were celebrating belowstairs or at the city inns and taverns.

The red claret he had been swilling was tasteless. Suddenly it came to him that he needed a stronger draught than wine this night. His palms itched to caress womanflesh. His lips burned to bury themselves in a soft, loose mouth.

"Marie," he whispered, staring south toward Dauphiné. "Why couldn't you have come to Orleans as Simone did?"

He knew the reason, of course. He himself had forbidden it. Now he cursed the timidity of spirit that had feared danger might attend her visit. If only she were here with him now, lying in the canopied bed behind him! Ah! Then might he celebrate his victory in all truth.

He flung the goblet from him.

Simone had been naked under that thin *camisa,* back there in late October when he had gone to visit her. He closed his eyes to blot out the vision of her pale breasts, of the soft fleshy thighs that trembled as she walked. It did no good. Her body leaped to life behind his eyelids and postured lewdly to his thoughts.

"The Tavern of the Three Crosses," he muttered.

An October wind had howled about his boots when he thrust open the door of the inn, those months ago. Now it was May, and mild, with the fragrance of growing things in the air. Six months is a long time. Surely the farm woman would not still be in that room, eternally waiting.

And yet—

His hand went out to his cloak. He threw it about his shoulders and went to the solar door. He wore leather jerkin and thigh boots, and under the jerkin a coat of fine mail. A longsword hung by straps at his waist. He might have been a soldier of fortune rather than commander of the Dauphin's army.

As such a soldier of fortune he had won Simone.

The halls were empty. Soldiers and servants, serving maids and scullery wenches, all were scattered this night across the city, drinking, making love, enjoying the taste of freedom from siege. He went swiftly between the shadows of the gallery and down the wide marble staircase.

The Tavern of the Three Crosses was not so far that he could not make it in the burning of a Paris-candle notch. Wrapping the cloak tighter about his middle, he began to walk. Twice he was stopped—unrecognized each time—by roisterers and forced to share a gulp of their cheap wine. Once a woman flung herself into his arms, and the touch of her soft middle and open mouth built a fire in his groin.

He had been tempted to take the woman into the nearest public house and hire her services. She was a pretty little thing, plumply fleshed and mature, but the image of the farm woman danced before his eyes, and he satisfied himself with pinching her thigh as he slipped a handful of silver *ecus* into her bodice.

Then the Three Crosses was before him, its wooden sign creaking on rusting chains overhead and its door opening to a push of the hand. The sweet smells of roasting meats and baking sweetbreads rose to tantalize his nostrils. An acrid air of wines and ales overhung everything.

The narrow staircase was to his right. Jean flipped a copper denier to a maidservant, then took the treads three at a time. He discovered that his heart was pumping rapidly in his rib case. He paused a moment at her door before he knocked.

A bolt was withdrawn. The door swung inward.

Simone stood with a candle in her hand, looking at him with those smoky eyes. She wore the same thin *guimpe* she had worn in October. With the candle flames behind her, her naked body showed clearly under the linen. There was a sense of unreality about the woman and the room that held The Bastard in its pall.

"Is it still the autumn?" he asked.

She smiled faintly. "I saw you coming up the street from the window. I took off my things and put on this wrapper. Last time, you liked me in it well enough to stare, at least." She stepped back to let him enter.

When he had closed the door and bolted it, she brought him wine, walking with a full stride that exposed one white leg from foot to hip. His arm hooked her soft middle and drew her against him as his free hand caught the goblet.

"There's no hurry," she whispered, staring up into his glowing eyes, knowing with the press of a soft hip that he was feverishly hungry for her body. "We have all night. I've been in this room for six months. Six more hours won't make any difference."

He drank and stared at her, and his hand roved over her slowly, gently, until she began to tremble. She moaned and slumped against him while he drank the claret she had poured.

"Hurry," she breathed. "Oh my God, hurry!"

"You said we have all night," he reminded her, but the goblet fell from his fingers and he clutched her to him.

Simone began to whimper like a lost, frightened child. Not for six months had this man sent these riotous emotions flooding through her body. Until tonight she had not realized just how much she missed his caresses.

"Love me, love me, love me," she breathed.

They fell on the bed, twisting and turning, seeking both to give and to receive in their madness of the flesh. Forgotten was Marie, forgotten also the long, empty wait in this room above the cobbled streets of Orleans. They were a man and woman starved for love; and until the dawn painted an angry redness in the eastern sky they glutted themselves with each other.

It was close to noon when Red Gui, standing in the shadows of a recessed doorway, watched The Bastard leave the inn of the Three Crosses. Jean walked slowly, like a man deep in thought, or as one who was very tired.

With infinite patience, Red Gui took up the pursuit.

135

CHAPTER EIGHT

THE WAR CAPTAINS were gathered on a hill that looked out over Jargeau. All were here—La Hire and Giles de Raiz, Pothon de Saintrailles, Florent d'Illiers, and The Bastard. Beside them, Jeanne looked small and helpless, even padded as she was in armor. Yet it was to her they turned as they discussed ways and means of attacking the city on the Loire.

"Do what you will, sires," she said at last. "My heart isn't in it. I ride to see the Dauphin, to encourage him to be Dauphin no longer but king of France."

"Jargeau would make a fine gift to place before him," Saintrailles murmured.

The Maid stared at him with her direct gaze. "Orleans is gift enough for the moment. You do what you will. I ride for Tours within the hour."

The Bastard was torn between attack and delay. Without Jeanne and her banner at their head, his troops would revert to their old ways before the English, he was sure. Jeanne had performed her miracle at Orleans. He needed her now in lesser battles.

La Hire pressed him to fight. "We have them on the run. Word of their defeat at Orleans is spreading all across Touraine. Strike now!"

Saintrailles and Saint-Sévere added their voices to the cause. Jean frowned, having no heart for this siege in which his beloved cannon would be forced to play a minor role. Besides, he did not want the Dauphin to be crowned king at Reims while he was in the field.

A dusty messenger had brought him a letter this very morning from Marie, who was on her way north from Dauphiné to rejoin the court. She had concluded, ". . . and now that our days of courtship are at an end, and since I feel that you have won me by your tender attentions, it is time for me to become— Your loving wife, Marie."

He took her words as a promise.

136

In his impatience to see her he gave consent to the attack on Jargeau. "An attack only, mind. There's to be no siege. If the city falls—*bien!* If it doesn't, we'll pull back and go on to Tours ourselves."

La Hire tossed his battle-ax high in the air. "Let me lead the first charge and I promise you'll sup in the city palace!"

La Hire was more enthusiastic than he was successful. The citizens of Jargeau fought with the bitter foreknowledge of what defeat would mean, with drunken soldiers overrunning their streets and homes, raping and stealing. Stones sailed through the air to batter at *trebuchets* and catapults. Huge javelins came stabbing to impale men and horses. From the walls, vats of boiling pitch waited for the first scaling ladders to be set against them.

By sunset The Bastard realized the city could not be won by a frontal assault in less than a week. Reluctantly, he agreed to wait one more day. If on the morrow the city gates did not open to them, they would by-pass the city and go southwest to Tours.

Once more La Hire failed in his promises. He came stamping into the tent he shared with *le Bâtard*, cursing fluently, ripping at his arming points, freeing himself of cuirass and vambraces.

"*Canaille!* I am forced to lead *canaille* into battle! They flee when the enemy shouts. They run when they see so much as a single arrow in the sky!"

"There is no Jeanne to lead them," Jean smiled wryly.

The Gascon paused, half out of his cuirass. "No Jeanne? That simple country wench? You think she's a great general?"

"No, she isn't a great general, but she's an inspiration. Men look at her and instantly they are giants. They forget they're fighting the *godons*. Sight of her changes them inside, somehow. I thought you realized that."

"You give her all the credit," La Hire muttered sourly.

"Credit she deserves, though she doesn't seek it. Jeanne and I see eye to eye on the most important thing of all. France must be free! To accomplish that Jeanne will do anything. As will I."

La Hire only shook his head.

On the morning of the third day before Jargeau, The

137

Bastard broke his tents and marched his little army westward toward Tours. When he arrived he learned that The Maid had pleaded with the Dauphin that he march with her to Reims to be crowned King of France, and that a compromise had been reached. The Dauphin would go to Reims, but he would go with the army so that the towns along the Loire could be overcome and brought once more under the lily banner.

The Bastard added his pleas to those of the girl from Domremy, but Charles dawdled and fretted, contenting himself with writing letters praising her to his friends. He appointed her good friend the Duke of Alençon commander of the army, overriding The Bastard and other war captains, such as Florent d'Illiers and Étienne de Vignoles.

There was no jealousy in Jean of Orleans. He served a greater cause than his own personal glory. His example and his words to the other warlords—heated words, at times—swayed them to this acceptance of a young, unproven nobleman to their command.

"You give up too much, Jean," Saint-Sévere told him, pacing before an illuminated map hung on the wall of the castle at Loches.

"So long as France is freed, who cares for glory?"

But, so that his friends should not think him too much the altruist, The Bastard insisted on immediate action and that he be given a place of honor during the first charge of lances at the next mixed battle.

Now The Maid and The Bastard acted as one person; The Maid, with her "Jesus Maria" standard, exhorted the common soldiers to attack with full fury. The Bastard browbeat the sometimes sullen and always jealous war captains into line.

With Jeanne at the van, Jargeau was captured in two days. Beaugency fell, four days later. The French army had become a whirlwind of destruction to the English strongholds along the Loire.

To meet The Maid in battle and to put an end to her successes against their veteran troops, Sir John Falstolf and Lord Talbot rode from Paris at the head of five thousand picked men. They would meet The Maid in the field rather than behind fortress walls. As they had done at Crécy and

Agincourt, they would shatter this latest French menace.

On the plains of La Beauce the armies came face to face, but when the *godons* saw how their opponents held the highest ground they refused battle and turned to depart. So large and vast was the plain and forest here at Patay that the French lost sight of the enemy—and no man can fight that which he cannot see.

"A stag," chuckled Jean. "Turn loose a stag in the woods. If there are any *godons* within ten miles, they'll set up a view halloo!"

He meant it as a jest but The Maid nodded, her serious eyes turned to him. "A stag it shall be, good Jean. And you other gentlemen, see that you wear sharp spurs this day. The battle will not be so much a French fight as it will an English flight."

As The Maid foretold, so it was. The English—scattered and marching away from battle—were in no position to form lines and defend themselves. French lances rode them down. French swords and axes split skulls and shoulder blades. There was even no need for The Bastard to bring his artillery into play. Two hours past noon, Lord Talbot was a prisoner and the English had suffered their greatest setback on French soil.

In his tent that night, The Bastard urged an immediate march on Paris. "The English are disheartened. Their commander is our prisoner. Falstolf flees to the Duke of Bedford. Paris will fall like an overripe plum into our palms!"

Jeanne d'Arc was of a different mind. "It is more important to make the Dauphin king. Paris will wait."

There was a discussion over tactics, but The Bastard, remembering his attack on Jargeau without Jeanne, remained aloof from the heated arguments that Saint-Sévere and La Hire threw at The Maid. With The Maid at its head, the French army was irresistible. Without her, it was something less than formidable.

After Joan departed for her tent, La Hire whirled on Jean in flush-faced anger. "You might have sided with us, since you know as well as I the military advantage we hold!"

"The girl is our military advantage, Étienne."

"She has you under a spell!"

139

"Not me, but the soldiers. God is with Jeanne. We all know that. Doesn't it follow that where she goes, He goes, too? And if Jeanne goes to Reims, is God with the French army attacking Paris?"

La Hire argued and grumbled but The Bastard stood firm. After a while, when wine was brought, La Hire contented himself with getting drunk.

Instead of Paris, Troyes became the marching point of the French army, and after Troyes, Châlons. By the middle of July they were before Reims.

On July 17, 1429, in the great cathedral built of gray stone and with stained glass windows and mosaic floors, the Dauphin became King Charles VII of France. Jeanne the Maid was beside him as the Archbishop touched his forehead with the holy oil from the tiny vial called Sainte Ampoule. The Bastard stood among the war captains, reflecting that the crowning of a king was a long step forward in the seemingly eternal fight for the freedom of his beloved France.

As the shouted *Noels* rang upward to the vaulted roof, The Bastard turned his gaze from his king to his wife. Marie Louvet stood beside the Countess of Claremont, ripely lovely in a crimson kirtle ornate with cuffs and hems of ermine. A pointed hennin, with a veil obscuring her forehead, was a scarlet beacon to his eyes.

Protocol demanded that he ride with The Maid through the cobbled streets, which were lined with cheering thousands gathered to honor their new king, but his heart was far behind him, with the woman in red who walked sedately among the ladies of the court. The Maid was anxious now to march on Paris, he found.

"Let Paris fall and the English are done forever in France," she assured him. "So the sooner we finish the task, the better."

The Bastard was in full agreement. However, a large party of Burgundians were in the city under a flag of truce, waiting an audience with Charles VII. The Duke of Burgundy claimed to be friendly with France once more, willing to let bygones be bygones, apparently ready to cast off his attachments with the English.

Already The Maid and his war captains had advised Charles to deal warily with these ambassadors. The Duke of Burgundy had profited handsomely by his English alliance. His sister Anne was the wife of the Duke of Bedford, regent for the child-king Henry VI of England. He held many cities and much territory that was normally French. He stood to lose much and gain nothing by alliance with France and her new king.

Yet La Trémoille, that grossly fat high counselor of the king, saw merit in the suggestions of these ambassadors. He was insisting that Charles give ear to their arguments. And so, for the space of these few days, the army was at a standstill in the great meadows south of Reims.

The Bastard said, considering all this, "If I could believe Philip of Burgundy, I should have no worries. Win him over and we win our war. Yet I think the man plays a deeper game."

"You mean he plays for time?"

"Time in which the English can reinforce Paris, gather fresh soldiers, mount an offensive against us."

"I'll speak to Charles this night," Jeanne promised.

At the palace grounds where the feasting was to take place, Jean wasted no time seeking out the crimson figure of his wife. For a little while he was content to forget war and the freedom of France. Enough for him now was the sight of her slim waist and swaying skirt, the round white shoulders lifting upward from the fashionably low-cut collar.

He bent over her hand as she sat on a marble bench before a white sea of flowering tuberoses. "You outshine the very flowers," he whispered, kissing the smooth hand she presented to him.

"Absence has taught you the art of flattery, my lord."

"The sight of you has touched my lips with truth."

She laughed, rose and walked with her hand on his arm, between courtiers and their ladies in the bright July sunlight. The Bastard knew an upsurge of gaity, an effervescent brightness of spirit that banished all his cares of state.

"I feel like a virgin boy with his first woman," he murmured. "Indeed, where you and I are concerned, I am a virgin."

"I like that comparison," she whispered. "It makes me less afraid of you."

"Does the thought of me inspire fear?"

"A very little. After all, I've never known a man."

To allay that terror, he drew her into the shadows of a stone arch and kissed her moist lips. Pressed so close together, he knew the softness of her loins and thighs while she realized the tautness of his powerful body and his honest need of her.

"We must wait until after the feasting," she murmured when she could. "It would not—be right for us to run to a solar bed—while the rest of France cheers—its new king."

"Love is greater than any king."

His kisses touched her smooth shoulders. Above his down-bent head she said softly, "You make it very difficult for me to remember that I owe a duty to Charles to be present when he— Oh, my love. My very love!"

His mouth was on the upper slopes of her trembling breasts. She clung with both hands to his head while her eyes roved the gardens. They were hidden by stone arch and tall flowers, but enough sunlight filtered through the leaves to make her apprehensive of discovery.

"Sweet Jean, enough! Oh, no more, I beg! Or else—"

His head lifted and he smiled tenderly. "Or else—what?"

She clung to him. "Or else I'll forget who and what I am and be the ardent doxy you seem to be expecting."

As if this were the answer he wanted, The Bastard put his arm around her slim waist and brought her with him along a secluded path and through a garden doorway. When she sought to protest their leaving the festivities—already they could hear the buzz of conversation that announced the approach of Charles and The Maid onto the palace grounds— he hurried her along the faster.

"Charles has waited to be king no longer than I've waited to be your husband. Tell me, which is more important?"

"To France?" she asked in mock seriousness.

"To you, sweet temptress!"

The palace was deserted. Even the cooks and servants stood in the buttery doorways, craning on tiptoes to see what they could of their new ruler. Now Marie could not protest when he caught her to him and kissed her red ripe mouth or so disordered her kirtle lacings that he could feast his eyes and lips on the ripe mounds of her bared breasts.

"I find myself shameless," she breathed as his mouth touched her. "And—oh my God!—so very much in love with you. Jean, Jean! Can you understand what you are doing to me? I've never—"

She twisted and writhed against him, hungry for his love. It was as if a floodgate had been opened deep within her. This was not the cool, remote Marie Louvet whom all France knew as the estranged wife of Jean of Orleans. This was an elemental woman, a female no better than a tavern maid or common *poule,* to whom the body of a man was the most important thing in her world.

"Do you want me? Do you?" she panted.

"More than life itself."

"Will you make up for all the years we've lost? Can you make up for them with your love?"

"Like this!" he cried, and would have caught her in his arms once more, but she twisted away and ran, skirt held high to free her legs.

Her laughter was a challenge as were the twinkling calves and ankles she revealed as she raced along the gallery. Some years before silk stockings had been created for the Queen of Spain, but they were still a rarity in France. The clinging black silk made her ankles slim and desirable as she fled before him on light feet.

Jean caught her two steps from a columned staircase, swung her up into his arms and carried her the rest of the way, until an open door hung with his insignia showed the solar that was to serve as his bedchamber. His foot kicked the door shut behind him as he set Marie on her feet.

She was flushed and laughing, shyly avoiding his eyes as she turned, whirling so that her skirts rose to her knees, well aware that he was standing with his back to the bolted door, staring avidly.

"Come here," he told her hoarsely.

"Ah, no. You shall come to me!" she cried. When he hesitated she took her skirt in her hand and lifted it slowly, past her knees, up to the middle of her smooth white thighs.

143

"Does this tempt you to leave the door, my darling? They are very latest fad, these hose made of Spanish silk."

Jean admitted the black stockings made her legs seem more than normally curved, made the whiteness of her thighs above them oddly sensual. His will was weakening. In another moment he would forget he had ordered her to come to him and yield to her demand.

"The Greek and Romans used to call silk, *sericus*," Marie went on, raising her skirt a little higher and bending forward so that she might also see her stockinged legs. "It's raised in China, I understand. Worms make it. Can you imagine that? It used to come by caravan to the cities along the Mediterranean."

"Marie!"

Her eyes were innocent. "My love?"

"You torture me, showing off your legs like that!"

"Are they so hideous?" she wondered, lifting the skirt to her hips and revealing the fact that, other than the stockings and red garters, she wore no underclothing.

A moment she posed so, before he gave a soft cry and leaped for her, and now Marie fled no longer but came into his arms with the needs of a woman grown amorous with play. Her mouth was wide open, her tongue as inquisitive as his own.

"This is why I have lived, my Jean. Just for this fevered madness! Teach me how very much you love me. Teach me!"

"I've dreamed of you like this!"

"Make that dream reality, my darling!"

With lips and hands he sought her body, showering it with caresses until she could stand no longer but must collapse against him, forcing him to carry her to the canopied bed and deposit her on top of the covers. There she lay, pasture for his eyes and lips.

She cried out brokenly as he drew her to him, cried out and then drew strength from some inner fountain of her being so that her arms held him strongly, even as she discovered that until this moment she had been like a dead woman. Her lips kissed him frantically as her hands clutched his back, and her murmurs were like honey drippings to the ear as she whispered her love and adoration of him.

144

Even as she cried out and twisted to his fancy, she told herself that, from this moment on, no other woman should so much as touch a finger of this man whom she was making her very own. The Bastard—what a silly young fool she had been to cavil at that name!—belonged to her alone. He was her property, as she was his.

Then she was whirling up and away in a cyclone of sensation, spinning higher and higher until they were alone in this heaven of the senses.

Three days were all they had to discover one another.

Only three days in which to learn the sudden touch of lips on tender flesh, the stroking caress of fevered palm, the raptured bliss of a kiss stolen between the visits of a page or tirewoman; this was their honeymoon. So long delayed, it became a maelstrom of fevered pleasures, a leaf torn from the book of paradise itself.

Jean must attend her bath in the huge wooden tub to wash her back as she bent forward, black hair piled atop her head. The fact that his kisses trailed the soapy cloth Marie accepted as a tribute to her beauty. Or when she dressed he would watch like a schoolboy with his first love, avid for every experience.

In turn, Marie must play the maid to him, running to fetch him cakes and wine only to be pulled down onto the bed, tousled and kissed until aroused to frenzy. She must learn to tease and torment by seemingly accidental glimpses of a white leg from hip to ankle as she bent to remove a stocking or permit the disclosure of her bosom when she unfastened a kirtle.

Time was a continuous paean to their love. They drank every minute empty of the delights it held. Where they could not escape the affairs of state—there were feasts in the great hall of the palace, and attendances upon the king—they were always side by side, touching one another at shoulder or hand as if to reassure themselves that this was everyday reality and not the figment of a dream.

It was during an audience with the king that Jean of Orleans was named Count of Dunois. "In some small token

145

of our gratitude and esteem for your military victories, dear cousin," Charles said with a smile.

"I did it for France, sire," Jean answered honestly.

Charles looked surprised. "Well? Am I not France? If I reward you, France rewards you. When you fight for France, you fight for me. *N'est-ce pas?*"

Jean laughed and bowed his head.

That night, as they lay in bed with the moonlight glinting through the open casements, Marie said, "A countess. I can hardly believe it. The Countess Marie of Dunois and Dauphiné." She turned over and lay on her front so she could look down into his eyes. "You'll have to treat me with more respect, Jean."

"Such as?"

Her fingertips traced the outline of his mouth. "For instance, when I come to the wars with you I'll need a wagon and—"

His eyes opened wide as his hand caught her fingers. "To the wars? You? Ah, no. War is a mean and dirty business. There's no part in it for you."

"I love you. I want to be near you all the time!"

"And I love you. More than life itself. Yet when I ride away to fight a battle I don't want to worry about your riding in the baggage train, subject to— God! The mere thought of those English devils finding you alone and helpless to their lusts—"

His arms held her so tightly she could scarcely breathe. Her thick black hair was scented as it trailed over his chest and shoulders, reminding him that this woman was the world to him. And he could not risk losing that world, once he had known its joys.

"We'll say no more about it," he murmured at last "You'll stay safe in Dauphiné."

Marie pouted and looked slantwise at him through her long black lashes. "So I'm to be tucked away safe and sound, am I? Like a reliquary wrapped in cloth to preserve the sheen of its gold? What about you, friend husband? *Hein?* You and that farm woman, that blonde hussy Simone, you'll be having yourselves a holiday in the Loire country. Maybe even laughing at me."

The more she talked, the more excited she became. She

wept a little, pitying herself, and only when Jean began the slow tide of caresses against which she had no defense did she forget the future for the present. Yet the shadow lay between them, vaguely glimpsed and disturbing. As they dressed to go belowstairs to the great hall she would sigh and glance at him, murmuring, "Three days is such a short time, isn't it?" Or as they strolled in the garden in the summer night she might whisper, "Is the moon ever so full above your battle tent, my love?"

And when he held her in his arms, as they stood at the oriel window of their bedchamber staring south toward Dauphiné and the blue Mediterranean coast, she would lean back into him, saying, "I shall be very lonely without you. You've taught me what a man can mean to a woman, here in Reims."

He kissed her white throat. "Are you suggesting that you might be unfaithful while I'm gone?"

She tossed her head. "Who knows? I'm a human being and a woman. You leave me a deserted wife, a new bride. There are very many attractive men at the court."

"I'll put you in a chastity belt."

"Ha! You wouldn't dare!"

"I would dare very much to keep you for my own, Marie," he said soberly. She turned and pressed against him. "Then take me with you, Jean! Take me as wife or camp trull— only don't leave me here alone!"

"Would you ride as did Simone? Live among crude soldiers, get used to the boisterious ways and lewd talk?"

"If it meant being near you, I would. Gladly!"

Her soft mouth touched his lips as she pressed closer, murmuring throatily, "You find it easy to forbid me now, while I'm here in your arms doing naughty things to you. Like this and—this!" She laughed. "It won't be so easy for you a month from now, or two months. Unless you plan on taking Simone with you."

It grew harder to talk with his wife displaying such affection, but Jean said, "I've told you I bought a tavern in Orleans for her, where she can earn a good living. What was between us is over and done."

147

"Words, just words," she whispered. "Hmmm? Aren't they?"

"Marie, Marie! Don't you believe I love you and you alone? These past few days together and our nights—"

"Prove you love me. Prove it by taking me along when you march out of Reims to fight the beefeaters."

He swung her up in his arms and carried her toward the bed. "I'll prove it in a better way right now."

With this devotion, with this ecstacy of flesh against flesh and fevered words whispered into her lips with his kisses, Marie had to be content. And since she realized that nothing could persuade him to risk her safety, she found a queer hunger to snatch at pleasure while she could. With strong young arms she clung to him, with kisses she sought to teach him that without him, she was nothing.

Later toward dawn, while he slept, Marie wept alone into her pillow, tears of mingled happiness and sorrow, of dread for the dull and empty days that would be her lot once Jeanne d'Arc lifted her banner in the city square to march the army into Champagne.

Philip de Basoches sat munching crayfish as he listened to the serving woman who stood so respectfully before him, bobbing her head every now and so often as she talked. In the cobbled streets below his solar windows they could hear the clatter of hoofs and the clank of metal, the creak of wagon hubs, as the soldiers of the army of France gathered to the harsh voices of their sergeants. From time to time his upraised palm would halt her flow of words to permit the passage of a courier on a galloping horse.

"Going to Châteaudun, she is, milord. The castle given to The Bastard by his brother Charles, the Duke of Orleans, for his victories over the English."

"Oh, yes. The old Palais de Thibaut. And you'll be going with her, eh? It will make a nice arrangement. I'll follow in a month or two, giving her enough time to miss her husband's attentions."

Lord Philip smiled with his thick red lips. To leave a bride of three days was the act of a fool. Only such a hotheaded patriot like Jean of Dunois could be so stupid. Ah, well. The mistakes of one man were the successes of another. He anticipated no trouble with the new Countess of Dunois once she became lonely enough to need a man.

His fingers closed on a small purse that was fat with silver *ecus*. He tossed it through the air and watched the woman catch it in greedy hands. Her name was Corinne. She was a widow, though still young and attractive. Watching her tuck the purse into her girdle, he toyed with the idea of bedding her.

"When I ride to Châteaudun, I'll need a room in which to sleep until I overcome what few prejudices against me Marie may still have," he said softly.

Her startled glance sought his face, and her eyes narrowed. He was a great bull of a man, this Count de Basoches. In her heart she had envied Marie the attraction she held for him. Partly for the money he gave her, partly because of her own admiration of him, she had consented to betray her mistress.

Now she smiled understandingly. "My lord need have no worry on that score. My own room will shelter him. None save myself will see him enter or leave."

Philip rose and moved past the table to stand looking down at her. "And you yourself? Until the time is ripe for me to bed the countess, where will you sleep?"

Her eyes were bold. "Wherever milord pleases. On the floor amid the rushes or—in milord's arms."

He patted her shoulder. "Until Châteaudun, then."

She went out with a rustle of underskirts. Behind her Philip de Basoches munched thoughtfully on a crayfish. He had been a very patient man, these past months while The Bastard was making such a name for himself. He had willed himself to calmness even when he knew that Marie was falling deeply in love with her husband.

Now, however . . .

Perhaps the gods of chance were about to favor him instead of his rival. With The Bastard away on the field of battle—let him be a hero, he didn't care!—Marie would be ready, like a ripe plum, to be plucked.

He munched with his eyes half closed, lewdly dreaming.

CHAPTER NINE

FROM REIMS the army of France marched west, pennons flying, to meet the English. Advancing against them came the Regent of England, John, Duke of Bedford; yet when the armies did meet, at Montepilloy in the middle of August, there were only a few sorties. It was as if each side dreaded to come to grips, for so much might ride on the result of one pitched battle neither quite dared to strike the necessary first blow.

The Maid was beside herself with fury, but she had insisted Charles come with them on this triumphal march on Paris; now that the king was in the field, she hoped he would help her achieve the victories *le bon Dieu* had promised. Yet it was Charles more than any other—he was *le roi* now— who persisted in these vacillating, desultory tactics. A fight at a stone bridge near Senlis, an exchange of arrows a few miles beyond La Ferté Milon, and the king was satisfied.

Though Bedford wrote insulting letters to the King of France in which he named Jeanne of Domremy as no better than a harlot, he was seemingly content to wage a war of outposts and patrols. As if assured that The Maid would be unable to throw her army into a decisive battle, he went back to Paris.

And The Maid moved into Compiègne.

The Bastard fumed and fretted at this living chess game. Bad enough to be away from his Marie! But also, to see his cannons turned into pack trains, to watch his lances grow rusty with disuse, seemed the insult of all insults. A dozen times he railed at Charles, together with The Maid, demanding he be allowed to match strength with England in a pitched battle.

"Let me throw my cannon against their bowmen! Just once, to prove what I can do! Sire, I beg—on my knees if you want—only give the word to fight!"

Charles could not say that word. So long unused to victory, so long accustomed only to the anonymity of the dauphinage, he had become drunk with importance. He saw such rich towns as Beauvais and Compiègne bow to his *oriflamme.* At the same time he was negotiating with his archenemy the Duke of Burgundy, Philip the Good, for a truce between them.

In September he permitted himself to be persuaded to attack Paris, only to call back The Maid and the army before little more than a single attack had been made. In Gien, then, he took up his royal residence and began to disband his troops.

"Are you mad?" asked The Bastard of his royal cousin. "Or are you a traitor to yourself? It may be you're only stupid."

Charles VII heaved himself up from his X-chair. His ugly face was flushed with fury. His crooked legs shook as if with ague, so great was his emotion. His hand hammered the chair arm viciously.

"I could have you racked for those words, Jean. As Thibaut roasted alive that poor devil, Lord Sulpice of Chaumont, over a slow spit—so I could also order you cooked!"

Jean laughed at him. "You utter fool! Must you put so much trust in La Trémoille and Philip of Burgundy that you hinder and delay our every attack? Arrest me, if you dare! See La Hire and Saintrailles and others—perhaps even The Maid—fall away from your standard. You are France, but you can die, Charles. Then someone else might be France. My brother Charles, the Duke of Orleans, for example. Do you think the English would release him as their prisoner long enough to have him crowned as you were crowned?"

The man who had been the Dauphin shrank within his costly ermine robes. His hand shook as he made a little gesture, half in anger, half in conciliation. "I—I spoke too hastily, cousin," he said. "God knows I owe you everything I am."

"Then owe me also the patience to listen when I speak. This treaty with Burgundy—your attempt to give Philip Compiègne when Compiègne wants only to belong to you—

151

is madness. Your destruction of the bridge at Saint Denis to prevent our return to Paris was more madness. Are you with the English or against them?"

The king twisted his long fingers together. Always weak, he was now revealing himself as a man who feared to be strong. The idea of command ennobles some men; others it shatters as a fall might shatter a vase.

"I don't know what to do! Burgundy promised me he'd withdraw from the English, refuse to support them any longer. Once the Burgundian party in Paris knows that, they will either turn against the English garrisons or stand aside while you and Jeanne march in."

The Bastard shook his head. "Too late for that. Bedford will have reinforced Paris."

Again the hands wrung together. "What shall I do?"

"Put the army in the field again! Forget Burgundy. Remember only that you must fight to drive the English out. It should be your only thought."

Charles promised, but his Council, who controlled the purse strings to such pitiful monies as were in the royal treasury, would not vote the funds necessary to send a strong force against the beefeaters. And so, as autumn passed, the court moved from Issoudun to Montargis to Bourges. Where the court went, The Maid went almost like a prisoner.

The Bastard left in disgust, took his five hundred lances and his artillery and went out to find someone to fight.

Along a country road ten miles south of Montdidier, The Bastard ran full tilt into a strong English force traveling south toward Paris. A hasty placement of his cannon—two bombardments were enough to decimate the beefeaters—a charge of lances, and the engagement was over.

In the supply train he found a packet of letters addressed to the Duke of Bedford. When he broke the seals and read them, he realized that fate had put a whip in his hands.

That night he began a hurried march toward Bourges.

It was late October when he faced the king and his council in an upper chamber of the *château* at Bourges, flinging the letters down before them with an angry hand. He made a fine figure in his silvered armor, his green jupon emblazoned with the golden nettles. His tawny hair was cropped close to his skull, and his blue eyes burned with battle lust.

"Read them, *monsieur le roi!* Read—and know that the boy-king of England, Henry VI, will land at Caen in March with a fresh army! That he will join with Burgundy to attack us all along the Marne. That, while he attacks our rear, Bedford will devote himself to our forces at Lagny and Senlis. We shall be between two armies, each of which will outnumber us."

If he wanted consternation, he found it in dramatic fashion. Charles wept with self-pity. His counselors cursed and would have given the lie to Jean of Dunois except that no man could deny the authenticity of the letters. Against its will, the Council voted to move against Burgundy by besieging La Charité.

Philip de Basoches surveyed himself for the tenth time in the little mirror of the bedroom, well content with his powerful figure clad in black cote-hardie and hose, each sleeve trimmed in martin. He was a handsome man. Marie of Dunois would trip over her feet running into his arms.

Corinne had assured him of this in terse whispers less than an hour after he had dismounted in the inner bailey of the *palais Châteaudun.* "She pines for *le Bâtard,* believe me! Her eyes grow sunken, her cheeks haggard. Every night she tosses restlessly and whispers his name. I've heard her with my own ears!"

Something about the widow told the Lord of Arnais that she herself might enjoy the ministrations he planned for the mistress. Her cheeks were flushed, her eyes bright. She took occasion to lean forward on the little faldstool where she sat so that her bosom might press pointed outlines into the thin stuff of her bliaut.

"*Assez!* You're done well, my sweet."

She shrugged. A secret smile touched her full mouth. As Philip had been patient, so could Corinne afford to bide her time. Let him take his Marie. After a little while, when the bloom had worn off, he would come hotfooting it into the servant's bed. Corinne had known more than one nobleman in her lifetime. Always they followed a pattern where it came to women.

She rose and shook out her skirt, touching his shoulder with a thigh as she bent to brush away a bit of lint. They were close enough so that all he need do was—

Ah! It began now, with his hand under her skirt, stroking her calf. She looked down at him, smiling lazily. "My lord Philip! Have you forgotten the Countess of Dunois?"

"Are her legs shapelier than yours? Or any smoother?"

Her eyes were wise, staring into his. *"Mais non!* But she is inside your head—" her finger tapped his forehead—"and that is a very dangerous place for a woman to be, with a man." She caught his hand as it foraged upwards. "Enough! Go lay with your Marie. Then when you've put her out of your head— Well, we shall see."

Philip grinned at her. A cocky piece, *par Dieu!* It was too bad he'd committed himself with the Countess of Dunois. This pert serving maid might prove to be the better woman between the sheets.

Half in amusement at his own inconstancy, Basoches permitted Corinne to lead him up the spiral stair toward the large bedchamber that looked out across the river to the old Church of Saint Jehan. The candle she carried in a brass holder cast shadows along the gallery, with its row of sculptured saints, and quivered with every footfall.

The woman pushed him through a partially open door. "Hide behind the standing screen. It's time for her disrobement. I'll have to attend her, of course. When I leave the rest is up to you."

Then she was gone and Basoches was inside the room, feeling like a character out of a tale by Giovanni Boccaccio. The standing screen was a tall one, reaching above his head, but there was more than an inch of open space at its hinges, which permitted him a full view of the room.

Marie stood before the fireplace unhooking her gown, arms bent behind her and fingers fumbling at the clasps. He could hear a little of the tune she hummed, but he gave small heed to his ears. The only sense that concerned him at the moment was his sight.

He found that, as she began lowering the kirtle from

154

shoulders to hips, his mouth became dry and breathing more difficult. With the red fire flames on her jutting breasts and round belly, she became a fabled succubus, one of those mythical women who come to men at night to place them under a fleshly spell. And, as if he were already enchanted by her, he could not turn away his gaze.

When she walked naked to pour wine, standing unconcerned and sipping slowly, Philip de Basoches almost tipped over the screen. His poulaine made a scraping sound on the floor, and Lady Marie swung about and stared into the shadows. After a moment she turned away, finishing the wine and crossing the room to throw open the casements to breathe a little of the mild October air. Behind her Corinne went from candlestand to table, putting out all the lights except a tiny oil boat beside the bed.

Then Corinne went out and closed the door.

The Countess of Dunois was not disposed to sleep. She moved about the room, hands ruffling her thick black hair, lifting it high above her head, letting it fall about her white shoulders down to her hips. She braided it standing before the mirror, head tilted to one side. When Marie was done, Basoches thought she looked almost like a little girl.

Twice more she drank from the silver wine pitcher, and at each sup the Lord of Arnais nodded his approval. A drunken woman was an amorous woman.

At last she moved to the bed and thrust back the heavy brocade drape to reveal the turned-down coverlets. Putting a knee on the sheet, she rolled between the covers and drew them up to her chin. The little flame in the oil boat flickered in the faint breeze. As far as Philip de Basoches could tell, she was wide awake. *Bien!* He would wait.

Not until a cramp moved in his leg did he stir from behind the screen, advancing softly on the tips of his toes. She lay with her eyes closed, faintly breathing. Philip de Basoches came to the side of the bed and stood a moment, looking down into her lovely face.

Her eyes opened.

For a long moment they stared at one another.

Marie thrust a hand beneath the cushion, and Basoches saw the muscles of her forearm tense. In almost that same motion the pillow was cast aside, and a long Savoyard dagger gleamed in her fist.

"My Lord of Arnais," she said harshly and he saw the disgust on her features, "come like a sneak in the night. A pretty tale this will make for Jean's ears. He'll seek you out and slay you, you know that."

Philip laughed thickly. "Then let me give him reason to kill." He moved forward toward the bed but halted when the dagger lifted. For a moment he paused, uncertain. The hate was livid in her eyes. He knew she would use the steel on him. It was there for him to read in her back-drawn lips and shallow breathing.

He had come seeking a woman in need of a man. He had not expected to find a woman so virtuous she would fight for her honor.

The Lord of Arnais sneered. "If you value your fidelity so much, keep it."

He drew away into the shadows, stood motionless a long moment, then was gone. Marie came to her feet, the linen sheet wrapped about her nudity. She listened to his footfalls moving down the hall.

She ran to the casement window, leaning out.

"Baptiste! Regnault! Come quickly!"

If Sieur Philip were still at Châteaudun—and he could scarcely have escaped so quickly—she would make him her prisoner and send him to Jean in irons.

Her retainers searched the castle from mews to barbican, but they found no trace of Philip. They invaded Corinne's little room but did not think to toss aside the rumpled covers from which their knockings had roused the serving woman. Clutching her nightgown tightly, she screamed curses as they moved about her bedchamber, examining a big clothes cupboard and thrusting back the tapestried hangings that kept out drafts and cold night air.

"Imbeciles! Fools!" she screamed. "What would a noble-man be doing in my *pièce?* He came to amuse himself with Lady Marie. Probably he didn't please her, so she sent you to run him down."

A tall man-at-arms grunted sourly. "I was winning at dice

when she called. Come along, you men. He's not in here. We'll try the other rooms."

As the door closed behind them, Corinne thrust home the bolt, then leaned her shoulders into the wood, closing her eyes in weak relief. Stupid fool that she'd been, to take such a risk. And for what? A purse of silver? God forgive her for being a clodpoll!

She opened her eyes and saw Lord Philip casting back the covers, stepping from the bed onto the stone floor. He was red-faced and his dignity had been ruffled, but he was safe enough.

"She'll pay for this," he snarled, setting his roundel belt more firmly to his hips. "I swear by God and the devil, she'll pay."

"You aren't safe out of her castle, yet already you make threats," the woman sniffed, moving past him. "Wait a little while, then go."

His hand stabbed her wrist and drew her in against him. "I've failed with one woman tonight. I won't fail with a second."

"While every man-at-arms in the place hunts for you?"

His thick lips smiled. "The conceit amuses me. They explore the castle, I explore you."

"And if I should scream?"

"I'll put cold steel between your ribs."

"You would, too, wouldn't you?" Corinne hesitated. Nobody would come to search her room a second time this night. As well enjoy herself as be forced. It wasn't every wench who got to lie with a nobleman. She let her body soften. "Eh, well. What's to lose?"

"Nothing's to lose, everything's to gain."

She eyed his hand, which had slipped down into the opening of her nightgown. "You make me feel like a Porte Saint-Antoine whore."

"I'm talking about gold pieces, not silver. It isn't only your body I'm interested in, but your tongue as well. You've been with your mistress a good many years?"

"Almost twelve. I know more about her than she knows about herself."

157

"*Bien*. You will tell me all you know. You understand? Hold nothing back, absolutely nothing."

She shivered to his handplay on her body.

The attack on the fortified city of La Charité was undertaken toward the latter part of November. From the beginning, as The Bastard grumbled, it was doomed to failure.

Money was scarce in the royal court in these early days of Charles' reign. At a time when there was not enough money even to buy the king a pair of poulaines, little wonder there was none to pay soldiers. Lack of money meant a lack of food, of proper arms and equipment. Hungry men do not fight well.

The siege lasted into December and was lifted.

The Maid went back to the Court.

And The Bastard, with La Hire and the other war captains, took their separate commands and marched along the roads to Paris, to Louviers, to Lagny. Filled with a fierce anger at his king and all his Council, he swore not to return home until the *oriflamme* was set above the towers of Notre Dame in Paris.

A courier from his wife found him in a crossroads tavern a week before Christmas. He had been raiding English supply trains moving east from Caen for Paris. Though he drove his lances hard, he drove himself even harder. Mud rimmed the edges of his armor, and the lines of his face were haggard as he stood before the inn hearth, spreading out the parchment that was filled with Marie's neat, precise handwriting.

A scowl darkened his features as he read. *"Douce Dieu!* Is Basoches mad, to throw himself at my wife? The fool! Didn't he know I'd pay him a return visit?"

Tiredness dropped from him as he whirled to face his officers. "Eat your fill, gentlemen. Tomorrow we march for Arnais."

One of his officers, a swarthy Italian named Jacopo Saltello, who had fought with Muzio Attandolo in his Neapolitan campaigns, rasped, "For Arnais? He's on our side. Men say he's good friends with the king."

"Good friend of Charles, bad enemy of mine!"

Dark Jacopo stared, then shrugged. "One enemy or the

158

other, what's the difference? We fight for the gold we steal. I just hope Philip has plenty." He watched Jean move to the fireplace and read the parchment over and over. Jacopo gestured with a wine cup. "That one, he isn't interested in gold, but a rope. I think when he finds Lord Philip he'll hang him on the highest gibbet in Champagne. It must be hell to love a woman that much."

The Bastard marched his lances the hundred and fifty miles to Basoches in a little more than four days. He ringed the curtain walls of the Château Arnais with his cannon and his siege engines, then sent word for Philip to surrender himself and spare his people.

The castellan came on quivering legs to reveal the fact that Lord Philip was not at Basoches but in southern France. "The last we heard, lord Count, is that he was visiting a friend in Nîmes. I don't know when he'll return."

"My quarrel lies with Philip alone. Yet I have hungry soldiers to feed, greedy soldiers to pay."

The old man drew a sigh of relief. "I'll send carts from the castle with barley bread and capons, geese and pigs. There will be tarts and sweetmeats, with many jacks of wine."

Jean smiled. "And fifty thousand *livres tournois.*"

The castellan blinked. "Lord Philip is a good Frenchman. This is an act of banditry."

Jean appeared to reflect. "Perhaps you're right. If I take the castle and put all its people to the sword, there'll be no survivors to run to the king with my name."

"The fifty thousand gold pieces will come with the food," he was assured.

The thought that Philip de Basoches was free to harry his Marie was like a whiplash laid across his shoulders. Jean grew haggard, fretful. It was, at times, as if he walked in a dream world. He laid plans for attacks and alarums against the English or the Burgundians, and his stratagems achieved complete succes; yet he accepted each victory with a casual air.

His officers watched him with brooding eyes. They were devoted to him and to his cause, yet they sensed a bemusement in him that worried them.

"Go to Châteaudun," one of them urged.

"What? When French arms are successful at every point? I here in Picardy, Jeanne d'Arc at Lagny and La Hire in Maine? No, no. Marie must wait. France is in more danger than she."

Later he was to realize how wrong he was.

And so he marched against the Duke of Bedford and against Philip of Burgundy, breaking their longbow formations again and again with his cannon. Winter had given way to spring, and everywhere the hyacinths pushed their purple buds into the April sunlight; hope was in the air, together with their fragrance.

He was encamped a few miles outside Pontoise when he heard that Jeanne the Maid had been captured. The early morning sunlight glinted on his armor as he stood before his tent, listening to the courier who had ridden fast from Compiègne.

"She was attacking Margny when she was dragged from her saddle," the messenger told him between long swallows at a winejack. "She was defending the rear guard so her men could pass through the gates to safety from the Burgundians when it happened.

"Some fool named Flavy gave orders to raise the drawbridge and close the city gate. She was left almost alone outside, fighting savagely. Even so, she almost got away. She yielded to a man-at-arms in the service of Jean of Luxembourg."

"God have pity on her," The Bastard said, fist clenched against the agony in his soul, "for the English won't!"

And France? he asked himself. What effect will Jeanne's capture have on France? Would she lapse into the apathy that had sapped her lifeblood before the coming of The Maid?

"No," he growled, "I won't let it happen."

Jeanne d'Arc was a prisoner of the English, but prisoners could be freed by a swift, surprise attack. She was lodged in the castle at Beaulieu only a little more than seventy miles from his own camp.

He told his men, "We march at once."

Spring rains had made a quagmire of the dirt roads of

160

Normandy. It took him three days to travel thirty miles, dragging cannon and his few siege engines through muddy bogs almost every step of the way. When he reached Clairoix he found the combined armies of England and Burgundy drawn up before him.

The Bastard ordered a withdrawal.

He swung around by way of Laon, but again he was intercepted in force. With only five hundred lances he scarcely dared hurl himself at the uncounted thousands behind the English lions. The Dukes of Bedford and Burgundy, appreciating the value of their captive, were determined to keep her at all costs. In capturing her they had captured the heart of France.

The Bastard moved into Normandy, where he set about recruiting troops. With enough soldiers he could defy the English, meet them in open battle, win through to The Maid. Never once did he doubt his ability. All he needed were the men to carry arms.

May became June and then early summer; and now the English, as if aware that danger threatened their hold on Jeanne, began to move her around the countryside. From Beaulieu she went to Beaurevoir. Twice she herself tried to escape, and both times was discovered. The Bastard found it hard to keep informed of her whereabouts. There were rumors that Holy Church believed her to be a witch and would petition Jean of Luxembourg to turn her over to the Bishop of Beauvais for trial.

Jeanne went to Arras and then to Crotoy during November. In December she was at Saint-Valery, then went on to Dieppe and to the old castle of Philip Augustus at Rouen.

In Rouen she was lodged in a castle tower and chained by the neck, by the wrists and by the ankles. These manacles were never removed. Five soldiers were always on guard to prevent another escape attempt.

The Bastard never gave up hope.

He offered silvier deniers and gold *louis d'or* for strong young men in Normandy. He trained them well—with his own hands, sometimes. His twenty cannon became fifty. He kept in constant touch with La Hire against the moment when they might unite their forces and move against Rouen.

When La Hire could take time away from his tavern women, he would pay Jean a whirlwind visit. "We waste our time," he would grumble on occasion. "The Maid herself is resigned to the fact the English will kill her. She's already said so."

"I'm not resigned to the fact."

"You're afraid that if she dies, France dies with her."

"Well, yes, since without her we seem to win few battles. Free her, lift up the *oriflamme,* march on Bedford and Burgundy! Imprison Henry VI as Jeanne lies imprisoned at the moment. Ha! We'd teach the *godons* a thing or two!"

"Jeanne might be more valuable dead than alive," said La Hire.

"I've thought of that, but I won't accept it."

"She'd be a martyr. She could be everywhere that Frenchmen fight then, not just in one place."

The Bastard scowled at him. "Are you trying to talk me out of my rescue preparations?"

"God forbid. I only point out facts."

They said no more on the matter of Jeanne d'Arc, these hard-bitten war captains, for winter was at hand and the snows that draped Normandy in white silence meant that armies in the field must put up at winter quarters.

Jean marched his men south, into Poitou.

Red Gui stamped across the common room of the Inn of the Red Feather, shaking dust and grime from his cordovan boots. His flaring cloak revealed a chain mail shirt and leather jerkin above the Spanish leather. He had ridden a long way since sunup, and tiredness was a cramp in every muscle.

The man who waited in the shadows of an arched room stirred at his coming, his hand falling away from a wooden tankard filled with claret. The flickering candle flames tinted black shadows at his jaw and beneath his sunken eyes. Philip de Basoches was a man so consumed by hate it showed in his every feature.

"Milord, I came as fast as I could but my horse—"

"Never mind that. You're here now." A ringed hand indicated a second tankard and a pitcher of chilled wine.

"Drink your fill. Then answer what I want to know. A long

162

time ago you mentioned a woman named Simone. A farm woman of Brie, you said she was."

"I remember. The Bastard made her his mistress."

"*Oui.* Now then—I seem to recall your having spoken about a black mass—it was near Sezanne, I believe. This Simone lay naked on a stone altar in an abbey court . . ."

The claret was good to the tongue. Red Gui rolled the wine about in his mouth, eyes closed, his weight full on the wooden bench in the arched cubicle. He swallowed and looked at the nobleman.

"A black mass it was, said to the devil himself." Red Gui shivered. "In return, Simone got a love potion."

Basoches relaxed a little, laughing harshly. "*Bien!* This cloak Simone wore, would you know it again?"

"Mmm, I think so. Blue it was, with red shields sewn onto its border. It was probably stolen from an English supply train, red shields being the device of the Erroll family."

"You'll ride to Orleans and steal it."

The outlaw goggled. "Steal a cloak? Name of God! If it's a cape you want, I can steal you a better one right here in Loches."

Basoches smiled grimly. "No, no. It won't do at all. For instance, when you swear that this cloak was at the black mass you saw four years ago, the ring of truth will be in your voice. *Hein?*"

"When I swear—God's love! What'd Simone ever do to you, you'd run to the Church about her?"

"Not Simone. Another."

He gave Red Gui time to think, sitting and sipping his wine. At last the red-headed man cried out thickly in understanding. "Ah, I see your plan. To strike at the man through his wife—through Marie! *Hein?* It shall be Marie of Dunois we accuse of sacrilege, not Simone. Marie who stretched naked on that altar. Marie who used the blue cloak to hide her nakedness."

"Can you lie convincingly enough before a Church court?"

The bandit chuckled. "Aye. I can. Give me a bag of golden *livres* and Simone for my own and I'll swear to anything you name."

Basoches scowled. "There may be need to torture the farm

woman to get her statement that she knew Marie was undertaking the black mass, that she tried to dissuade her . . ." His shoulders moved. "If there's enough womanhood left in her when my tortures are done—why, take her in any way you like."

Red Gui nodded. "I'll ride for Orleans at dawn."

The great bells of the Orleans cathedral were bonging out the midnight hour as Simone stirred from her stool beside the cask rack. Her back ached and she stretched, letting her eyes run the length of the common room with its oak benches and heavy trestle tables. In the past year and a half she had become a well-to-do woman, here in the tavern of the Three Crosses.

The wine casks flanking the east wall bulged with tart claret and sweet port. The *aumonière* at her waist was heavy with gold and silver coins. When a customer could not pay for a hanap of wine or a small mug of ale, he left such garments as he wore to cover their price hanging on the wall hooks. There was enough confiscated clothing on those hooks to feed her for half a year.

Several of her pretty barmaids also served those customers in other ways than by carrying winejacks to the tables. Simone was a realist. She knew well enough that most wayside taverns in this year of God 1430 were little more than brothels. Besides, a proportion of their body-earnings went into her money sacks.

She rapped now on a keg with a length of wood.

"Closing time, closing time. Move along, all of you. I don't want the city guard in here, shutting me up."

A few men rose to their feet and began to lurch for the oaken door. One man lay snoring over a wet tabletop. Simone gestured with her hand, and a burly servant came to heave him over a shoulder and toss him out onto the cobblestones. In the shadows close beside an enormous wine tun a well-dressed merchant sat with pretty Caroline, his hand out of sight under her skirt.

Simone rapped again, louder. "Caroline! Don't you hear the bells? On your feet, girl."

164

The merchant turned a flushed face in her direction. "A few more minutes, Simone. Just—"

"You men," she laughed. "Are you never satisfied?"

"A room, then. Abovestairs," he muttered.

"*Peste!* Be off with you. Come earlier tomorrow night."

Grumbling, the tradesman pulled free of the girl, gathering up his thick woolen greatcape. Standing, he draped it over his shoulders and wrapped it about him tightly. It was cold in Orleans in this late February of the year.

Simone watched him go, waiting for Caroline to straighten her rumpled clothes, for little Gai and pert Isobel and languid Claire to join her in the nightly procession to their cellar beds. When burly Roger had thrust another log on the hearth fire, Simone moved to the door and stood breathing deeply of the crisp air a few moments.

There was a strange dissatisfaction in the farm woman. She knew well enough that The Bastard had been more than generous in buying this tavern so she might earn her livelihood with it. It was not material matters that oppressed her so much as it was—

"Well, *ma petite fou?*" she asked of herself and the cold winter moon high above. "What is it that troubles you, *hein?* The lack of a man? No, no. I gave all that up when Jean went back to his wife. The fact that I grow reasonably rich from my wine casks and the bodies of my servants? No, not that, either."

She closed the door and leaned her forehead against it, shivering slightly. She was a lucky woman. Farm life was hard life. She had escaped that servitude with The Bastard. Her palms were smooth and soft now; as a farm wife they'd have been cracked and gnarled and dirty long ago. She was still pretty, still slimly attractive.

"I'd have been a dumpy sow if Red Gui hadn't killed my husband those years ago. Strange how life works itself out. I must be tired, to stand here brooding so." Her hands moved the iron door-bar into its slots.

She went from candle to candle, lamp to lamp, extinguishing the flames. This was a nightly ritual with her. Always she paused in the hallway door to turn and give the common room one last glance, as if with that look to reassure herself that she owned what she saw. Then she turned and, skirt in hand, mounted the narrow little stair to the second floor.

She knelt in prayer beside her bed before undressing, whispering her *Ave Marias* with bent head, thinking, I pray for you, my Jean, night after night and every night. Do you ever pray for me? Do you ever even think of me, wherever you are, out there somewhere fighting the *godons?* And from Jean her thoughts went to The Maid, cold and lonely and afraid in her iron manacles; and she breathed a little prayer for her, too, to give her strength to endure the trial that she was undergoing.

For all the world knew now that the English sought to have Jeanne condemned as a witch. Daily they questioned her, daily they threw the evidence of witnesses at her.

Simone shuddered. They burned witches at the stake.

She arose and undressed, moving naked to the bed, clambering between the thick quilts and coverlets. A tiny candle burned on the table beside her in case she might wake and need to move about the room. Its pallid beams danced a little on her closed eyelids like ghostly fingertips before she fell asleep. . . .

A hand touched her throat. Fingers closed down savagely.

She came awake threshing and fighting, trying to claw the hairy forearms and thrust aside the weight of knees and shoulders that pinned her so helplessly into the rope mattress. Her wide eyes saw a grinning face, a lock of loose red hair, a thick chest where a leather jerkin fell away.

"Sweet mother of Christ," she whimpered. "I dream!"

Those hard fingers biting into her windpipe, making breathing next to impossible, this heavy body holding her helpless was no dream! No! This was Red Gui, come to life out of past nightmares!

"There's no Bastard around to stop me now, is there?" he taunted her, enjoying the terror that bulged her eyes, that distended her ripe red mouth. "Philip said I could have you before his torturers went to work on you. I like you like this— naked under the covers, warm from sleep—"

His free hand yanked at the quiltings, sent them flying. His eyes raked her nudity, and he licked thick lips. Laughter rumbled in his chest.

166

"You're even better than I dreamed, farm woman. Big breasts—wide hips—fine legs!"

She tried to scream and could not. His hands were on her, pinching cruelly, slapping, turning her body this way and that for his amusement. And when he took her with vicious strength, as if she were a mare and he a stud, she found that she could not even mercifully faint.

Only when he was done with her, when his lusts were momentarily sated, did oblivion come, in the form of his big fist across her face.

Red Gui grinned as she slumped unconscious. "This is the beginning, you blonde baggage," he told her relaxed body. "You're my prisoner now. Until Philip gives you to his hot irons and the rack, you're mine to do with as I want."

He chuckled and slid off the bed. Now he must find the cloak with the red shields of Erroll, wrap the woman in it and carry her down to the drayman's cart waiting below. He had come up hand over hand to the casement windows of the inn; he would leave by the front door, the woman over a shoulder.

By dawn they would be miles beyond Orleans.

CHAPTER TEN

THE SCENTS OF SPRING were in the air again. The netted iris in a panoply of blue-purple and gold, the yellow jonquils and purple hyacinths made fragrant blankets in the fields and along the roadside ditches as The Bastard unfurled his nettle standard.

Jeanne The Maid was a prisoner in Rouen and the English were in France. These were his goals—to free the one and oust the other. Until then he had no life as a man, only as a soldier.

He marched north into Normandy, and now there rode with him a full thousand lances, with five hundred crossbowmen and five hundred pikes, with nearly three hundred

167

artillerymen to fire his fifty great cannon. Sunlight glinted on lance point and gun barrel as leather creaked and metal clanked to the plodding hoofs of their war horses. Their voices lifted in song. The Maid was a prisoner, but there was a new stirring in the breasts of Frenchmen. She had taught them what it meant to be a free people. And so, as they walked or rode, they sang.

Jean listened to the bawdy verses with a grim smile. He rode with his tawny head bare to the spring breezes off the foothills to the west, his fine silver armor seeming light to his rested body. Now the winter was gone, with all its pleasures and delights, and it was time to strike, to hit the *godons* again and again until they retreated across the channel and into their own land.

"Rolf!" he shouted suddenly.

His esquire jabbed spurs to his mount and came galloping.

"Rolf, we're coming into Poix shortly. It isn't much of a town, but an old enemy of mine has his *château* there. His name is Robert de Berri."

Robert de Berri was the only one of his father's murderers whose deed on that long-gone night outside the Hôtel Barbette was still unavenged. Raoul d'Anquetonville was alive, but his wife Alix had paid for his crime with her body. Jean sighed, remembering her ecstasies.

Too long had he placed France above his vengeance. It was time now to resume the war with the beefeaters and his own personal vendetta.

"We pause a little while to speak with de Berri. Tell Jacopo to surround his *château* but not to launch an assault until I give the word."

They swung slightly to the west at Senlis and moved north into Poix, skirting the town and the forest and the fields cultivated with cabbages and cucumbers, beets and barley until they came to the gray stone walls of the *château*. Here and there at the merlons they could see a few pinched, frightened faces peering down. An old man appeared above the donjon and called to them, asking what they wanted.

"The death of your master," Jean yelled back. "Only ask him if he wants to die in single combat or in his burning

168

castle after I've smashed its walls and my men have slain its garrison."

The old man went away but soon enough was back, and by his side stood a tall knight, already half cased in armor. The Bastard knew him for Robert de Berri.

"No one can get through these walls," he said, gesturing around him. "Tomorrow I ride out to join my lord Stafford to harry you French at all points. By Midsummer Night we'll have your king as we have The Maid."

Jean waved a hand, and several of his cannon came trundling forward, to aim their long barrels at the portcullis and donjon gate. The drawbridge was raised, but this would splinter fast enough after a few stone balls came crashing through its plankings. At a called word five squat bombards, their thick noses pointing almost skyward, came to flank their bigger brothers.

"You bombardmen, sweep those walls clean above the gate with canister shot. You cannoneers, get me entry into the *château.*"

The cannonading began within minutes. Before midday the drawbridge and oaken gate lay shattered and the iron bars of the portcullis were bent and twisted beyond recognition. Now it was the turn of the sappers to race forward with wagons of dirt and branches and stone, to fill in that part of the moat normally spanned by the drawbridge. As they ran in close to the walls, the bombards opened fire.

Scraps of metal swept the wall walks above the moat. Those defenders who had run with boiling oil and pitch, with longbows and huge rocks to throw down on the sappers, screamed in agony as they were torn apart under that awesome hail.

The moat was covered. The gate lay open.

"Forward!" Jean shouted.

He himself led that first charge of bristling foot-long lance points, pounding over the dirt and rocks and twigs of the breached moat, under the portcullis and into the open bailey. A man-at-arms went down with his lance thrusting a yard out his back. Then his sword was in his hand as he brought his fighting men the length of the courtyard to a flight of short stone steps leading upward to the great hall.

"De Berri!" he roared. "Get me De Berri!"

His lances made short work of the defenders. More than sixty lay stretched in death on the wall walks and the bailey cobbles, while another forty stood hangdog and unarmed as prisoners. The womenfolk were screaming now as the victors began their search for loot and valuables. A young girl ran past The Bastard and, seeing his rich armor and the golden nettles of Orleans, screamed and went to her knees, clinging to his armored legs.

"Mercy, lord. Don't let— I'm virgin and—"

Pity moved in him. These were hard times for the weak and the helpless, who were so often only pawns in the larger game of statecraft played all around them. The common soldier went to war for what he could loot from the conquered and for the fleshy joys which the enemy women could bring him. In a sense, the tall young trooper behind the girl, waiting patiently while she sobbed, was doing no more than collecting what was his due.

Jean could have bought her, but it would have meant buying all the other women and—

A door at the top of the stair opened, and Robert de Berri stood framed between its jambs, clad in armor, the stag's horn that was his device worked in golden thread on his jupon. He held a long, two-edged battle-ax in a hand.

"Be gentle with her," Jean told the young soldier, and shifted his grip on his sword.

He could hear the girl screeching as he went slowly up the stone steps, his eyes never leaving the visored helmet above him. "This is to pay for the night you visited my father," he said, his voice booming inside the heavy helm.

The glinting helmet nodded. "I thought as much when I saw your nettles. I must be the last of them."

De Berri lifted his axe. His was the advantage, being above. A strong enough charge and he might sweep *le Bâtard* off his feet, send him tumbling heels over head to the bailey cobbles. He would be easy victim then for the great war ax.

The nobleman roared and sprang, but Jean was no fledgling soldier to be caught by such a stratagem. He fell to a knee and drove straight ahead with the point of his blade. Armor dented as the point drove home between *bracconière* and

170

thigh plate. Then De Berri was on top of him, stumbling, hitting his shoulder-pieces and falling forward.

The Bastard knelt a moment, sobbing for breath, his sword arm numb from shock. Their collision had been at full speed, and in his armor Robert de Berri was a formidable weight. He turned and clawed at the stonework balustrade to rise.

His opponent still lay stretched out on the ground. From every doorway and window, looting soldiers were pausing to watch and shout suggestions to their commander. A knot of them had gathered about three women and were stripping them; these, too, paused, holding the women motionless, almost completely exposed to the sunlight. Two others, belaboring a fat merchant, also halted to stare.

Jean came down the steps slowly.

As if the clanking footfalls of his mail sollerets were an alarum bell, De Berri stirred and sat up. His hand went to his ax shaft. He got up just as Jean reached the bottom step.

They rushed together, sword and ax flailing. Sparks rang where the steel edges met and screeched. For a few moments neither gave a step. Only the sword and the ax moved, back and forth in thrust and parry, sparkling in the sunlight.

Then the sword hit home on a shoulder, cutting into camail and pauldron. A wet red stain appeared on the riven metal, and De Berri staggered. The ax lowered just a little.

Jean guessed at the pain lancing into the man, at the weariness that made his ax arm fall. All around him Robert de Berri would see his people slain, about to be robbed or raped. There was no hope of rescue in him. The candle of his life was guttering its last.

"You die alone, my lord," Jean grated, "as died my father with your dagger blade in him! To Hell, De Berri!"

His sword came down in an overhead blow, slicing into the weakened chain mail. The blade came away red and wet. It fell again and again. De Berri groaned and fought back, but his eyes were glazing behind the visor and the stiffness of death was already in the muscles of his legs.

Where the stone wall of the buttery made a shadowed angle with that of the chapel, The Bastard laid his sword edge deep into his throat. Blood spouted and broken lengths of

171

chain mail went flying. De Berri slammed back against the wall. His body stood a moment braced by the stones, then lunged forward.

His fall brought a roar from the onlookers.

Jean lifted his visor. Victory was his, and this *château* and everything in it, according to the usages of war. But all he wanted at the moment was a pitcher of chilled wine.

Rolf came to undo his arming points, to lift off his helm and loosen his armor. The cool spring wind felt good on his flushed face. He breathed deeply, slowly.

"We camp here overnight!" he said at last. "Pass the word to my captains. After that, come to me in the great hall. I want an accounting of whatever treasure De Berri may have amassed."

A man-at-arms brought him a silver wine cup as he entered the great hall. He stood sipping, eying the battle standards hung from their wall poles, the heraldic shields below them. A good fortress, this one. It might have held out indefinitely against siege engines.

"Cannon," he said meditatively. "Cannon can do anything! With cannon and The Maid—"

He was almost strong enough to rescue her. Double his forces, equip each man with a horse for speed and mobility of movement, and he could surprise Rouen, and within a day enter it as he had entered here. An all-out attack on the old castle of Philip Augustus, a metalworker to remove her manacles, and Jeanne d'Arc would stand at his side once again.

Impatiently he waited for his men to bring the money chests, stalking the dais with long strides. There was so little time in which to do what must be done! The days were lengthening in this springtime of the year, but they were not nearly long enough. Time was running out faster and faster, like the sands of an hourglass.

He could not buy time as he bought recruits.

On May 30th, 1431 the English and Pierre Cauchon, Bishop of Beauvais, their trial concluded, caused Jeanne d'Arc to be brought to the marketplace of Rouen and there mounted upon a high, plaster scaffold and tied to a stake.

Faggots had been piled at her feet, and these were lighted by torches in the hands of soldiers.

She died in the consuming flames, staring at a crucifix.

The news of her death came to The Bastard while his army was in the field near Beaulieu. At first he did not believe the messenger.

"Are they mad, these beefeaters? Don't they understand that a dead Jeanne can be a thousand times greater inspiration than if she were still alive? A martyr for France! Her life in exchange for French freedom!"

When he was alone, he wept bitterly and unashamedly, for he was a sensitive man and there was a trace of guilt in him that he had aided her in her military career by his encouragement and counsel. Then he swore never to rest until her death was avenged in full, by complete victory.

Simone lay naked on the rack, her slim white wrists gripped so tightly by leather thongs that they bled where the skin was torn, her ankles held by cords wrapped about a wooden spindle. She was stretched out on a flat surface mounted on rollers. As the spindles at head and feet were turned, her body lengthened.

She was quivering with pain now, her head moving to left and right with a maniacal steadiness. Saliva had run from her mouth, mixed with blood from a bitten lip. She was moaning steadily.

Philip de Basoches sat in a curule chair at his ease, watching her suffering, gauging it to the breaking point. A clerk was at his elbow, writing materials on the desk before him. In the shadows behind them stood Red Gui.

Basoches said softly, "Learn wisdom, my dear. All you're being asked to do is sign the deposition Martin here has written in his clerkly hand." He leaned forward, making a signal with his right hand.

The burly executioners gave the spindles another turn. Simone screamed thickly, mouth wide open. Her pallid flesh rippled with the pain that ate at her joints.

"Mercy," she whimpered. "Ah, sweet Christ, have mercy!"

"The deposition. All you need do is sign the deposition.

173

Martin has read it to you a dozen times. We merely ask you to back up Gui's statement that Marie of Dunois is a witch, having offered herself in the black mass to the devil."

"No! No, I—"

The melodious voice went on serenely. "Marie is being charged with witchcraft, not you. Are you so enamored of The Bastard that you'd burn yourself rather than see his wife given to the flames? Come, woman. Sign the deposition while you're still pretty and all your limbs are straight. In time the rack will deform you. You must understand that.

"Or would you have me apply the boot to one of those pretty feet, breaking the leg bone and crippling you forever? Hmmm? What about a hot iron pressed against your belly?"

"Jesu, have pity!" came the broken whimper.

Lord Philip made a sign with his other hand, and now a third man in the purple tunic of the executioner came forward with a whip fashioned from flexible metal wires. Twice he laid them with all his strength across her thighs; twice she screamed and would have convulsed, had not her wrists and ankles been stretched to breaking.

"Now will you sign?"

"Oh, sweet Jesu—forgive me! Yes! Yes! Yes!"

The leather thongs were undone, and she was lifted to a sitting position on the rack. Her hands were shaking so fitfully that Philip had to assist her to scrawl her name at the bottom of the deposition. When it was done, she crumpled and fell unconscious to the floor.

Red Gui came forward from the shadows, loosening his cloak, throwing it about her nakedness. One of the executioners chuckled. Lord Philip smiled and nodded.

"She is none the worse for her experience. The welts on her legs will fade before long. Her joints may ache on raw days, but she'll still be serviceable enough in bed."

The red-headed bandit bent and lifted her in his arms.

Jean of Dunois was encamped at Grandvilliers when a passing merchant, displaying bolts of Amiens velvet and *cramoisi* stuffs from Lille, brought him news of his wife's arrest. At first The Bastard did not understand what he heard.

"—even such a woman as a countess, a witch!" the heavy-set mercer muttered, shaking his head. "Can you believe it? Well, maybe she is, at that, if The Maid was. There's enough of a to-do about—"

Jean had been studying the new roping on a siege catapult. He turned to survery the tradesman. "A countess, you say?"

"*Oui*, sire. The Countess Marie, The Bastard's wife."

Dunois laughed. His men were playing a crude jest on him. In plain leather jerkin and jackboots, with only a sword at his hip and no rich cloak thrown about his shoulders, the merchant thought him merely another trooper.

"It's no joke," the man grumbled, shaking his head. "Philip de Basoches is hot to have her burned, the way The Maid was burned. Already he's secured depositions from some female tavernkeeper in Orleans—there's gossip he racked her to force her to—"

Jean stabbed outward with his hand. He caught the tradesman by his furred cote-hardie and dragged him forward so swiftly that the man stumbled and went to his knees.

"A jest," Jean rasped. "Say you jest, man! Say that Jacopo Saltello put you up to it!"

"No—it's God's own truth! I know not this Jacopo fellow!"

The fright in the man's face told Jean he was speaking the truth. And in that realization a cold terror crept like a river fog into his veins and crawled along his flesh. Twice he tried to speak, and twice his tongue remained frozen in his mouth.

At last he blurted, "Speak out, man. There's no need to fear me. Here!" His hand loosed a plain purse from his sword belt, thrust it into the shaking hands of the seller of velvets. "Know me for Jean, Count of Dunois."

"Sire, I never knew. As sweet Jesu is my witness, I never realized!" His hand dragged a square of linen across his sweating forehead. "All I did was speak the truth. My life on it!"

"Tell me all of it," Jean said gently.

The words came babbling out like the waters of a stream running over bottomstones. The accusation had been made by the Lord of Arnais more than two months before. The Countess Marie had been arrested at Châteaudun and taken to Chinon, where the king had interested himself in her case.

Depositions from Simone had been read to the judges. An

175

officer of Basoches' army named Red Gui had told of seeing the countess on a stone altar in the ruins of an old abbey in Brie and *la messe noire* being celebrated on her flesh.

A blue cloak hemmed with the red shields of Erroll had been produced and offered in evidence. This was the cloak she had used to cover herself when she walked to the altar. The forsworn priest had been found, he who had been the celebrant, and his testimony was to the effect that the countess had laid a spell on him, by which he had been robbed of his reason.

"Oh, God," whispered Jean.

"Not only that, lord. There were other witnesses, too, some of the men and women who had attended the mass. They said they also had been bewitched by Marie and forced to take part in the orgy afterward."

"Two months ago, you say. How long was the trial?"

The merchant shook his head. "Two weeks. Maybe three. Who knows? Basoches had a lot of witnesses. He paraded them all. Last I heard, the judges had voted the death sentence on her."

Chinon lay over two hundred miles to the south.

At full gallop a man could not reach it before three days were gone. His only chance was to set out now—as he was, with no more than a sword at his side—and ride until his horse collapsed, then buy another mount and go on. With luck he might arrive at Chinon by the third morning from now.

Ah, and then?

Would the naked body of his beloved be shown to the populace, charred and burned as the body of The Maid had been displayed, to prove her dead? The sweet flesh he had caressed with hands and lips! Would it be blackened and—Jesu!

He made a fist of his right hand and drove it again and again against a catapult beam, knowing that madness was stirring in his veins. Already she might be dead! But no, he must not have such thoughts. He had failed to rescue The Maid. He must not fail to rescue Marie!

He ran through the camp roaring for Jacopo Saltello.

"Follow me to Chinon! Take command in my absence.

176

Don't turn aside for anything, you hear? God, if Basoches has won, I'll kill him so slowly it will take him a year to die! I vow this on the true Cross!"

Rolf came with a bay mare, the fastest mount in the army. Jean paused only long enough to fling a brown wool cloak about his shoulders and snatch up a purse of *livres tournois.* Then his boot was in the stirrup and he was swinging into the high-peaked saddle, touching the mare with a toe, taking her into a canter and then a gallop.

He rode like a man in a nightmare, without eyes to see the Abbey of St. Gervais past which he flashed on the road to Breteuil or the hermitage carved from solid rock by monks five hundred years before, just beyond Mortagne. He grudged the pauses for rest that he had to give the mare and ignored the emptiness of his stomach while he rode hour after hour without food.

At a crossroads inn near Rémalard he feasted on roast duck and berry tarts, starved almost to exhaustion. His own dizziness and the staggering gait of the bay told him that, unless he slowed his headlong pace, he might never reach Chinon at all. He fell asleep in an upstairs room of the inn with his clothes on, his sword naked in hand against possible robbers.

Up at dawn, he found the mare somewhat refreshed. He would have exchanged her for a fresh mount, but the innkeeper had nothing but big clumsy beasts, better fitted for farm work than for running.

Before noon of the third morning, he was within sight of the Loire close by Tours. The wind off these ancient hills, which had been known as St. Symphorien in Roman times, flapped his greatcloak and laid a coolness across his cheeks. He rode more easily now, searching the riverbank for a ferry, discovering the low, flat boat near an abandoned water mill.

The slow polework of the ferryman and the lazy gurgle and wash of the river waters underkeel made The Bastard fret. It seemed that he would never get to Chinon, never be there in time to help his wife in her need. As soon as the wooden prow thrust into the reeds before the river bank he was tossing a few copper deniers to the ferryman and leaping his mare into shallow waters, clambering up onto the high bank.

Now the run to Chinon lay through the great forest to its north. Far ahead he could see the pointed turrets of the castle and hear the slow bonging of the bells of the Abbey of Fontevrault. Yet he paid no need to these, nor to the rush of the river Vienne, wide at this point and turbulent in this early summer of the year. All he could think of was Marie.

When he saw a black smudge of smoke on the horizon, his heart seemed to cease its beat; as he galloped closer he saw it was only a haystack burning, with a score of peasants casting well water over it. Relief was a weakness washing through his blood. How clearly he had envisioned his wife, hung in chains and ropes at the stake, flames billowing and smoking about her! His spurs raked the mare. She drove forward with the last of her strength.

Now he was at the outskirts of the town, now passing through its streets, scarcely seeing Le Grand Carroi where Richard Coeur-de-Lion, King of England, had died of wounds, or the Chapel of Saint Melaine where his father, Henry II, had passed away, naked and abandoned.

Hoofbeats clattered on the moat bridge. His lathered mare clattered into the cobbled courtyard close beside the soldiers' quarters. Jean dismounted in the shadow of the great donjon, the Tour du Coudray, and the mighty keep with its groined roof.

Two pages came running, believing him to be a royal courier. A box on the ears convinced them he was indeed the Count of Dunois and in no mood to play at games. He went at their heels up the outer stone stairway and into the *grand salle,* where Charles VII was at dinner.

"Jean!" said his king, looking up from a plate of truffles.

The Bastard strode forward. Anger made him more hawklike than ever, and there was a tenseness about his muscles that threw a hushed silence across the assemblage. "I see by your guilty face it's only too true."

"Jean, I—"

"How did she die? Did she suffer much pain?"

The king looked surprised. "Why, she isn't dead. Not yet. The burning's set for three days from now in the town square."

"Not dead? She lives? Ah—*merci à Dieu!*"

A graybeard on the other side of the king shook his head slowly. "No need to thank your God, young sir. You cannot alter the decree of Holy Mother Church. Who has been declared a witch must die as one."

Jean smiled mirthlessly. "Even though such judgment were secured by lying heretics, forsworn and damned in God's eyes?"

"Why, as to that, testimony would have to be heard, another judgment given. Even then it would not change the case. Three days is much too short a time in which to hear such testimony, and in three days Marie of Dunois must die."

The Bastard loosened his blade in its scabbard. "There is another way. Marie and I are of royal blood. Not even Charles can deny her the right to have a champion or the opportunity to prove her innocence with trial by combat!"

The table buzzed with excitement. No man could remember the last time anyone had insisted on trial by combat. It was an old law, dating back to the early tribal days when Frank and Visigoth had roamed the forest world of Gaul, and was closely related to the trial by ordeal. Could a woman find a champion to espouse her cause, her guilt depended on the outcome of the battle.

The graybeard looked doubtful. "The Countess Marie has already been found guilty," he intoned sonorously. "Her trial is over and done with."

"But not the trial of Philip de Basoches for the lying testimony he's presented to the king and his council on which her fate was decided! I declare the Lord of Arnais to be a liar, a perjurer, a traitor knight. He may answer this charge by any weapon he may name."

Charles VII looked hopeful. He was in no position to have The Bastard turn against him as he must surely do if his wife were to be burned as a sorceress. To have his trained lances, his famed cannons, his footmen and archers go over to the boy-king Henry might be tantamount to making England victorious.

He turned now to the sober old man by his elbow. "Well, Arnaulf? What do you say? Can you order such a combat to decide the merit of the testimony we've been hearing these past few weeks?"

"It can be done, yes."

The king leaned forward. He whispered vehemently, gesturing often. Twice Arnaulf de Barrois scowled, twice he shook his head, but the king was adamant. At last the jurist nodded slowly.

"So it shall be, then. His Majesty has decided that, because of his prerogative as ruler, he shall order such a battle combat decreed, according to the laws laid down in that treatise of law called the Mirror of Saxony."

Relief made Jean close his eyes. Everything must depend, then, on his right arm and sword. He asked, "And my wife? Am I permitted to speak with her? To see her?"

"The Countess of Dunois is imprisoned in the West Tower. A page can direct you there."

At the door Dunois turned once more. "This trial—the sooner the better, if it please your Majesty and his court."

Arnaulf de Barrois bowed his gray head. "Tomorrow, at the hour before midday. A messenger is even now on his way to find the Lord of Arnais."

His heart made muffled thunder in his chest as The Bastard mounted the spiraling stone staircase of the West Tower. On his long ride from Grandvilliers he had cursed the stupidity which had made him decree that Marie Louvet must remain behind while he took the road to war. None of this would have happened if she had been with him!

The little page brought out a key, inserted it in the huge iron lock. The door swung inward. Impatiently Dunois pushed the youth aside and entered.

A shaft of noonday sunlight illumined the little tower room, revealing a *prie-dieu* close beside the arrow slit and the slim figure of the woman kneeling there. Her black hair was bound up about her head in simple fashion, exposing the gracefulness of her white neck and throat. Her face lay buried in her hands, where a rosary of wooden beads was wrapped. She wore a simple gown that clung tightly at hip and bosom. To the staring Jean she seemed a young and innocent girl.

The Bastard could not speak. Only when the page cleared his throat did the woman put a hand on the illumined psalter open on the *prie-dieu* and turn her head.

Her mouth opened. Her eyes widened. She gave a low cry and swayed. Jean was across the little room in two steps, bending to lift her in his arms and draw her up against him, covering her cheeks and eyes and lips with kisses.

"My darling! My most precious one! Ah, God—to think how near I came never to seeing you again!"

She wept stormily, clinging to him, the courage that had sustained her during the nightmarish days of her trial deserting her before the frenzy of the moment.

"Is it you, in truth? They wouldn't let me send word to you, fearing you'd come with an army and lay siege to Chinon. Jean, Jean! Is there any hope at all? It's been so terrible!"

In broken sentences she told him of armed men appearing in her bedchamber before dawn, insisting she rise and dress and come with them in a creaking wagon across the length of Anjou to Chinon, a prisoner. During the unreal hours when she had stood before her accusers, listening to perjured testimony, hearing the deposition of Simone the farm woman read before the Court, staring at a grinning Red Gui as he described the black mass, she had all but lost her mind.

"So Jeanne d'Arc must have felt, as I felt. Nor had I her strong faith to sustain me. When you didn't come, day after day—"

"I never knew," he groaned.

She smiled through her tears and ran gentle fingertips across his wide brow, high cheeks and the firm strength of his mouth. "I know, I know. Only that would have kept you away."

"When I learned what had happened, I came more than two hundred miles in three days."

"Then you are tired!"

She made him lie on the little bed that occupied a length of the tower room, and here he told her of the coming trial by battle on the morrow. She wept in relief and then in fear that he might be slain by Basoches.

"God gives strength to the just," he told her. "The entire idea of the trial by combat is based on that idea."

She laughed through her tears. "I pray your strength is that of Du Guesclin, then."

181

He drew her down beside him, but she flushed and shook her head, twisting free. "Not now—your strength mustn't be dissipated in any way."

His shout of laughter was echoed by his hand on her wrist. She could not fight his muscles, so she felt herself drawn down onto his chest, where she could hear the pounding of his heart. She loved this man with all her being; without him, she was nothing. Even now, with his hands adventuring down her back and finding the clasps of her kirtle, she could refuse him nothing, though her own life would be the prize for the fighting on the morrow.

"Silly goose," he smiled, kissing her thick black hair. "I want only to have you sleep beside me. I've slept but once since leaving Normandy."

Her palm stroked his cheek. She began to sing softly, an old Provençal love song. His eyelids were heavy; it was a strain to keep them open. After a while he let them close and lay there, smelling her perfume and listening to her crooning voice.

He never knew when he fell asleep.

According to the Mirror of Saxony, the contestants in the trial by combat are to be armed by swords, and are to be clad in leather and linen in any fashion and as much as each may wish to wear. The hands and feet shall be bare, and they shall wear a cloak without sleeves. At either end of the field, each contestant shall have a pole man, who, when either contestant falls, shall thrust his pole between them as a signal that the combat has been concluded.

The Bastard was reviewing all this in his mind as he walked across the grassy plat that had been designated as the field of honor. At the far end of the field, close by the high-backed oaken cathedra where the king sat surrounded by his courtiers on tiny faldstools, he could make out Philip of Basoches.

The Lord of Arnais was garbed in the traditional leather cuirass and cloak, with a twist of linen about his middle. He wore leather chausses on his legs as far down as his ankles. He turned as The Bastard approached, scowling darkly.

"You claim I lied about the testimony, my Lord Dunois?" he asked haughtily.

"I not only claim it, I know you did. I'll prove it this day on your body." Jean was coldly angry, and pronounced each word with a vicious ring to his voice.

Arnais laughed nastily. "As you die, remember how your wife will suffer in the flames, Bastard."

Arnaulf de Barrois had been appointed judge by Charles. He stood now with his robe blowing idly in the wind, looking from one man to the other. "Peace ban has been proclaimed on this field," he announced. "Should any meddle in the fighting, his punishment is death." His wise old eyes looked at both men, studying them. "It is agreed that a bloodletting shall be the signal of defeat. The pole will be thrust between you. Anyone who continues to fight after that can be done to death without penalty for him who does the deed."

He gestured with his wrinkled hand, and Philip drew his sword from his scabbard, casting the gilt and leather receptacle from him so that it fell in the high grass off to one side. Jean carried his own blade wrapped in linen. He freed it now to the morning sun.

They faced one another with their blades held to one side. Each man scorned the use of the wood and leather shield that was permitted. One stroke of such swords as these and a wooden shield would split from rim to grips. The Mirror had been written before 1200, when swords were not the splendid weapons they were today.

They circled one another warily. The sun was on the left side at first, for according to the Mirror it must be equally shared by both at the beginning of the battle. Somewhat to his surprise, the Lord of Arnais put up little resistance when The Bastard charged him, so maneuvering his swordplay that Philip faced the sun after the first interchange of strokes.

The Lord of Arnais was a good foeman, Jean realized. His handling of the blade was sure and deft. He used it, as did Jean, both as sword and shield. Sparks flew when the edges met and scraped. Twice Philip came in, hammering so hard with his blade that Jean was forced to give ground to retain his advantage.

For ten minutes they fought before Jean saw his chance—

Arnais dropped his sword slightly after each overhead stroke, leaving an opening for The Bastard to thrust home. When he did it a fourth time, Jean cried out and leaped, his blade held straight forward in the thrust—

An instant before his point was about to plunge home, a brightness exploded in his eyes. Momentarily blinded, Jean could only stagger and cry out. He heard the muffled exclamation of triumph, the swift beat of feet on the grass, saw the uplifted sword that would cut him almost in two when it fell.

He twisted aside, still blinded, aware that Philip de Basoches had used some trick of the devil to drive sunlight into his eyes even though the sun was behind him. His sword arm came up. He deflected the blade once, twice—the last time it almost buried itself in his forearms as it came bounding off his blade—fighting with vicious fury, knowing that Marie burned in the fire flames if he failed her now.

It was close, but he drove Basoches back away from him with flailing slashes and overhead molinellos. Now, as he fought, he risked a glance over the nobleman's shoulders. There was a movement of sorts in the high grass near the river, and a glint of sunlight.

Jean smiled grimly. The Lord of Arnais had prepared an accomplice then. *Bien!* Once warned, The Bastard would be twice careful; and now, as he fought, he looked for an opportunity to turn that treachery to his favor.

The ten minutes of the battle became twenty, then thirty.

The clanging blades were almost the only sound in the meadow below the castle walls. Now and then a man might cry out at some brilliant sword stroke or a woman scream when it seemed that blood might flow. Once a bird screeched high overhead as it sought to elude a hunting hawk.

"You die, milord," said Jean at last, pressing the attack. "You die this day for your trickery, for your dishonor."

Arnais was having trouble with his breathing. His face was flushed, his forehead wet with sweat. The weeks and the months of his own idleness, while Jean had been active in the field, were telling on him. His body was soft beneath its leather, not hard and fit as was The Bastard's.

Yet he managed to gasp, "Not mine the corpse, but yours!"

184

The swords wove in and out. They screeched and clanged together. Closer and closer they came to the tall grasses, so the pole men had to run to keep up with them. Now Jean was employing slashes at thigh and arm. He stepped back, gathered himself with his swordarm lifting high as he leaped—

As he had expected, the flash of reflected sunlight came stabbing for his eyes. But now he was prepared. He shifted slightly so that Philip's head blocked off that blinding ray, even while he pretended panic and blindness.

Seeing his helplessness, Philip roared to the attack.

The Bastard dropped to a knee and a toe. His blade shot forward. Taken by surprise, the Lord of Arnais could not halt his headlong lunge. He ran right into that sharp point, the weight of his own body driving it deep—through leather and linen into his middle and then out behind his spine—until he hung impaled on its bloody length.

For an instant Philip de Basoches hung so, eyes wide and a bloody froth showing at his back-drawn lips, dead on his feet and suspended only by Jean and his sword. Then, as The Bastard stepped back and wrenched his blade free, the Lord of Arnais fell face down into the grass.

The pole man came running.

Jean paid no heed to him. He was racing into the tall grasses, crying out harshly. The king and his court—all of them were standing now, straining their eyes to see what was taking place—thought him mad as he went tearing into the reeds.

Ahead of him a man bounded up from his hiding place. The Bastard recognized him instantly, and his hand tightened on the haft of his sword. He ran on, following the other in his dodging flight until, close beside an old horse-tow path, Jean brought his steel down on top of the red poll.

Red Gui fell face down like a poled steer and lay there with legs and arms twitching uncontrollably. A small hand mirror rolled from his nerveless fingers. The Bastard bent, picked it up and tossed it in the air.

The king was seated in a cathedra facing the fire flames in the open hearth, turning the mirror over and over in his fingers. Now and again he sighed and shook his head, turning

185

to eye the man and woman who stood beside him in the shadows.

"He blinded you with this the better to overcome you?" Charles asked at last.

"Aye, sire. Blinded, I would fall easy victim to his thrust—or so he thought. I marveled that he let me place him with the sun to his eyes so early in the fight. He knew my strategy and was prepared to meet it in his own way—with trickery."

Jean smiled down at Marie. "I suppose now there's no question of my wife's innocence?"

"*Non!* None at all! The bandit—Red Gui, I think they call him—has confessed everything under the hot iron and the boot. There was no need for the rack. He named Philip traitor knight and told him he schemed to do injury to you both."

Charles went on, "The real witch—or should I call her a victim of her own lusts?—was the farm woman, Simone. It was she who had the black mass said, she whom Red Gui saw. He and Philip forswore themselves, naming the Countess Marie for Simone."

Jean looked embarrassed. "This Simone, now. Can your majesty forgive her? Or must she stand trial, too?"

"The woman's dead by her own hand. We found her hanged in an inn room where the outlaw imprisoned her. Mayhap she's better off. Her body bore the marks of the rack, and of certain other devices that Red Gui had used to force her to his lusts.

"Ah, well. He shall not go unpunished, this Red Gui. My orders are that he shall be placed in an iron cage, in which he shall be able to neither stand nor lie nor sit, and shall be hung as a warning to all evildoers in the public square. Unfed, he'll die within a fortnight or howsoever long he can go without food."

The king smiled grimly. "I learn how to rule, it seems. Perhaps France shall be grateful for me, after all." His hard eyes raked The Bastard. "And you, my Lord Dunois? Go you back to the wars?"

"Tomorrow at noon, sire. And with my wife safe beside me. I think I fear the *godons* less than I fear traitor Frenchmen, after this."

Charles smiled wryly. "I had it in mind to cause a *fête*

to be made this night to celebrate my cousin's victory. Instead I think you two would rather be alone, to enjoy Marie's freedom in whatever way you both think best."

The royal eyelid fell in a heavy wink even as his hand signaled their dismissal. For a long moment the king of France continued to stare into the flames, aware that this trouble between Jean of Dunois and Philip de Basoches was only the first of other and more serious problems that would be his lot as king in France.

Sometimes he felt that men asked too much of royalty. And yet, for the power of absolute command over life and death, men killed and lusted. He wished there was peace between England and France so that he could speak to Henry VI as man to man. Yet Henry was only a child, and would not understand.

Charles VII felt very much alone.

The Countess of Dunois was in an impish mood.

She stood naked before the massive ambry, lip between her teeth, holding a fashionable kirtle at her shoulders, staring down at herself with twinkling eyes, well aware that, while her front was modestly covered, her husband could see her from the thick black hair piled atop her head to her heels.

"Well, my lord count? Will this gown do when I ride into battle with you?"

Dunois grinned. "It might be modest enough for the enemy, but the soldiers who follow me may find it hard to look at the *godons* with your pretty rump waggling before them."

Marie bent double with laughter. Jean reached out from the settle where he sat to clap a hand to a bared buttock. She screeched and jumped.

"The Maid wore a man's clothes. I can't have you doing that, though. So bring them all, every last gown you own, my love. We'll ride to battle with the finest dresses in all Europe in our train."

"You only tease," she pouted.

When she saw the dark hunger in his eyes she laughed and backed away slowly, past the standing candle holders toward the darker shadows of the room. She held the kirtle up before

187

her, but in such manner that she gave her husband fleeting glimpses of a slim white leg from toes to rounded hip.

"My lord is tired," she whispered, "from the fighting this day."

Jean rose to his feet. "Is he? Are you so very certain? Don't you know that the mere sight of you does away with fatigue?"

"You should rest in bed," she breathed.

"Mmmm, I had something of the sort in mind."

"Alone!"

"I've been too much alone of late. So've you."

The wooden panelings of the solar were cool against her shoulder blades as Marie pressed into them. Her husband was moving toward her slowly, smiling gently, until he was so close she could have put out a hand to touch him.

"I—I think I need my own rest," she breathed.

"The bed is very soft."

His hands were on her, now, moving up her sides to her shoulders, and he was thrusting against her, forcing her back into the panelings with gentle insistence. Marie was finding it very difficult to breathe.

"Milord—"

His lips were on her throat, branding her skin with wildfire. They touched her ear and spilled their kisses under the thick black mass of hair, which had tumbled down about her shoulders with her movements. She arched suddenly, in spasmodic response to his stroking fingers.

"I thought we agreed to look at dresses," she murmured.

"I saw them all."

"Scarcely half!"

"Do you own so many?"

"Not so many that— Oh! Jean!"

"Mmmm?"

"I cannot think when— If you don't stop I—"

There was a little silence in the room. The countess let her head sink back against the wall panelings, and now a curious little smile twisted the corners of her mouth. From time to time she shuddered, but it was a pleasant shuddering.

"Well?" he whispered at last. "Aren't you—"

"Don't talk. Oh, don't talk."

188

She put her bare white arms about his neck and searched with closed eyes and open lips for his mouth. When she found them she crushed herself against him, clinging, whimpering very faintly. Her heart was spilling over with love for this man, her husband. In her own way, she would teach him what it meant to be her beloved.

She laughed. "Do you think me shameless?"

"I like to think you're inspired by Eros!"

The kirtle lay beneath her bare feet, crushed and rumpled. Those feet moved suddenly. The samite of the kirtle tore.

"Oh sweet Jesu!" she whispered.

Their dark shadows were one in the candle flames. A voice cried out thickly, almost hysterically. Bare feet rustled in the rushes on the floor, and then a rope mattress creaked.

Marie muttered, "You're a devil. You know that, *hein?*"

"Only for you, my love."

"Hmpf! I should hope so. Now I'm coming to the wars with you, there won't be any tavern maids to keep you awake nights."

"You're thinking of La Hire."

Her eyebrows arched. "And you, Jeanne d'Arc? Were there no women in all the months we've been apart?"

His hand touched her soft thigh. "Why, come to think of it, there was a maidservant in Montdidier, with black hair and eyes the color of your own— I did this to her—"

"Mon Dieu!"

He grinned, bending to kiss the soft flesh he was caressing. "And kissed her so, a great number of times until—"

She squirmed angrily, cheeks flushed.

"How dared you! That caress I thought was mine alone!"

"—until, as I say, I woke and realized I was dreaming of you."

"Jean! Ahh—truly?" Tears glimmered in her eyes.

"Do you think any other woman could take your place in my heart?" he growled. "Did you?" His big palm clapped her soft flesh. "God's love! You should be punished for your lack of faith in me."

She hid her face against his chest. "If it would please you—I don't think I'd mind so very much. . . ."

They laughed and whispered and made love, and it seemed

to both of them that all the years of their life had been no more than prelude to this night. Behind them were the despairs and the hatreds, the lustings and the slayings of those yesteryears. Ahead lay only their happiness and the fruition of the love each one bore the other.

With his countess at his side, Jean rode to the wars once more. As The Maid had inspired the common people, rousing the foot soldiers and the lances to rash courage, so Marie inspired the latent military genius which slumbered in The Bastard.

His sorties upon the English grew in daring and destruction. During the year following the burning of The Maid he captured Chartres and drove the Duke of Bedford before him as he willed, with terrible sweeps of his thundering lances and smoking cannonades of his artillery. And when the *godons* retired from Lagny, the road to Paris lay wide open.

When that grossly fat and slyly evil counselor of the king, La Trémoille, was slain in 1433, Arthur of Brittany, Count of Richemont and Constable of France, assumed command of the government as adviser to Charles VII. Peace was made between the king and Philip the Good, Duke of Burgundy, by the treaty of Arras, in September, 1435.

Now Jean of Dunois swept the countryside like a spiked flail.

The English reeled under his blows, staggered and retreated.

In the middle of April, 1436, by way of the St. James Gate, Jean and the Constable galloped their war horses side by side into the city of Paris. The white lily banner of Valois followed, in the hand of Henri of Villeblanche. L'Isle-Adam, *marechal* of France, planted those lilies on top of the great stone gate.

Paris was once more a city of France.

The war was not yet over, though the truce of Tours suspended the fighting until 1449. Then Charles VII threw Jean The Bastard into Normandy, where, with miraculous speed and thoroughness he captured Rouen—weeping a little in his heart in memory of The Maid—defeated the English in the field at Firminy and took Cherbourg. In a single year

190

he had accomplished what no other Frenchman had been able to do in a hundred.

The year following, Charles ordered The Bastard into Guienne.

Here too, his lances and his cannon were irresistible. Bordeaux fell to his nettle standard, as did Bayonne. The *godons* moved against him, determined to wipe out this military wizard. They met at Castillon in the middle of July, 1453 and the victory for Dunois was complete and decisive.

Nothing remained to the English in France but Calais port. The Maid had been avenged.

In his later years, The Bastard served his country as ambassador to England, to Burgundy, to Savoy and Rome. He assisted in the financial and military reforms by which Charles VII strengthened his country, so that, when Louis XI came to the throne, the way had been cleared for him to begin his series of moves destined to result in the absolute monarchy of Louis XIV, the Sun King.

When The Bastard died in November, 1468, Louis XI was present at the funeral. Jean was buried in Notre Dame de Clery, though later his heart and that of Marie were disinterred and placed in the little vault below the altar in the chapel of the castle at Châteaudun.

They are still there today, side by side.

It is as they would have wanted.